MEET MATHEW S

"Sometimes, wh
hot summer rain st
breath of a concrete dragon, the smell of death rolls
down from Old Town and hangs over the living like a
hammer over an anvil—waiting. There's life in death, I
suppose; the knowledge of the rind makes the taste of
the melon sweeter. But then, I suppose a lot of things.
That's why I make my living solving other people's
problems . . .

"Venitas Boulevard was a carnival as I hummed my
bullet through its misty innards. Midday whores, young
ones who had to look good in the light of day, roamed
the jungle paths looking for lunch money. Lean, tall
studs in color-changing tunics and street-parade hair red
as West Texas mud, prowled like panthers; their heads
set firm, and their eyes ever watchful. Pack hunting
brown cubs with black, tangled manes and guts full of
government dope leaned against the hulking ruins of
dead brownstones and called with primal elegance to
those unfortunate enough to be passing by. It was
Tuesday—garbage day."

THAT'S JUST THE BEGINNING OF *HOT TIME
IN OLD TOWN*, THE FIRST IN A RIVETING NEW
SCIENCE FICTION MYSTERY SERIES STARRING
MATHEW SWAIN, A HARD-BOILED PRIVATE
EYE. IN THE TRADITION OF SAM SPADE AND
THE CONTINENTAL OP.

BEFORE THE UNIVERSE by Frederik Pohl and C.M. Kornbluth
A CANTICLE FOR LEIBOWITZ by Walter M. Miller, Jr.
THE CARNELIAN THRONE by Janet E. Morris
THE CENTAURI DEVICE by M. John Harrison
CROMPTON DIVIDED by Robert Sheckley
CRYSTAL PHOENIX by Michael Berlyn
DISTANT STARS by Samuel R. Delany
ENGINE SUMMER by John Crowley
FANTASTIC VOYAGE by Isaac Asimov
THE GATES OF HEAVEN by Paul Preuss
THE GOLDEN SWORD by Janet E. Morris
HIGH COUCH OF SILISTRA by Janet E. Morris
THE HUMANOID TOUCH by Jack Williamson
JEM by Frederik Pohl
MAN PLUS by Frederik Pohl
THE MAN WHO FELL TO EARTH by Walter Tevis
MATHEW SWAIN: HOT TIME IN OLD TOWN by Mike McQuay
NEBULA WINNERS THIRTEEN Edited by Samual R. Delany
ON WINGS OF SONG by Thomas M. Disch
RE-ENTRY by Paul Preuss
THE REVOLT OF THE MICRONAUTS by Gordon Williams
SPACE ON MY HANDS by Frederic Brown
STARWORLD by Harry Harrison
THE STAINLESS STEEL RAT WANTS YOU! by Harry Harrison
THE STEEL OF RAITHSKAR by Randall Garret and Vicki Ann Heydron
A STORM UPON ULSTER by Kenneth C. Flint
SUNDIVER by David Brin
TALES FROM GAVAGAN'S BAR by L. Sprague de Camp and Fletcher
  Pratt
THE TIME MACHINE by H.G. Wells
TIME STORM by Gordon Dickson
20,000 LEAGUES UNDER THE SEA by Jules Verne
UNDER THE CITY OF THE ANGELS by Jerry Earl Brown
VALIS by Philip K. Dick
WHEELWORLD by Harry Harrison
WIND FROM THE ABYSS by Janet E. Morris

Mathew Swain:
Hot Time in Old Town

by
Mike McQuay

BANTAM BOOKS
TORONTO • NEW YORK • LONDON • SYDNEY

MATHEW SWAIN: HOT TIME IN OLD TOWN
A Bantam Book / September 1981

ISBN 0-553-14811-7

Published simultaneously in the United States and Canada

Bantam Books are published by Bantam Books, Inc. Its trademark, consisting
of the words "Bantam Books" and the portrayal of a bantam, is Registered
in U.S. Patent and Trademark Office and in other countries. Marca Registrada.
Bantam Books, Inc., 666 Fifth Avenue, New York, New York 10103.

PRINTED IN THE UNITED STATES OF AMERICA

0 9 8 7 6 5 4 3 2 1

This entire series
is dedicated to the memory
of Raymond Chandler,
who understood.

1

Sometimes, when the wind blows just right and the hot summer rain steams the streets like the last foul breath of a concrete dragon, the smell of death rolls down from Old Town and hangs over the living like a hammer over an anvil— waiting. There's life in death, I suppose; the knowledge of the rind makes the taste of the melon sweeter. But then, I suppose a lot of things. That's why I make my living solving other people's problems.

The rain had come hard that afternoon, hard like a young fighter who seems never to weary. It did weary though, then rolled on to the northeast, to the Oklahoma-Arkansas conglomerate and bayou Louisiana, leaving behind the smell of death and the steaming streets.

Venitas Boulevard was a carnival as I hummed my bullet through its misty innards. Midday whores, young ones who had to look good in the light of day, roamed the jungle paths looking for lunch money. Lean, tall studs in color-changing tunics and street-parade hair, red as West Texas mud, prowled like panthers: their heads set firm, and their eyes watchful. Pack-hunting brown cubs with black, tangled manes and guts full of government dope leaned against the hulking ruins of dead brownstones and called with primal elegance to those unfortunate enough to be passing by. It was Tuesday—garbage day.

I sat out the light at Tremaine Street, then turned north, heading away from the center of town. Away from the decay. Fifteen minutes earlier I had been counting the cracks on my office wall and trying to think of even a bad excuse to get out of working on a follow-up insurance job, which I had been foolish and hungry enough to take, when a priority police blurb juiced through my vis. I only listen to those things with half an ear, but a familiar address drifted through the marmalade that passes for my brain. It was Phil Grover's. Now, I've never chased an ambulance in my life, but Grover was a former client who had paid me in cash, and I like to hold on to people like that. I'm funny that way.

I had been to Grover's once, to deliver some poop on the whereabouts of an ex-girlfriend. At least I had supposed she was a girlfriend. Grover was a queer duck. He lived in the penthouse of a middle aging high rise on the edge of the dying part of the city. He was smart and careful, but had the kind of eyes that chould go wild on you, like those of an animal that senses danger to its life. It made me nervous just to be around him. He seemed on the edge, and not sure what to do about it. That had been two months ago, and now there was a police call.

The traffic was sparse on Tremaine. The people who lived within its rotting towers of steel and broken glass couldn't afford transportation, and those who traversed it out of necessity usually opted for the protected heli-buses that floated at bird level above the broken, pitted streets. I never felt much like a bird.

As I moved along Tremaine, away from the bankrupt decay, its face physically changed the farther I went. The road itself lost its scarred jigsaw look; the buildings were cleaner, more imposing. Newscreens dotted occasional corners showing, to anyone who cared to look, just how crazy things can be when we really work at it. Holoprojections changed in store windows, displaying in unstealability whatever luxury items those with the means couldn't live without that day. There were street lights that worked, and Fancy Dans in security guard-with-permit uniforms stood like pompous statues beside the electronic maws of fortresslike department stores. Fancy Dans with guns bothered me. Like left-handed boxers, you never knew where they were coming from.

Just about the time I started looking for Grover's building, three armored police cars beaconed me in. They had pulled up slantways on the four-lane street, blocking one whole line of traffic that had thickened to safe-area proportions. My position was not so privileged. I had to drive around the block twice before finding a legal parking space. I was out of the bullet and into the heat before the engine's magnetic whine had hushed to silence. I slipped my waistcoat on over my rumpled gray one-piece with the hole under the left armpit, and tried to look like something other than a back-alley P.I. who had to work insurance follow-ups just to keep himself in cigs and booze. Uselessly running a hand through hair that had a mind of its own, I swung the door closed. It made the sound of a tuna can falling on a wood floor. Then I grubbed my pockets and fed the meter enough silver to keep me in the building all day if need be. It was wishful thinking.

I had ultimately managed to get the bullet within a block of the Marmeth Arms, Grover's apartment building. I hoofed the rest. Once I got the jacket on, a minute in the smog-bottled humidity had me sweating like a fat man at the Turkish bath. The Marmeth was wide, unwindowed, wood-grained concrete that rose thirty stories into the smog bank. Its front entrance was straight, riveted steel that wouldn't open unless a little card with all the right holes punched into it was pushed into an eye-level slot. I didn't have one of those. A two-way vis perched just above the doorway, angling down to check keyless visitors. A policeman's face occupied the screen, in place of the usual doorman. I didn't have to ask to know they wouldn't let me in.

There was a public vis at the end of the block. I took the hike down there and used my Beltel card to get inside the thing. I punched up information, and a projection of what a computer thought would be a pleasant female face appeared on the concave screen.

"Good afternoon," I said, and smiled. "Do you have a listing for a Mr. Brown at the Marmeth Arms?"

The face went blank for a second, then became pleasant again. "No sir, there is no Brown listed at that address."

"How about a Mr. Smith?" I asked.

"No, sir."

I tried some other names. Finally, they gave me the listing for a Richard Rodriguez. I punched up the number, hoping that someone would be home in the middle of the day. A plump, cheeky Mexican woman faded in. She had puppy-dog eyes that might have been inviting twenty years ago, and enough flesh on her face to cover a canoe. She was chewing vigorously, which reminded me that I hadn't had lunch yet. A thin coating of greasy residue clung to her chin for dear life.

"Wa' you want?" she asked.

"My name is Swain," I answered. "Is Mr. Rodriguez at home?"

"No," she said and began picking her teeth with a long-nailed finger, "he's at the office playing around with his programmer."

"Perhaps you can help me. I'm a lawyer representing the estate of his late aunt, Clara Diaz . . ."

"I don' remember any Diaz," she returned rudely and wiped at the grease with the back of her large hand.

I smiled solicitously. "Well, she remembers him. She left him quite a large amount of money in her will."

The woman's eyes, previously lost in her cheeks, came popping into view like twin moons cresting the horizon. "Money!" she gulped, nearly choking. "How much?"

"Around eighty thousand, give or take."

"Madre de Dios!"

"There are a few papers that have to be signed. I thought I might drop over to deliver them. I'm only a few minutes . . ."

"Come ahead, what are you waiting for?" she said, her face bobbing up and down the screen like a bingo ball in an air chamber.

I blanked off and stood for a few minutes in the dark coolness of the armored vis booth. I lit a cig, watching the gray-white smoke defy its natural inclination by getting sucked at a right angle into the ventilators.

After about ten minutes, I left the booth and walked back to the Marmeth. I moved into the viewscreen's sensors and hoped that the cop on duty didn't know me. "Mr. Swain to see Mrs. Rodriguez."

"Just a minute." The screen blanked.

He came back on after the required time. "Identification?"

I held up my driver's license and smiled angelically. There was a loud buzz, then a click, and the door swung open. I saluted the screen, walked through the potted-palm lobby that looked old the way lobbies shouldn't look old, and went right up to the elevators. Setting my weight on the up-tube, I rode it all the way to the penthouse.

2

The up-tube hatched open, and I found myself face to face
with a uniformed cop a good head shorter than me. His black,
form-fitting, kevlar uniform hugged his frame like a surgical
glove. He had his thumbs hooked in his gun belt so that his
elbows stuck straight out like bird wings.

"Let me guess," I said. "You're a loving cup."

I looked over the top of his head. The tube opened into an
entrance foyer, then Grover's front door. The door was open
and enough cops to fill a moron's football team were moving
around inside the apartment.

"Tube off," the loving cup said, and his face was puffed
up like a sponge in a bathtub. "This place is restricted."

I reached out and pinched his cheek. "Go home, Junior, I
hear your mother calling you."

I saw Mack Watershed's corpulent frame move past the
door space. Homicide was here; I had just lost a client. "Fat
Mack," I called, as the irritated tube cop tried to shove me
back into the motivator.

Watershed stuck his head around the door. "How the *hell*
did you get up heah?" he bellowed in a drawl that sounded
like his mouth and nose had exchanged places. He jellied
through the door and up to the tube, pushing his man out of
the way in the process. He walked right up to me, so that his
immense belly was touching mine.

"We've got to stop meeting like this," I told him.

Fat Mack glared at me with his slit eyes, his flat nostrils
flaring in and out. He worked his purple lips, and I won-

6

dered if he had indigestion or just didn't like the company. "I asked you a question, Swain. What are you doing heah?"

"I live here," I answered, "and you're trespassing."

His dough face tightened and his thick lips worked double time. I realized it wasn't indigestion. His usual bucket of sweat rolled down his cheeks like sap from a maple tree. "Don't push me, boy. I'm in the market for suspects right now."

"What kind of suspects?" I asked, and eased him away from me with my fingertips.

He stepped back and eyed me suspiciously. I could see the terminals clicking inside his simple mind. "What *are* you doing heah?" he asked quietly.

I moved out of the tube and tried to get to the door. He blocked me with his body. "Take it easy, would you? Grover was a client of mine."

He brightened. "Was?" he said. "How'd you know he was dead?"

"Well, you aren't exactly the maid, now, are you?"

He took a deep calm-down breath and jabbed my chest with his index finger. "You wait right heah," he said, then turned and walked into the apartment. I followed him in. The place was crawling with homicide people.

The room itself was tastefully elegant, telling me that Grover had money, but wasn't rolling in it. He chose his lifestyle too carefully. It was a nice apartment, nice like a cold beer on a hot day—but no nicer.

Harrison Jenkins, head of homicide, was parked on an overstuffed sofa that sat squarely in the middle of the living room. He was locked in deep conference with his pocketcom. He'd grumble and the little thing would beep in return. It was a surprise to see him there; I didn't know that Grover was big-time enough to rate the first-class treatment.

Watershed turned and saw me behind him. His face flushed crimson and he balled up his fists, threatening. "You son of a bitch," he whispered, and stretched himself up to meet me eye to eye.

"Now, Mack," I smiled, "you know what it does to your blood pressure when you get all excited like this."

He cocked a beefy fist.

"Watershed!" Jenkins said sharply from the sofa. Mack turned to the man. Jenkins shook his head and continued his man-to-machine talk. He motioned for me to join him.

I grinned cutely at Watershed's contorted face and walked past him. Jenkins chuckled without smiling as I walked up and eased myself next to him on the couch.

"You need a muzzle for your dog," I told him.

He rolled his eyes till just the whites showed. Jenkins looked tired all the time. I guess that balancing politics and a job could do that to a man. His face was glossy ebony, darker than that of most Africks, and his droopy, heard-it-all-before eyes belied a man who had compromised himself too many times. He had come down from Chicago to run the department ten years previously, and had almost immediately acquired the nickname, Jumpstreet Harry, which everyone called him—but not to his face. He had an amiable look about him, but with a slight hardness exaggerated by his slick eyebrows and thin moustache. His clothing was dapper, as always. He wore a dull-sheen silver one-piece that hung from his lean frame as if he had been born to wear it. A black silk ascot, imprinted with a myriad of tiny yellow fleurs-de-lis, was wound around his neck and tucked into the collar of the one-piece. Over all that he wore a thigh-length dress tunic, black as the ascot. The tunic was open down the front, and when he moved a certain way, his nickel-plated laser could be glimpsed in its simple leather strap holster. He was always cool and collected and good under pressure. I almost liked him.

"What brings you up here, Swain?" he asked.

"Is that all you guys know how to say?"

"Grover a friend of yours?"

"Business associate."

Harry held the pocketcom up in front of his face and punched up a couple of terminals, grimacing the whole time. Then he got intent as something appeared beeping on the readout screen. He closed his eyes like he just got kicked in the balls and lowered the machine. "The only business he's going to conduct now will be with the angels," he said.

"Can I see him?"

"Why?"

"Morbid curiosity."

A uniform came out of the bedroom and approached us. "Jordan wants to do a residual reading," the man said.

"Does he think we're made out of money?" Harry snapped.

"He says you've got to get residuals early," the man answered apologetically.

Harry shook his head. "We're already . . ." he punched up his pocketcom, ". . . thirty-seven hundred over budget for a prelim."

The man shrugged.

Jenkins put up his hands. "All right, tell him to go ahead," he said. "But tell Jordan that if we can't sell this one, it's coming out of his salary."

The cop got away while the getting was good.

Harry looked at me, wide-eyed. "What's another few hundred bucks, huh?"

"It's only money."

He laughed the way people laugh when something's not funny. "Money," was all he said.

"Can I see him?" I asked again.

"Who?"

"Your overbudgeted prelim."

His face said, why not, and he tilted his head in the direction of the bedroom. "I want to talk to you after you've looked," he said, and raised his eyebrows to emphasize the point.

I stood up, nodding, and went to the bedroom. Several plainclothesmen in bargain-basement suits droned around the room, scanning with wave recorders, trying to reconstruct the crime. The polelike cambot moved methodically, its hundred cameras continually whirring, taking infrared and heat-keyed photos of the entire place.

The room was spacious and all done up in white, like a mausoleum looks from the outside. The furnishings were low-slung and had an oriental flavor: sweeping peaks and ornate filigree. But the albino coloration made it look odd and disjointed. This furniture didn't fit the scheme or taste of the rest of the apartment and made me wonder if Grover or someone else decorated it. The plush carpet was off-white and worn, and stretched all the way to beige walls that could have used a couple coats of paint. White drapes hung from ceiling to floor and alternately displayed or covered a view of the rotting part of the city according to the tenant's whim. The drapes were open. This had to be the only window in the entire building. A two-meter-square vis screen sat squarely in the center of the room facing the stasis bed. The stasis was still turned on, making the satin pillows on it look as if they were floating in mid-air a foot above the solid black base. I never cared for that kind of luxury; I liked to rub up against things when I was sleeping. To each his own, I guess.

Grover, or what was left of him, lay on the floor next to the stasis. I recognized the white knee-boots that he was so fond of wearing and the tight pants that tucked inside. Except for his head, which lay halfway across the room against the wall, that was all that remained of Philip Grover. The rest of him was gone. I walked up and examined the leftovers. There was no blood, or even the cauterization one would expect from a heat-producing weapon. He had been cut off cleanly at the hips, the internal organs and tissues being instantly preserved. I'd never seen the like. I moved over to the head, which was grinning broadly up at me from ankle level. It was the same story—no blood or apparent damage.

Mo Johnson, from the Medical Examiner's office, sat on the stasis staring dumbly at the floor. I moved to him and stood.

"What's it look like?"

He glanced up at me with a weathered squirrel face, as if he had just noticed my presence. "Was it this hot last year?" he asked, and his voice was older than his face. He put a hand to his rapidly thinning, combed-forward hair, just to see if it was still there. "Honest to God, Swain, this damned humidity just runs me into the ground. And now this bullcrap." He pointed to the body. "What in the holy hell is *this* supposed to be?"

"You tell me," I replied.

"It's a bag of worms, that's what it is." He hunched his shoulders and sighed, looking for all the world as if he wanted nothing more than to lie back on the bed and take a short nap. "I've seen it all," he said. "Poisons, drugs, electric stimulations, ultrasonic scrambles that would turn your stomach . . . hell, I've found laser burns in places where *I'd* never stick a gun, but this is the cork in the pig's ass." He smoothed the sleeve of his weathered brown toga. "I've never seen anything like this." He shook his head. "You think you've seen everything, you think you can keep up with the changes, then something like this crops up. Why do people have to get fancy? A knife will kill somebody just as dead and it doesn't even make noise."

"Do you know anything of what happened?"

"I don't even know what I'm looking at. Ask Jordan." He arched a creased eyebrow in the direction of Nardy Jordan, the department's electrex.

Jordan was standing to one side of the room, his white one-piece dangling electronic gadgetry like a melting reactor. Spider legs, perched on his shoulders, housed powerpacks that fanned a belt of readout screens in a semicircle in front of his face. He was neither young nor old. His head was shaved as were his eyebrows. His lips were a thin slash, practically nonexistent, and his expression, as always, was completely lifeless. When I walked over to him, he stared through me with color-poor eyes.

"How's my boy?" I asked him.

"You only talk to me when you want something," he answered in a monotone. "So, if you'll excuse me. Time is money, and I have very little of either."

"Is that nice?" I answered. "Here I am, ready to volunteer information as a concerned private citizen, and you give me a tough time about it."

"What sort of information?" His eyes continually watched the changing patterns of lights and wave lines that moved in sequence across the screens around him.

"For instance, have you figured out yet that Grover was killed by a woman?"

He looked up from his mesmerizing patterns and took me in for the first time. "How do you know that?"

"Un uh," I said. "You tell me your dream and I'll tell you mine."

His brows furrowed and he looked back to his screens. "I've recorded disturbances in the wave patterns of the room and tried to scale them down and separate them into a time-

11

reference grid. The way it looks is that Grover came into the apartment about ten last night. He came directly into the bedroom and turned on the vis. After a time, he moved through other parts of the house, then came back and lay on the bed with the vis still on. Someone else came into the apartment around eleven, give or take, apparently without his knowledge, for he didn't go to the door to answer a bell.''

"Maybe it was somebody he knew," I added.

"That's a possibility. Anyway, he got out of bed and went to the bedroom door just as the other party reached it. There was a tremendous expenditure of energy then, and Grover's remains were knocked across the room. Whoever did it went directly to the kitchen afterwards, then left. That was it. The maid discovered the body this morning. She came in to shut off the vis, and that's when she saw the body.''

"There were no records of anyone calling on Grover last night?''

"No.''

"Well, how did the killer get in?''

"Came through the keyhole.''

I looked at the room one more time, then turned to go.

"Hey," Jordan called after me. "What about my information? What makes you think it was a woman who killed Grover?''

"Intuition," I answered with a wink, and got a sampling of his middle English in return.

I moved back into the living room. Harry was still sitting on the couch, rubbing his face and yawning. I stopped by the long, low bar, set against a wall occupied by a neon sculpture of two turtles copulating, and looked for a little lunch. For a rich boy, Grover didn't keep a very good bar. I found a decanter of cut glass that seemed to be about half-full of scotch. There was a row of dusty cordial glasses lined up like soldiers on a shelf in the back of the bar. I filled one to try the stuff out. It was fair, but no earth-mover. I filled the glass again and went back to talk to Harry.

"He's dead all right," I said, and sat down next to Jenkins, putting my feet up on an imitation-mahogany coffee table. I could see Fat Mack glaring at me from across the room. I pulled my arms back to rest on the back of the couch and sipped my whisky like a country gentleman.

"Make yourself at home," Harry said.

"Thanks," I answered, and took my shoes off.

He shook his head and showed me non-nicotined teeth. "You're a strange one, Swain."

"Just uncomplicated."

"Tell me what you know about Grover."

"Well, he won't be doing any more singing in the church choir," I replied. "This is a little off the beaten track for you, isn't it, Harry?"

He half-smiled. "They're complaining downtown about prelim teams going over budget too often. I'm supposed to go on some of these damn things and show them how to do it properly."

"What you need to do," I said, wiggling my stockinged toes, "is to get people to die in the station house, so that you can save transportation costs."

He turned up the corners of his mouth. "You said he was your client?"

"Yeah, he was. I did a little job for him a couple of months ago, but that was all finished."

He turned and sat sideways on the couch, so that he was facing me. "Then why are you here?"

"Like all my packages tied up nice and clean. Grover was in trouble when I knew him, although I didn't know what it was. When I heard the call to come over, I thought I'd show up just to see what was going on."

"What sort of job did you do for him?"

"Played locator service. I scared up a certain party for him."

"What was that certain party's name?"

I turned and looked hard at him. It was a policy of mine never to give more than I was getting. "That was a long time ago, Harry. The name has slipped my mind."

He didn't buy it. "The man's dead. You can't claim confidentiality on this. In case you've forgotten, there are laws against hampering a murder investigation."

"You find any drugs in the apartment?" I asked.

"No, why?"

"No liquor, no drugs—hardly the lifestyle of someone who lives in the penthouse."

He sat there for a minute and tugged on his lower lip. "Okay," he said. "I don't know why, but I'll go ahead and tell you. The only information we have on Grover in our data banks is that he'd been picked up three times in the last ten years for publicly tubing-out on booze and mind expanders. Had to be committed all three times. That stuff does something to his brain."

"No wonder he stayed away from it. What did the doctors say?"

He shook his head. "No record. Whatever it was, the family suppressed it. You know what he did for a living?"

"He never said," I answered, and finished the scotch, "and I never asked. I knew there was money in his family, but I don't know if he was on the pipeline or not. He paid in cash, for what that's worth. You going to run the investigation?"

"Naw," he stood up, straightening the front of his tunic. "I'm just the social director. Your old friend Watershed's running the show."

I slipped my shoes on and stood also. wiping my glass with a handkerchief—I knew how Fat Mack's mind worked. A man in my line of work can't be too careful.

Harry motioned for his driver, Goetz, who was trying to blend in with the wallpaper. He took a few steps then turned back to me. "I sure hope that somebody can foot the bill on this one," he said. "We got stuck eight times last month."

"Some people don't care how they inconvenience you when they die," I answered.

"How well I know. Try to remember that name, would you? Call me back some time today."

He smiled his political smile and smoothed his already smooth hair. While he headed for the door, I made one more trip to the bedroom.

Jordan said that the vis was turned on when Grover died. I wondered if he had asked it any questions during that hour that it was operating. They were just finishing up in there. The bits and pieces of Grover's body were being loaded on a stretcher that was made for some whole person. Jordan was

14

packing up his equipment, and Mo had, in fact, curled himself up on the stasis for a cat nap.

I juiced the vis screen. It was showing unedited scenes of bullet wrecks, one after another—going for the straight emotion. I punched through the memory terminals to see what, if anything, the machine had been asked. It was a long shot, but one worth trying. The screen blanked, then three readouts appeared. There were two vis numbers and a recipe for soy casserole. I committed the numbers to memory, then shut down the machine.

A pudgy hand grabbed my shoulder and spun me around. "Hit the streets, blood money." It was Fat Mack, back in control after his boss left.

I jerked away from his grasp. "Keep your paws to yourself, Rover, or I'll have to teach you how to heel."

Blue veins throbbed on his temple; he wiped the sweat off his face. "I don't know what your connection with all this is, Swain, but this is my baby and you'd better stay out of my way or I'll roll right over you."

"You're just the man who could do it too," I said and patted his stomach.

He knocked my hand away and began sputtering again. I took that as my cue to leave. I moved out of the bedroom and lit a cig, watching the cops tramp through the apartment like Sherman through Atlanta. Murder was always a nasty business, but there was something particularly gruesome about this one and it wasn't the dismemberment either. I think the efficiency bothered me. Efficient murders are calculated murders. Calculated murders are usually professional murders. Grover had gotten himself involved in something that was beyond his ability to accommodate, and I had considered Grover an able person. Only one thing seemed out of place, and that was the murder weapon. Exotic means of destruction can certainly be dramatic, but tend to be more easily traceable. A professional killer would never have used a weapon so bizarre to do a job. If I were handling the case, I would key in on that point.

I smiled sweetly at the guard who had blocked my entrance when I first came up, and gently moved him aside so I could leave. When I got downstairs, Mrs. Rodriguez was running crazily around the lobby, looking for the man who was going to make her rich. I hid behind a potted palm, then slipped past her when she wasn't looking.

When I reached the street, the steam was gone from the pavement, leaving only the heat. I slipped off my waistcoat and slung it across my arm, then walked back to my bullet. The inside felt like a blast furnace. I slotted my contact key and felt myself rise a half-meter off of street level, the engine humming like a tone-deaf baritone.

I still hadn't had anything to eat that day, and it was beginning to get late. Maxey's sounded good for pastrami sandwiches, and it was close to the Marmeth. I nosed into the early rush traffic, heading in that direction.

I thought about Grover for a while. My one overpowering impression of him was that he was a total loner, not the kind of person that anyone would go to so much trouble to kill. I tried to fill in some blanks in my mind, but eventually the ache in my belly superseded the intellectual process and I thought instead about pastrami on rye.

With mustard.

3

It rained again while I was at lunch. It came down pretty good and convinced me that I really didn't need to do any more work that day. So I sat in my bullet during the busy time on Tremaine, watched the rain drool down my windshield, and drained the innards of a fiver of my old friend Black Jack in memory of a file that had just become permanently inactive. I hated to lose Grover. Not that I had any special love for the man—quite the contrary, in fact—but anyone in the age of fluidics who needed the services of an old fashioned P.I. was okay in my movie.

While I sat there, the police department's blue and white mutant-removal van pulled up to the curb across the street. Three people in bulky burn-suits jumped out of the cab of the thing and ran into an unmarked brick building. Apparently they had gotten word that one of the Old Town mutants had busted quarantine and was hiding in the city. I watched the building's front, wondering what in the world was going on behind that calm facade. Several Fancy Dans with their hip boots and shiny buttons had also detected the arrival of the van and had congregated around the building's entrance.

Just about the time that I thought nothing would happen, a woman came running out of the building. She looked normal to me at first, but as she ran her wig fell off, and I could see that she was hairless. She tried to cut across the street, but the Fancy Dans had pulled their guns and gleefully used her for target practice. There wasn't much left when they were finished.

The rain and the go-home traffic let up about the same time. The cops across the street were arguing with the Fancy

Dans about just who was going to clean up the mess they had made as I pulled away from the curb. I guess nobody likes to straighten up after the party.

I decided that I'd better go back to the office and check my message playback before calling it a day. I operated a little farther back in the decay; it suited my personality. Humming through the safe area, I moved out of Fancy Dan territory and into the rot. I pulled up in front of the lean tall building whose entrance began at the top of a flight of stone steps. 2313 was lettered on a half-moon transom above the doorway. I walked the two flights up and let myself in the frosted glass door on which my name was stenciled at eye level in glossy gold paint with the suggestion of black shadow behind each letter. My one concession to merchandising.

The office was simple, which suited my taste and financial disposition. The desk was old, but real wood. It sat in front of venetian-blinded windows that could bring in the afternoon sunlight, such as it was. There was a coat-and-tunic rack in the corner, and a small settee with purple- and violet-flowered upholstery waited against the wall for clients to make themselves at home. They rarely did. Occasionally, when it got drunk out, I tried to use it as a bed, but it was a lot like trying to stuff a three-pound foot into a two-pound sock. I had a swivel chair for the desk, and several folding chairs for heavy conferences that never occurred. My vis screen took up most of the wall opposite the sofa.

I sank into the desk chair and leaned back, sliding back and forth a couple of times. Then I pulled open the big bottom drawer of the desk and took out Black Jack's twin brother and a glass. I poured a slug, and eased back to sip it while waiting to see who was missing me. The screen focused on Foley down at Continental Insurance, and I didn't need to see it to know what he was going to say. He had that disgusted look on his face that he always wore when talking to me. Continental had hired me to do some follow-ups on death claims that involved large amounts of cash, stuff that couldn't be cleared through the regular computer channels. I was doing them a good job, but worked at my own pace. Foley ran the computer claims department, and it infuriated him to have to deal with someone who didn't work on a time schedule.

"Damn it, Swain, where are you?" the projection said. "You're supposed to be in your office working on the MacGruder case."

I lifted my glass and toasted the image.

"The casebooks should have been turned in three days ago. I'll bet you haven't even started on it yet."

He was right. An overdose-of-aphrodisiac case was something that I was having a hard time getting myself up for, if you'll pardon the epigram. Foley was shaking his tiny, manicured fist at the screen.

"Get that thing done, Swain, or I swear by my rectifiers that I'll demodulate you. Get it in here tomorrow—Thursday at the latest."

"Roger." I snapped off a stiff salute. "Over and out." I hoped that the next message would be more interesting. It was. The picture blurred into focus, and the entire screen was filled with a naked female breast. Nice looking, too. The breast stayed on the screen for a time, then backed up ever so slowly, until its twin appeared, jouncing seductively.

"Hello, Ginny," I said, and poured another drink.

Presently she backed up enough so that Virginia Teal's face came into view. A red-nailed finger came up to wisp a long strand of honey blond hair to her mouth, where wet lips held it fast. Her pale blue eyes stared at the screen as if she could count the hairs on the back of my head right through my skull. She smiled, a white-toothed demon. Even in a recording she could get to me.

"Mathew," she purred, and her voice was sweet as milk and graham crackers. "Yours truly has just returned from the wilds of San Francisco and Angel City. I'm officially reclaiming my rightful property—you. So kick the rest of the flower-of-Texas womanhood out of bed and call me, you bastard."

She blanked off.

I sat and looked for a minute at the screen, the buzz center of my body in complete turmoil. Since Ginny had left for the West Coast three months before, my female companionship had consisted of two dinners with my Aunt Gertrude, and daily cuddle sessions with my cat Matilda. I was glad she had come back; it was touch and go there for a while.

The meter showed another message on the board. I keyed it and saw an unfamiliar form take shape. A long, wrinkled face was looking out of the screen with eyes that shone out of that weathered casing like floodlights at a munitions factory. His hair was like the top of Mount Fuji, and he had a long, straight nose that came out of his face like a ski jump.

"This message is intended only for the ears of Mathew Swain," he said, in a voice that was firm, yet pleasant. He stopped talking for a time, so I could clear the room of my staff, I suppose. Then he began again. "My name is Barnett, and I am calling on behalf of Silas Grover."

I sat up straight and leaned on the desk. Maybe my Grover file wouldn't close after all. Reaching out, I juiced my typer and hoped for the best.

"Mr. Grover requests that you take dinner with him tonight at seven to discuss matters of a highly . . . personal nature. If you choose to accept the invitation, you will be well reimbursed for your time and trouble."

He gave me an address on the near edge of town, which meant old money. It certainly sounded like a job, which brightened my disposition considerably. I wondered how Phil's father got my number.

It was already five-thirty. I couldn't make it by seven, so I gave them a buzz to say I'd be late. Barnett, who turned out to be old man Grover's manservant, took the call and my message, but wouldn't discuss any details over the airways. That was okay with me.

After finishing with Barnett, I called Ginny to see what she was up to. She was gone. Her vis asked if I'd like to leave a message, so I dropped my pants and returned hers in kind, saying I'd be around her way sometime before the witching hour. I didn't bother with Foley; he had enough problems without dealing with a gumshoe who didn't care whether Mr. MacGruder screwed himself to death or not.

I only lived about a kilometer from the office. Usually I walked it just to keep my feet grounded in something solid, but tonight I was in a hurry. As my bullet moved through the streets, I saw that the garbage hadn't made it after all. Trash was strewn all over the streets. That one-of-a-kind odor drifted through my open windows. It was no worse than pungent now; another day would turn it rancid. Scroungy four- and two-legged animals rummaged through the stuff, vying haunch-to-haunch and elbow-to-elbow for the choicest portions. And in this neighborhood, that wasn't saying a whole lot.

My apartment was a converted basement of a fifteen-story also-ran in the race of durability. It wasn't much, but it beat living in my bullet. The landlord couldn't be depended upon to do anything in the way of maintenance, except for maintaining my rent money in his bank account, so I pretty well took care of the place myself. If the detective business ever got any worse, I'd probably make a pretty good janitor; I like things neat and clean. The place was quite livable with paneled walls and cheap but wearable carpet covering a cement floor that looked like a remnant of the San Francisco earthquake. The only really bad point was the red brick pillars that ran, in double rows, through the entire length of the flat. I couldn't ignore them, so I hung dart boards and pictures and mirrors on all their sides and did the best I could. The place was naturally cool in the summer, and my windows opened up to sidewalk level, which gave me and Black Jack a pretty good leg show whenever we chose to pass the time just watching.

Matilda greeted me with her usual charm when I arrived. She ran between my feet, rubbing her sleek blackness against my legs while staring lovingly up at me with her black-dotted yellow eyes. She wanted something.

"Hungry aren't you?" I said, and reached down to stroke her internally-clicking body. "You broads are all alike."

I gave her what she wanted, then went in and showered. I even shaved, and I'm not a two-shave-a-day man. But then, working for old money was not something I did very often either.

I put on my best suit: a black, form-fitting polyester one-piece that opened in the front down to the sternum. Over that went a tan waistcoat that stayed open. The collar from the suit overhung the lapels of the coat. Boots the same color as the coat climbed to mid calf and zipped up tight. I checked myself in the full-length in the bedroom. I couldn't have been more dashing if I'd been running the two-minute mile.

4

It was a long drive over to the Grovers; the money lived as far away from the death as possible. As I drove, I wondered what they could possibly want with me. The rich boys usually only used my kind for divorce investigations, and I didn't take that sort of junk. I didn't get into the money end of town very often. I'm a very elementary kind of guy, and the electronic limbo of the rich boys went right past me. Life was people to me—a shiv in the throat I could understand; good whiskey I could understand; crying and laughing I could understand. The city, even crumbling and financially crippled, was real to me. Everything else was just confusing.

I got through the crumble, and into the money. You could tell by two things: the condition of the streets and the sophistication of the security systems. The farther I went, the better the defenses got. It began with floodlights and barking dogs, moved to electrified fences and armed guards, and ended with high walls with solid steel gates and heat-sensitive laser turrets. And all the people inside their walls were worrying about what the people outside were up to. I think it was because the people inside knew what they did to get what they had, and didn't want the same thing to happen to them.

The only difference between rich crooks and poor crooks is that the poor ones don't kid themselves about what they're doing.

I reached my destination about seven-fifteen. The Grover house sat on a huge lot that was dotted with a lot of good smog-growing trees and strange, smooth statues done in solid blacks and whites. They were in the high wall category, but their turrets had been shut down and replaced with armed guards. They must have been in something of a financial decline. I hummed up a gravel drive that terminated after a time at the big steel gate. A small, head-sized door slid open at eye level within the gate. A roadmap face with a droopy moustache gouged through the cut-out.

"Name and business," the face said in a voice that sounded the way a broken mirror looks.

"Swain to see Mr. Grover."

The big door creaked to the welcome position and I drove in. The house was large and elliptical, like a grapefruit cut in half and lying on its cut edge. It had no windows. The drive circled in front of the house, coming close to the secured front door at one point. I stopped there. Another guard stood at the front door.

"Leave it running," the man said from the porch. He was a Fancy Dan, with a uniform that was all brass buttons and twined cords and flag patches. He wore a patent leather belt and bandolier, and on his hip rode a boxy-looking frump gun, the messy kind that exploded pellets on impact and left nothing but a pile of warm goo on the ground. His patent leather boots rose almost all the way to his hips as he crunched across the gravel to meet me.

"I'll park it," he said.

I climbed out and stood next to him. "Don't tear the upholstery with those buttons," I told him.

He wanted to say something clever back to me, but either he couldn't think of anything or his job demanded he be nice to visitors. He got silently into the bullet.

"Take good care of it, and don't chip the paint, and maybe I'll give you a nice tip so you can buy yourself a shiny whistle."

"Shove it . . ." he started to say through sneering lips, but instead he set his jaw and drove away. He was a punk. He had a Fancy Dan uniform and a frump gun and patches of flags . . . and he was still a punk.

I wandered up to the door; it spoke to me.

"Name?"

"Abraham Lincoln."

The door was silent. Then, "Could you spell that last name please?"

"Certainly. P-l-e-a-s-e."

"No, no," it said. "The last name from before."

"F-r-o-m . . ."

"Just a minute, please."

Approximately sixty seconds later, a human voice drifted through the door's speaker. "We seem to be having some difficulty," said a familiar-sounding voice. "What is your name please?"

"Swain to see Mr. Grover."

The door opened. Mr. Barnett stood there. He was tall and stooped and dressed in a butler's tunic. He ushered me in. "I'm sorry for the delay," he said, and sounded as if he really was sorry. "I don't know what happened to the door."

"Aw, you know how those gadgets are," I answered.

He looked at me; there was the hint of a twinkle in his eye. "Could you wait here for a moment?"

"Nothing but time."

He shuffled away. I stood in an entrance foyer that reminded me of the Luray Caverns. The ceiling went all the way up to the top of the building, a good three stories straight up. A large chandelier hung on an immense chain all the way down from the ceiling to within touching distance. The floors were marble, or something close to it, and ran in a swirling pattern out from the center point like a pinwheel in motion. Stainless steel stairs extended upwards from my right and left, reaching the second floor rooms that ran around in a circle from an open hallway. There were more rooms to be seen on the third floor, proceeding from stairs on the second. A vast amount of Minimal sculpture done in alabaster and chrome steel sat everywhere, sprouting from every nook and cranny of the room like deformed vegetables. Every blank wall contained a view screen, all of them showing variations on erotic themes. It was cold in there, and it wasn't the kind that could be shut out with an overcoat.

"Are there any more like you at home?"

I turned to the sound. A young woman had moved into the room. She appeared to be in her mid-twenties, short, but nicely constructed. She had a round, olive-complexioned face and large dark eyes that looked the way all women want their eyes to look. Her long black hair, parted in the middle, hung straight down her head, covering her ears and framing her face like a simple yet elegant stage curtain. She wore a diaphanous white gown that hung to the floor, making it look as if she were floating more than walking. The gown hid very little of her dark-skinned body, of which she didn't have a thing to be ashamed.

"Broke the mold when they made me," I said.

She began walking tight circles around me, sizing me up and down like a coat on the rack. "I'm Sheila," she said after a moment.

"Marco Polo," I responded.

She shrugged, then cocked her head to one side. "You're not too bad for a street person."

"Congratulate my mother. I'm looking for Silas Grover."

She stared at me hard for a few seconds, wide-eyed, the way my cat does when she's hungry. "He's having dinner," she said finally, and smiled the kind of smile you put on for the photographer. Then she played will-o'-the-wisp with her fingers. "Come on, I'll take you to meet the old bones."

She turned and led the way through a corniced archway, wiggling her behind enough to throw it out of joint as she walked. We moved down a dark hallway. It was quite narrow, and a rolling pattern of lights slid around the walls and ceiling, making the entire hallway seem to be rotating. It destroyed my equilibrium, and I staggered as I walked, reaching out from time to time to steady myself against the wall. Cute little Sheila kept looking over her shoulder and giggling at me. Cute little Sheila needed her fanny burned.

The hallway ended in a large dining room, although that place could have ruined even the heartiest appetite. The place was done up like a cave. The walls were black, jagged rock, with thick stalactites and stalagmites alternately dripping and growing from the horizontal planes. Thick, verdant moss hung everywhere, and the room smelled cold and musty. Holoprojections of cavemen and various prehistoric rodents and lizards roamed freely through the room, chasing each other and hiding behind rocks. I turned back the way I had come in. The doorway was the cave mouth, and through its opening a projection of a constantly erupting volcano could be seen in the distance. The table sat at the center point of the room. It was a long, rectangular affair that glowed fluorescently from within, providing the only light in the whole room. It was black and very basic, as were the seats, rooted to the floor like tree stumps. This was a change. The last time I'd gone to the fun house, I had to pay for it.

An old man, a taxidermist's dream, sat at the head of the table. He was frail and bent like a twig, and I could have believed for a moment that he was a preserved corpse perpetually fixed in the dining posture. Then he moved, taking the smallest piece of mush on the end of a fork, and bringing it ever so slowly up to ancient, withered lips. He chewed slowly, with great care, as if he were counting the individual bites.

"A street person to see you," the girl said.

He looked slowly up at me, appraising. His eyes held the knowledge and weariness of a thousand years. He carefully raised an arm and motioned for me to sit at his right. I took the seat, and noticed that Sheila sat a little farther down the table. Up close, his face looked waxy—unreal. He was wearing a robe of black silk that seemed to be sporting a proliferation of mechanical devices: small black boxes, mostly, that occasionally flashed tiny colored lights and made whirring noises like tapes rewinding. He had a slight odor of petroleum about him.

"How do you like my house, Mr. Swain?" he asked, and his voice came in a flat, tinny monotone from a circular metal disc attached to his neck.

"I hate it."

A smile just barely touched the corners of his mouth, as if the gesture was painful, but his eyes were laughing. "So do I," he answered. "This is my daughter's gaucherie."

I turned to Sheila. She was watching a burly caveman drag a naked woman across the rock floor by her hair. It figured.

"I can't deny her," Grover said. "She's more like a granddaughter. Dinner?" He smiled again when he saw me appraising the grayish glob that occupied his plate. "I can

26

provide better for you than the fodder my failed health forces me to eat.''

"No, thanks," I answered. "I had some pastrami not too long ago."

He painfully rolled his eyes heavenward. "Ah, pastrami," he said, then took a deep breath. "The things we do to stay alive."

"It's the only game in town, Mr. Grover."

"If you won't break bread with me, how about a drink? I have some thirty-five-year-old scotch."

"You twisted my arm."

"Good." He looked to his daughter, who still sat, pretending not to be listening to the conversation. "Be a good girl, Sheila, and on your way out have Mr. Barnett bring our friend a drink."

"I thought I'd stay," she said, pouting her lower lip.

"No, no. We have personal business to discuss here."

She folded her arms across her chest. "I want to stay," she said, and gave us a I'll-hold-my-breath-till-I-turn-blue look.

"Be a good little girl," I said, "and go play. If you do what Daddy says, I'll give you a piece of candy when we're finished."

She stood up. "Go to hell," she spat, and stamped out of the room.

"Gets her feelings hurt easily," I said.

"You're fresh air, Mr. Swain," Grover said. "I think we can do business together."

"What sort of business? And call me Swain."

"I lost a son today, Swain. Do you have any idea what it feels like to outlive your children?"

I shook my head.

"I feel like I'm gone. I feel like the life has drained out of me and just left the outside crust. I've got all the symptoms of death, with none of the peace of the grave."

He coughed. It was a rasping gut-wrencher that made my skin crawl just to hear it. A white linen napkin came up from his lap and dabbed at his trembling lips.

"I'm old," he said, "older than I thought I'd ever be. I've watched life around me change so that I can't even understand what it's about any more. My habit . . . my routines

27

are all I have to keep me grounded in reality. My body has failed me; my children despise me; my mind tells me things I know can't be true. I'm afraid that if I don't have dinner at seven every evening and a bath at nine, I'll find myself moving around in a maze that I can't get out of. Look at me. I'm half mechanical.''

He lurched several times, very slightly, his already ashen face going completely white with pain. I watched his lips tighten to an angry slash and the muscles of his jaw knot up as his skeletal hands picked up his plate and flung it discuslike across the room. The plate sailed through a projection of a baby dinosaur and crashed loudly against the rock wall.

Grover breathed deeply a couple of times, the pain and the anger subsiding. ''A plane crash started it years ago. There were prosthetic limbs and internal complications. Then my perpetually weakened condition brought me cancer and Parkinson's and atrophy and heaven knows what all. It's all very complicated, I'm afraid, but there's very little of me that doesn't need to be serviced by a mechanic every six months.''

Mr. Barnett shuffled in through a rock-hidden door, with a crystal goblet of scotch in his hand. He placed it before me on the table, then moved to the wall and began picking up the pieces of the broken plate. While the man went about his business, I sat staring at the booze and the way the bottom lighting made it glow like a firefly. I wondered what I was doing there.

''Thank you, Mr. Barnett,'' Grover's mechanical voice intoned when the man was finished cleaning up.

Barnett almost smiled, then wordlessly left the room, his stooped shuffle grating on the rock of the floor.

''What exactly do you want from me?'' I asked when we were alone again.

He shook his head, and pointed with a liverish hand. ''Try that first,'' he said, and watched me expectantly.

I took a sip. It was a spoiler and I told him so.

He nodded happily, vicariously enjoying my delight. Then he saddened. Very slowly, he brought his arms up to rest on the table top. ''I'm not a nice man,'' he said and stared with rancor at the diffused light. ''My life has been one prolonged bout of selfish dissipation. My father was an inventor who made a fortune with some cheap holo patents, a fortune that I've spent my every waking moment trying to squander. At some point along the way, I married, for no other reason than it seemed like the thing to do. My first two children were twins—Phil and his brother Mike. I found them to be an annoyance to my lifestyle, and chose to ignore them to death.''

He looked at me. "Are you condemning me, Swain?"

I shook my head. "Very few people on this earth don't make mistakes.''

Phil and Mike were raised by their mother, and, understandably I suppose, they idolized her. Sheila came later, conceived on one of my infrequent visits home.'' His hand came to his mouth. "God, I was so foolish.'' He shook his head. "Sheila was still young when Maureen died.''

"Your wife?"

He nodded. "The plane crash that left me like this : . .'' he stopped so I could appreciate his infirmity, ''. . . killed Maureen. It was my fault; I was drunk. It took that accident for me to realize just what my life was worth. But it was too late. The boys blamed me for their mother's death and left home as soon as they could. I overcompensated with Sheila, and you can see how she came out. I tried with Phil, tried to get him back. I gave him money, which he took, but it couldn't buy his love . . . or salve his hatred.''

He stopped, his thin lips tightening—quivering. His eyes began to mist over. It was a moment before he could speak again. "Now he's gone. They tell me he was dismembered.''

"Yes,'' I said.

"You saw it?" He found my eyes and held them.

"That's why I was late this evening.''

"I can't bring my son back, Swain. I lost him a long time ago. But can't I be enough of a father to bring some reason to his death? I don't have a lot of time left. I've got to spend it seeing that justice is done. Do you understand any of this?''

I understood. "Why do you want me?" I asked. "I can't begin to compete with the police when it comes to evidence-gathering and investigation.''

"To be perfectly honest with you, I can no longer afford the police.'' He folded his hands on the table top. All at

29

once, a tiny light began flashing angrily on his chest accompanied by a barely discernible buzzer. He jerked back in his chair, his hands shaking uncontrollably.

I jumped up and moved to him.

"P-Please," he rasped. "Please."

"What can I do?"

"Knob . . . on my chest."

"The one with the flashing light?"

"Y-Yes." His tongue protruded grotesquely and his eyes rolled backwards. "Turn . . . it . . . clockwise."

I turned the numbered knob; he relaxed immediately.

He nodded, gulping air. "Thank you, Swain. I always wonder if Sheila would . . ."

"Just take it easy," I said.

He nodded again and relaxed for a few minutes.

"Maybe we should do this some other time," I said, after he had regained his composure.

"No," he said flatly. "I'm a realist, you know. There may not be another time." He took one more deep breath, then began again. "As you no doubt noticed, my fortunes are not what they used to be. Since goods and services in a financially busted city depend solely upon the individual's ability to pay one-to-one for those goods and services, I'm in a bad way. Murder isn't a very high priority item at police headquarters anymore. The estimate for investigating my son's death was astronomical—much more than I could afford."

"But you can afford me."

"Yes." He looked down at the floor as a projected lizard scurried across his foot. "Disgusting," he said softly. "I spoke with Captain Jenkins on the vis this afternoon, and he gave me your name. He said that you had an interest in my son."

"I did some work for him."

He nodded, as if he understood it all. "Will you help me find my son's killer?"

I tilted the glass of scotch and finished it in one gulp. Setting it back down, I looked over at an old, broken man who was desperately looking for something he could believe in, in a world where nothing was real. "I'll need some operating capital."

His eyes lit up. "Would five thousand be all right?"

"Three thousand will do," I said.

Moving slowly, mechanically, he reached into his robe pocket and extracted a check. Setting it on the table, he slid it over to me. It was already made out to my name, only the amount remained blank. "Fill it in yourself, Swain," he said, the corners of his mouth turning upwards. "We haven't discussed your fee yet."

I folded the check and put it in the pocket of my waistcoat. "I usually get three hundred a day plus expenses, payable upon completion of the job to your satisfaction. I'll deduct the expenses from the three thousand."

"Whatever you think," he said. Grover wanted to like me, wanted to trust me, wanted to treat me like he never got to treat his son.

"I want you to understand," I said, "that I can't guarantee anything on this. Chances are, we're dealing out of a cold deck."

"Do what you can," he said.

I shrugged. "What did you know about Phil's habits?"

He frowned. "Nothing at all. He came by the house once a month to pick up his check. He'd have dinner with me, just as you are doing now. We'd try to talk, but it never worked. He'd stare at his food, or look at me as if I wasn't there, then he'd pocket his money and leave. The last several times I saw him, he seemed highly agitated—nervous. Then on his usual day the last time, he didn't show up. That was three weeks ago."

"When you did talk, what was it about?"

"Money, always money. He was concerned about our financial problems and, I think, angry that there wasn't going to be anything left for him when I die."

"You mentioned a brother."

The old man coughed through his disc. It wasn't as bad as the last one. "Mike hated me even more than Phil. He refused to accept any help from me at all after his mother died. He left home as soon as he was able and I never heard from him again."

"How long ago was that?"

"Twenty years."

31

"What about Sheila? What was her relationship with Phil?"

"They didn't get along," he said. "Phil left home when she was small. To her, he was just a stranger who came by for money, like a bill collector."

"There's something that I don't understand," I said. "If you treated your wife so badly, why did she stay with you all those years?"

"She loved me," he said, and I didn't believe him. "I'm getting tired now. I think I'd better take a nap."

"Just one more question," I said, and watched him carefully. "Why was Phil committed to a mental institution?"

"Stress," he said, and his eyes got hard. "That subject is totally unrelated to the problem at hand. I don't wish to discuss it further." He reached out a coarse, spastic hand. I shook it. His grasp was weak as yesterday's coffee grounds. "You'll have to excuse me. I'm getting quite tired."

He tried to stand. "I can see myself out," I said, and made my way back through the cave mouth.

"Thank you, Swain," he called weakly to me.

"Thank me later," I replied, and plunged headlong into the rotating hallway. When I got to the foyer, Sheila was waiting for me by the front door—blocking it. "Isn't it past your bedtime?" I asked.

She moved to me as seductively as she could. Being beautiful and rich made seduction a game she didn't have to play very often. She plastered her body against mine and, entwining those rich girl fingers around my neck, tried to pull my mouth down to meet hers. "You're a dangerous man," she said huskily when we were nose to nose. "That excites me."

"Was your brother Phil dangerous?" I asked her mouth.

"Phil was a self-righteous bastard," she said, and physically tried to climb up my body when I wouldn't meet her lips. "I'm glad he's dead."

I pried her arms from around my neck. She was off balance and fell heavily to the floor. She glared up at me, rubbing her wrists. "What are you, some kind of fag?" she said, and her voice was as hard as a slumlord's heart.

"Yeah," I answered, "I'm a fag."

Her eyes traveled down to my crotch. There were some

32

things that savoir-faire couldn't disguise. She smiled with her full mouth and stood again, tongue running across her lips. "So, you *do* like what you see."

"I like you just fine," I answered, "but I work for your daddy, and you weren't part of our agreement."

Her eyes narrowed. "What exactly *was* your agreement?"

"I'm just the hired hand. You'd have to ask the boss about that."

"Did you discuss the rest of the family?" she asked and leaned her back against the door.

"We discussed a lot of things."

"Did he tell you about my sister Angie?"

"You tell me," I answered.

Her black eyes smoldered, as she kissed the air four or five times. "Make me." She giggled, pushing her way past me to run up the stairs. She reached the landing and ran around the hallway to disappear behind one of the doorways, her shrill laughter drifting back like heartburn from a ballpark hot dog.

I shrugged and turned to the door. It had no knobs. I pushed it this way and that, but couldn't budge the thing. After a minute of frustration, Mr. Barnett shuffled in, the train of his tunic draped over his arm. He hummed a certain pitch into a tiny speaker and the door swung open.

"Thanks," I said, and he responded with his usual smile. "Say, what's the story on Angie Grover?"

Barnett looked surprised. "Mr. Grover told you about Angela?"

"The subject came up. I was wondering about how I could talk to her."

He shook his old, white head. "There's nothing she could tell you . . . about anything." He changed the subject. "Thank you for helping Mr. Grover. It meant a lot to him."

"Yeah. I'm a regular guardian angel."

I got the feeling that Barnett wanted to tell me something. I gave him a few seconds then started out the door.

"Mr. Swain . . ."

I turned around.

He looked behind him, then at me. "I didn't tell Mr. Grover this, because I was afraid it would upset him."

"Go on."

"Phil Grover called here yesterday. He didn't want to talk to his father, but to Sheila."

"Do you know what they talked about?"

He looked indignant. "I haven't kept my job here for thirty years by being a snoop," he said.

I nodded. "Good night."

"Good night."

I walked out the door and it closed right behind me. Mr. Barnett wasn't a snoop, but he sure knew that I was helping the old man, all right. The door wished me well as I went down the two-step landing, but I didn't answer. It had gotten dark while I was in there, and a full moon was spilling dull light through the smog cover.

My bullet was parked a little way down the drive. The Fancy Dan wasn't anywhere in sight, so I walked to it. My hand was on the door handle when I realized that something was wrong. I was still toying with it in my mind when I heard the crunch of gravel behind me. As I swung around, I saw the punk guard as a blur of arm and I knew I was going to get hit with the butt of his frump. I wanted to get my arms up, but instinctively knew it to be a useless gesture. In that second, I was sure that the thing was going to clip me good. I tried to move with it, roll with the blow. It caught me on the temple, and the whole world went bright white as I went backward with the force. The bullet was behind me; I banged it full force and gutted over and pain rattled my ribs.

Somehow I kept my feet and saw the punk rearing back again through a bleached haze. My right eye, where the frump had hit, still wasn't any good to me. He tried to swing, but I slumped forward, jamming him so he couldn't get a good lick. I caught him in a bear hug, still too hurt and weak to fight back, and his next one banged me, without apparent effect, on the upper back. I just pushed and lifted, bringing him up off his feet, and anger was the only thing that kept me moving. All I did then was fall. I fell like a dead man right on top of him, and when we hit bottom his private parts were wedged between my knee and the gravel.

A choking sound came out of his throat, as if his insides were all trying to get out. His eyes bugged so much I thought they'd unsocket. I wanted to lie there and pound the face

34

below me and let my own hurt subside, but I knew he wasn't the only punk on the grounds.

I rolled off him. He was gurgling and puking as I tried to get to my feet. My vision was blurred and blood was streaming down the right side of my face. The loss of equilibrium made my stomach go butterflies and I fell back to my knees twice before I could get up.

The wide, moon-glowing yard was tilting crazily, like the deck of a hurricane ship, and two dark forms were coming across it. I looked around for the punk's frump. He must have rolled on it. I fell upon him and roughly rolled him aside. The gun was on the ground. The punk grunted once and began puking some more.

"Right there, right there," I said, pointing toward the running forms. They stopped ten meters from me. My vision was still twisted, and free-flowing blood was getting in my eye. I wiped it off with the back of my hand. "On the ground," I yelled. "On your stomachs."

They did as they were told.

"Hands behind your heads."

They did that too. I quickly moved to them, as the ground danced a mazurka beneath my feet. They were guards, too, but they didn't look like punks. They both had Class III, nonlethal lasers on their hips. I took their guns and threw them as far as I could.

"Now just lie there like good little boys," I told them, "and everybody's head will stay on his shoulders."

I looked toward the house, which looked as if it were getting ready to roll away. I didn't know what was going on, but it seemed to me that going back in there might be something like Daniel reentering the lion's den. I opted for the front gate.

Stumbling back to the car, I stopped only long enough to kick the punk who had hit me. When I climbed in, the key was still in the ignition. I started the thing and tried to drive it down a double-vision gravway. It was weaving badly; I kept shaking blood out of my eyes. The frump lay beside me on the seat. As I neared the gate, I picked it up and made sure the safety was off.

The guard wasn't in his station by the gate, and the steel

doors were shut tight. I swung my gaze quickly, and caught a moonlit glimpse of something metallic from behind a large mimosa tree to my right. I pointed and fired. The first frump blew my side window to the place I hoped that punk guard would go when he died. The second reduced the mimosa to a year's supply of toothpicks. I figured if the guard was behind it, he was either buried in sawdust or halfway to Hoboken. I transferred the frump to my left hand and, sticking it out the open driver's side window, pumped what was left in the gun at the gate before me. There were explosions and the sound of rending metal. When the smoke cleared, the gate was halfway open, one side contorted and torn part way off the hinges.

I bumped the bullet through the demolished place, wiped off the frump, and threw it out the window. I was beginning to feel as if my stomach had been used as a welcome mat for Hannibal's army.

I nosed off the private drive onto the streets, feeling like I might lose consciousness. Ginny's place was a lot closer to this end of town than mine, so I headed in her direction. She was a semi-rich girl, but I didn't hold that against her.

I moved slowly, trying to figure out which of the streets I saw before me was real, and wondering where I'd get the money to fix the busted glass of the bullet's window.

Then I remembered the check in my pocket.

5

I was leaning against Ginny's door when she opened it. I didn't intend to fall on the floor that way, but I guess the door was supporting me more than I realized. Everything was really sporadic then anyway, so I wasn't too surprised or even embarrassed about that turn of events.

"Thought I'd drop in," I managed, as she bent over me making concerned noises. It must have been time for me to take a nap. I probably said something to that effect just before it all drifted away in visions of Virginia Teal with floating hair and laughing eyes and love up to here.

Pain replaced sweet dreams after a while, and I knew it was time to wake up. My eyes didn't feel much like opening, but eventually I convinced them that getting things moving again was necessary, and they fluttered to light.

I was able to focus this time, and the first thing I saw was Ginny's face puckered in disapprobation.

"When I told you to kick the girls out of your bed," she said, "I didn't realize they'd kick back." Her accent had just a touch of the South that raised her, like Tabasco in a bloody Mary.

I tried to grin. My brain was playing print-out typer on the inside of my skull. "What round is this?" My hand went to my temple; it was wrapped in bandages. "Well, did I knock all my brains out?"

"That's the least of your worries, sweetheart," she replied, and kissed me lightly on the cheek. "You didn't have any to begin with."

I sat up slowly. My head felt like a half-packed suitcase at first, but after a minute it cleared somewhat and the pain centered in the area of the cut. I held up my watch and read its face. It was 3:00 A.M.

"Bad?" she asked.

"Nothing that a drink and a smoke won't cure."

Ginny shook out a cig, then went into the other room to find the bottle. She was wearing a white body stocking that fit her like a second skin. There was supposed to be a flowing robe that went over it, but that was nowhere to be seen. Maybe I had died and gone to heaven.

I had the fag, but no fire. So I stuck it in my mouth and chewed on the filter until she returned with a tumbler full of Black Jack and cold ice. She found a match, and I got underway.

After a few drags, I tapped the large bandage. "What does it look like?"

She sat next to me on the bed that she had somehow managed to get me into. My blood-soaked clothes lay in a ball on the floor. "You've got a pretty good gash. I closed it with a bunch of Domine butterflies, so it should heal within a couple of days. You're going to have an ugly bruise for a while, though."

"Concussion?"

She shook her head and lightly ran the palms of her hands over my bare chest. "Don't think so. You just passed out from the shock before. What happened anyway?"

"The guards on my new client's estate aren't the friendliest in the world."

"With friends like that . . ."

"Yeah. But you should've seen the other guy." I took a sip of the booze. It made me feel better immediately.

"I've got some pain killers you could take for that," she said. "Make you wish you busted your head open every day."

I leaned the glass against my forehead. "No, thanks. I like to remember my mistakes."

"Masochist."

"Yeah. How was your trip?"

She shrugged. "I bought some art from some Austrians

and sold it to some Japanese. Then I traded a boat load of cocoa beans for a space-freighter load of Martian iron, then sold the iron for an undetermined amount of francs with which I purchased a tanker full of Iranian oil.''

"What are you going to do with the oil?''

"Not sure yet. I'm thinking of letting it spill off Martha's Vineyard, so that I can sell them my laboratory full of oil-eating microorganisms, which are eating *me* out of house and home.'' She replaced the hands on my chest with her red, red lips. "You didn't vis me once while I was away, you naughty boy.''

"Neither did you,'' I answered. I took another drink, then emptied both of my hands. Moving over, I made enough room for Ginny next to me on the bed. She slid up until we were both touching all over, and I remembered why dinner with Aunt Gertrude was never a very satisfying experience.

My mind was whirling with several strange happenings at once, not the least of which being my treatment at the hands of Grover's people. Ginny's lips came up to nibble on mine as her fingers gently spider-danced up and down my body. I needed to get my perspective on the Grover case, but there was really nothing I could do until the morning. Besides, at the moment I was drowning in a sea of tender loving care that would have made Hippocrates' bedside manner pale by comparison.

I hoped that I had given Matilda enough to eat, for I didn't expect that I'd be getting home any time soon.

Ginny began to growl down deep in her throat.

6

So I sat leaning on her formica table top drinking real coffee laced with Black Jack for the ache in my head, watching a fag consume itself in a metamorphic rock ashtray, and wondering why my new clients beat me up.

Ginny sat on her hanging couch, glued to her mammoth vis screen, enrapt in the readouts of the morning's stock market quotations. Parmoth, her man on the floor, appeared as a small insert at the upper right hand corner of the screen. His smooth, multi-lifted face remained porcelain smooth, except for occasional head bobs in response to orders.

I took a long drag of the smoker, then laid it back in the ashtray. "Does it make any sense to you?" I asked.

She turned and glanced at me quickly over the back of the sofa. "Nothing you do makes any sense to me," she replied, then turned back to the screen. "Sell that Merriweather junk when it gets to forty and buy into that aluminum reprocessing thing." Back to me. "I only keep you around because you're good in the sack."

"You think I overreacted?"

"Probably." She turned. "Whatever became of those mining expeditions on Venus?" Her screen switched to a progress report on mechanical mining operations on that planet's surface. "Parmoth, get us out of U.S. Steel and into the company that's making the drill bits on those diggers."

I finished my coffee and got some more, holding it under the mike-rod to heat it up. My head felt a little better, but my pride was still damaged. The more I thought about it, the more I was convinced that the Grover family had nothing to do with the attack on me. But what did that leave?

When Ginny had finished her dealing, I moved over to sit with her on the couch, bringing my coffee with me. She looked good in the short terrycloth robe that had been mine at one time. My business couldn't be so casually handled. I was wearing a loose-fitting tan one-piece. After the mess I had made of my clothes, it was fortunate that I kept things at her place.

"Use your vis?" I asked, setting my coffee on the floor.

"What's mine is yours," she returned and lay down on the sofa resting her legs on my lap.

"Business call," I said, and shoved her legs out of camera range. "You wouldn't want those people to think that I was playing around on their time?"

"You," she said, and pointed a red-nailed, accusing finger, "are an old fogey."

I called the Grover house. Might as well make sure my job was intact before doing any work. Mr. Barnett came on the line. His eyebrows wanted to take out a pilot's license when he saw me.

"What happened?" he asked.

"That's my line," I answered. "What the hell's going on out there?"

He shook his head. "Two of the guards came and told us you forced them to the ground at gunpoint. When I went out to check, the gate was demolished and you, along with the other two guards, were gone. What's wrong with your head?"

"One of your boys used it for batting practice. How long those guys work for you anyway?"

He thought for a minute, his crystal blue eyes floating in his aging face like diamonds in a nickel-plated setting. "The two who stayed have been with us since we got rid of the turrets, about two years ago. The other two started about three weeks ago, when two of our old hands quit on the same day."

"Let me talk to your boss," I said. Ginny began tickling my ribs with her big toe. I slapped it away.

"Mr. Grover doesn't talk on the vis."

41

"He will this time," I answered. "Tell him it's me and what happened."

Barnett blanked his screen. His story made some sense to me. If that Fancy Dan had wanted to do me in at the old boy's order, there sure as hell would have been a lot of easier ways of doing it. First, they would have used all their lousy guards, not just that one punk. Second, he would have just frumped me to shards and let it go at that. No, that clown wanted to take care of me quietly, then get me out of there and dump me someplace. The gate guard was in on it too. It began to look as if the guards who pulled the disappearing act had been planted on the Grover place. But why?

Mr. Grover's mechanical face appeared on the screen. He looked tired. "Mr. Barnett told me that the guards attacked you last night," he said. His face looked like it was lost out in never-never-land somewhere. "I don't know what to tell you, except that I'm sorry."

"I just wanted to make sure it wasn't some eloquent way of taking me off the case."

"You're my only hope, Swain."

He wore a look of quiet determination, like that of a three-legged dog trying to catch a rabbit. I wanted to ask him about the things he had kept from me the night before, but I thought I'd follow up what leads I had without prying until I had to.

"I'll keep in touch," I said, and blanked off.

Ginny got on her knees and scooted over next to me, going after my ear with her tongue.

"The meter's running, lady," I said, standing up. "Some of us poor slobs have to work for a living."

She smiled up at me, letting her robe part dramatically to reveal as nice a birthday suit as ever came down the pike. "Give it up, Mathew, and move in with me. I promise to keep you busy."

I headed for the door. "I already invested in a new pair of walking shoes," I told her over my shoulder. "Let's talk about it when the leather wears out."

"Bastard," she called after me.

"Flatterer," I returned, and got out the door.

Ginny lived way up in one of those top-security apartments; the kind that made the Marmeth look like a public toilet. I went down the tube and entered the scan booth that checked my voice and fingerprints and EEG before letting me through four double-steel doors that led to the parking garage. The underground car park was large enough to hold a soccer stadium and tiered out the same way. It glowed sterile white from unseen light sources, so that monsters couldn't hide in recessed shadows. Most of the precautions in these places were unnecessary, but crime-fear was the major preoccupation of the rich, and the safer something looked, the more they liked it.

Somehow, I had remembered to keep my token from the night before. I walked over to one of the railed platforms that lined up like secretaries at the automat on a bare wall, and stepping inside, stuck the flat card in the slot on the rail. The platform rose hesitantly from the floor and moved straight up. Row after row of bullets stacked one upon the other slid past my gaze, and I realized that I had no idea of where I had left mine.

The platform stopped on row thirteen, then moved horizontally until it reached my home away from home. Then it slid between the bullets to a wide berth that sat behind. I got out and the thing glided back to the central pool. I was seventy meters up and still below ground level.

In the garish light, I examined the bullet's damage. The window needed to be replaced, and the body was dented somewhat from cause or causes unknown. It had probably happened getting through the Grovers' gate. Getting inside, I reached through the window and laid my hand on the lighted panel that was positioned next to the parking slot. There was a sound like an arcade bell and the bullet slipped backwards on teflon runners. A section of the wall climbed away behind me, and I was plopped on a dark, winding, cement-surrounded roadway just large enough for one vehicle.

Humming the bullet to life, I drove through the man-made cavern at an ever-increasing angle, until it terminated in a cell-like grating. The grate opened with a sandpaper sound as soon as I pulled up.

"Have a nice day," a voice said, and I drove into the smog light.

7

It was going to be another scorcher, and the threat of rain was still handy, like alleyway limb strippers. Police toured the streets in force, and Fancy Dans were everywhere the coppers weren't.

I didn't like the nice neighborhoods; everyone carried guns as if they were walking sticks.

My first stop was the bank. I made it back to my end of town by ten-thirty and got to the bank a few minutes later. Before driving into the womb, I filled in the three thousand dollar amount on Grover's check, then endorsed the thing.

I pulled right up to the car-sized womb, and it opened its maw to admit me. It was pitch dark in there and body-temperature warm. The door clanged loudly behind me.

"Deposit or withdrawal?" a sympathetic mechanical voice asked.

"Withdrawal."

"Do you have an account with us?"

"Yes."

"Is this your personal check?"

"No."

"Have you written your account number under your endorsement on the reverse of the draft?"

I sighed. "No."

A tinny buzzer sounded, as an arm extended from the wall nearest my window. Red holowords floated in the air before my windshield. They read: ENDORSE CHECK PROPERLY, USE LIGHT TO EVALUATE ENDORSEMENT, DO NOT ATTEMPT TO STEAL PEN.

I reached out and pulled the flexible arm into the bullet. A pen was attached to the arm on a chain, and the arm itself terminated in a penlight. I pulled the light down to look at the check, then used the pen to fill in my account number.

The writing changed. SOUND HORN WHEN FINISHED.

I beeped once, and the penlight arm retracted back into its niche. To my left, a picture of a check lit on the wall. "You may affix your check if everything is in order," the voice said.

I stuck the check in the little gripper hands below the lighted picture. It was time to check me out. The womb immediately filled with a cool, foglike mist, and I passed out at once.

When I came back around, three grand in tens and twenties lay on my lap in a plastic folder. I stuck the bills in my wallet just as the wall in front of me opened and requested that I leave quickly for the convenience of customers waiting to use the facility.

I sat around for a while.

When I left the bank, the office was my first stop. The bullet needed to be taken care of, but I didn't have time to mess with it right then. The garbage still hadn't been picked up from Tuesday, and most of it lay strewn across the sidewalks already scavenged by the local vultures. The smell was as I had predicted. I rolled my driver's window up, but the rot odor oozed through the passenger side and made me curse the sanitation department.

Street crowds were sparse. It was still close enough to the first of the month so that everyone was narcotized from the government's monthly welfare drug rations. If it remained this hot, though, by the time the dope ran out near the end of the month, there'd be blood on the streets. It was going to be a long, hot summer.

Just like last year.

And the year before.

I hummed up to the crumbling curb in front of the office. A Mexican kid with eyes that were fifty years older than his body, sat on the stoop, probably waiting for me. I gave him a fiver to watch the bullet for me, with the promise of another if he made sure nothing happened to it. Then I trudged up the steps.

The office window faced east, so that I could catch the morning sun. But the smog cover was too thick, and it was already near eleven, so all that rolled onto my desk top through the slatted blinds was a fuzzy gray glow that made me think of dingy underwear.

The bandage was beginning to bother me. I sat in my swivel chair, the springs creaking their good-morning song, and pulled off the taped gauze. There was some blood on the head side of the thing, but it was dried and inconsequential. I flipped on my vis and turned it to monitor what the desk camera saw. My face came up on the screen immediately. The gash was there, but it was closed well and healing nicely. Ginny had done a good job. I magnified my face until the wall was filled with my right temple. It *was* going to leave an ugly bruise, but nothing that I couldn't live with.

I opened the big drawer and brought out my old friend. Pouring a good-sized shot, I set to work. There wasn't a lot I knew about Phil Grover. He was about five years older than me, lived in relative comfort in an almost nice part of town, apparently got his lifestyle from an old-money father who was on the skids, and was dead because he got into something over his head. He was also interested enough in the whereabouts of a woman to hire a private digger to find out about her. I put that file up on the screen, the one that Jumpstreet Harry was so interested in yesterday. A film rolled of a statuesque young woman with auburn hair cropped short and high arching eyebrows that roofed oriental-looking eyes. It was a mosquito cam film taken by my sometime associate, George Wesley, and showed her shopping for video stimulators in various electric marts. Her stats appeared as readout inserts at the bottom of the video.

Her name was Mina Goulding. That much info Grover gave me. The rest was a lot tougher. I went through the vis directory, and talked to thirty or so Gouldings without any satisfaction. A little fancy footwork with the vis people and I got the names in the unlisted category. Of those, one family refused to talk to me. I checked with their neighbors and found that Harry and Marabeth Goulding did indeed have a daughter named Mina. She was around twenty, and had left the Goulding home two years previously, never to return.

I talked to my friends at the Social Security then, and found that she had used her card to work as a cocktail waitress the first year of that time—then nothing. I went to her old boss at the Zanzi-Bar and found that she had abruptly quit one day without notice. One of her friends from the club was still working there. I oiled her jaws with a few dollars, and found that Mina had been sleeping with a very rich man who had offered to put her to work in his organization. She said it was strange, but the man had Mina change her name to Helen Trent. He then moved her to an uptown hotel, the name of which the girl couldn't remember. A few more dollars cleared up the temporary amnesia, and I found out that Mina Goulding alias Helen Trent was living in the Richmond Hotel. I had staked myself out across the street and watched the place until I saw her coming out and recognized her from a photo that her friend at the bar had showed me. With her new name, I found out that she was working at the Bermax Corporation, a privately run research foundation that tried to peddle its discoveries to the government or private industry. I had George take the films and give them to Grover, which ended my connection with the whole business.

The interesting thing about the Goulding case, besides the name change, was that in all my digging for the girl, I never found anything that linked her to Grover. But she was the wild card, the one obvious short circuit on the board. If I needed an earful, Mina Goulding was the front-running set of gums.

I was convinced that old man Grover had told me everything he thought was important about his son, but I wasn't sure about Sheila. She had apparently been one of the last people to talk to Phil before he died. Sheila and I were going to have to have a little heart-to-heart—and soon. Then there was Angela, who couldn't tell anyone anything about anything. I'd have to chew on that one for a while.

There were two other things: the readouts on Grover's vis. The simplest way to check those out would be to buzz them and see what happened. I punched up the digits on the first one, and set Black Jack on the desk in front of my return camera to block it off. After a few rings, a young person of doubtful gender appeared on the screen.

"Good morning," it said. "Bermax Corporation."

"Sorry, wrong fiber," I answered and rang off.

Bermax. The name had come up twice already, and I had myself a focal point. It may not have meant anything. Not knowing Grover's connection with Mina Goulding, I didn't know his connection with Bermax. Perhaps he just wanted to call her there to say hello. Although ten at night was hardly the time to be calling a business vis.

I tried the other number. A small, grizzled man with a rodent face focused on my screen. He was hunched over a stainless steel control board as if he were trying to burrow into its top.

"I can't see you," he said urgently. "I can't see you."

I moved the bottle out of camera range. "Sorry," I said.

He breathed a sigh of relief and brought a handkerchief up to wipe a many-furrowed forehead. "I thought it was something on this end." He sat quietly for a few seconds, then looked up at the screen—startled. "Central Data," he said. "May I help you?"

Central Data was the net connection for every vis in town. If you needed information not programmed into your home vis, you got it from there.

"Yeah," I said. "I've got a small problem here. Last night a friend of mine used the data pool from my vis. I was wondering about the cost of that call so I could, you know, charge him for it."

The little man squinted at the screen. "We don't give out free information here."

"Oh, I'd be willing to pay for it."

"The cost to find that out would probably be as much as his usage."

"I like to keep everything on the up-and-up."

He eyed my image suspiciously. I smiled broadly back at him.

"Highly irregular," he said. "Unprecedented. Foolish. Wasteful."

"Please."

"It'll cost you eight dollars."

"Just tag it on my bill."

"Oh, all right," he said, darting his little mole head around. "What was the number?"

I quickly punched Grover's file into my typer, and his vis number read out on my screen. I told it to the little man.

"What time?"

"Between ten and eleven last night."

"Just a minute." He began intently punching buttons with his stubby fingers. He worked his mouth as if he were talking to the machine as it went about its business.

Within seconds, a sound like marbles dropping into a tin can came through my vis, then a moving line of writing marched across the screen accompanied by a sonorous male voice reading the text. It was the transcript of what was known as the Emergency Quarantine Act of 2023, the bill that legally kept the mutants in Old Town. There were also summaries of pertinent court challenges stemming from that bill. Strange.

"That was a . . . ten dollar question," the man said.

"See, I saved two dollars."

He raised his bushy eyebrows. "You want that charged to the same number?"

"Absolutely," I answered. "Bye."

He frowned and blanked off.

I sat and looked at the empty screen. What in the hazy world could be Grover's interest in a sixty-year-old law. Most people tried to ignore the existence of Old Town. Phil Grover was researching it an hour before his death.

The story of Old Town and Ground Zero was not one that many people were proud of. Ground Zero used to be the city. In the middle of the twentieth century it had been a thriving little community that was distinguished only by the number of cowboy hats its inhabitants wore, and the three gargantuan cooling towers connected to the primitive fission reactors that provided power for Texas in the 1980s. Then there was the meltdown, and life in south-central Texas would never be the same again.

The government blocked off a large section around the meltdown area for a time after the disaster, but after several years they could no longer keep out the curiosity-seekers, and they were allowed to enter at their own risk. It became quite a tourist attraction, I suppose, for tourist-oriented businesses began to sprout up around the outskirts of the poisoned areas. A city grew from those businesses—a large city that crawled, then stumbled, then walked, then chewed up land by the thousands of acres. Industry settled because of antiunion sentiment and the usually nice weather. When the northern cities all began to go under, everyone moved down to the promised land of plenty. Soon, the original idea of the city was swallowed up in the jaws of progress.

All except for one thing.

The people who set up those original businesses, and their descendants and their descendants' descendants had all been exposed to concentrated doses of radiation for long periods of time. Their life expectancies were short; there were birth defects and mutations; there was congenital insanity. The people from there couldn't leave to work anywhere else, for no one wanted to hire those who were exposed and contagious. Finally, the Quarantine Bill forced them to stay there under penalty of law. So they stayed, serving what was left of the tourist trade and living off government handouts. The tourist trade disappeared eventually, as did the age of prosperity, which terminated the same way that the northern industrial state fell. The city went broke, and Old Town just got crazier.

I really hoped that Grover's interest in Old Town was purely scholarly.

I needed more than the sketchy information I had about Grover. Taking another drink, I leaned down and punched up the Credit Bureau's number. A woman came on. She had red-rimmed, staring eyes, and her mouth was set in a permanent frown that had deeply etched her face, giving her premature jowls. She looked at me, unblinking.

"Yeah?"

"Albert Lee," I told her.

Her hand came up and slid a thin, pink reef in the side of her slash mouth, the color clashing with her maroon lipstick and cantaloupe complexion. Her hand freed, she got me Lee's extension.

Her face dissolved and the happy moon-face of Lee appeared. He was smiling with a mouth so big it could chew on a pocketcom and still have room to whistle the National Anthem. His cesspool-brown skin shone with highlights, and his eyes widened to umber-speckled ivory pools when he saw me.

"Swain," he said, and laughed low. He brought his voice down to a mumble. "Baby wants a new pair of shoes."

"Philip Grover," I said. "Marmeth Arms."

"The rich stiff?" he asked, and I thought his smile would crack his cheeks.

"Not so rich after all," I answered.

"Or they wouldn't hire you," he laughed and his eyes got bigger.

"Now remember your Christian charity, Albert."

"Rich stiffs who make the news cost extra," he said, and winked.

"How much?"

"Hundred."

The amount didn't bother me, even though it was twice our usual figure; but I didn't want him to think I was easy, or we'd go through the inflated prices every time I called him. So, we haggled back and forth for a while, finally deciding on seventy, which was probably ten more than he expected to come away with. He perked up like a sheik with a new harem.

"It's a wonderful life," he said, while punching something on his typer. "The bank's open."

I used my typer to clear the seventy through my account and transfer to his. After a moment, a readout on the bottom of our screens informed us that the transaction had been completed. A moment after that Phil Grover's data was reading out on my vis.

I didn't get much for my investment. Usually the Credit Bureau knew everything from your shoe size to your favorite breakfast cereal to how many times you screw your spouse a week, but Phil might just as well have been the little man who wasn't there. He had no credit on his own; his bank account was guaranteed at five thousand a month by his father's credit. He had lived at the Marmeth for nearly ten years in the same apartment. He had no police record, save the incidents already mentioned, conducted all his business in cash, and had apparently never worked a day in his life. He had no bad habits to speak of, never spent his jack in the local nightspots, or in the liquor or dope stores, or the electrosex parlors. There was one note of interest, though. Grover had built up a savings account over the years of nearly thirty grand. He had cleaned out the account one day, drew it all out in long green. It was the same day that I turned over my file on Mina Goulding. That withdrawal was the last record of account listed to Phil Grover. The period at the end of the sentence.

I blanked Lee and lit a fag.

8

As much as I hated the smell of police stations, it looked like I was going to have to program myself over there. I'd worked on charity murders before. Usually the cops were happy to turn over their preliminary work on a case, just to clean out the files and get it out of their hands. Murder was in the high financial risk category with the police because they couldn't collect from the victim. Fewer than ten percent were ever investigated; fewer than one percent were ever brought to conclusion. It was just too costly and time-consuming a project to be worthwhile to any but the very rich.

On the open market, my friend Black Jack was worth more than human life.

It was eleven-thirty. If I was going to get to the station house before everyone became embroiled in a two-hour lunch, I had to leave then. Standing to the spring song, I moved out of the office and down the wood-rotted stairs with dirt-smeared paint on either side because there was no banister and people supported themselves by groping up and down the walls.

The big white- and red-crossed meat machine had floated down when I got to the streets, and was blocking the road next to my bullet. The fusion-waste helium trucks roved the skies, keying on sudden drops in human body temperature. Two black-garbed attendants had picked up a body and were sliding it down the chute in the truck back, into the acid pit below. It was the kid I had hired to watch my bullet. His throat had been cut from ear to ear. It was jagged, a bottle slash. He had probably been murdered for his five. His old man's eyes stared vacantly at the smog bank as he swooshed down the slide to be eaten away by popping, bubbling liquids.

The van was efficient, if not overly romantic. It was finished and gone in a matter of minutes. Meat-machine people didn't waste time—they had quotas. I silently watched it climb back into the sky like some mechanical grim reaper and hide itself in the smog bank. When the time came, I'd take that last slide and go out the same way. It was perhaps the only return I'd ever see on my tax dollars. Just my luck that I wouldn't be around to appreciate it.

The ride to headquarters was eventful only in my brain. I thought about the dead kid with the air-conditioned throat, and wondered if the bottomless pit might not have a bottom after all. Life seemed to me a forest where the tall-growing trees overshadowed the smaller ones, cutting off their sun and sustenance, leaving them to rot and finally die, and eventually to crash to the ground—alone and unwanted. What would I be watching when I went down the chute?

Tenth Street Station was firmly entrenched in the decay, a good five blocks from any sign of the living city. When I started in this business ten years ago, Tenth Street was still thriving and breathing. Ten years could change a lot of things.

I found a parking spot about a block from my destination, next to the rusted hulk of an overturned letterbox. It started to drizzle just as soon as I got out of the bullet, and I wished that I had gotten the window replaced first thing. The sprinkle was warm and iron-oxide red. Instead of cleaning the streets and air, it just made everything seem dirtier.

The station was a three-floor stone building built in the neo-Gothic storybook style that had been so popular with the pseudo-Utopians of the early twenty-first century. It was gray on gray, with two cylindrical castle turrets near the apex. Its high, pointed roof was a ruddy brown—the Mecca, apparently, for every pigeon within crapping distance. One day the whole roof would collapse from the weight of bird shit.

A long flight of quarry stone steps led up through the cathedral-arched doorway and into the station. I took the steps two at a time and went into the monkey house. The noise rolling out was overpowering, like an overweight soprano belting out an aria in a portable toilet.

The lobby was jammed with people, all of them yelling to make themselves heard over the others who were yelling to make themselves heard over them. Around the room, uniformed police sat at desks or stood behind partitions, listening to whoever was yelling the loudest or flashed the most money. The rate schedule was flashing on a huge neon quotation board that occupied an entire wall, but everyone thought his was a special case that didn't fit the regular payment category.

I pushed my way through sardine central, and up to the desk sergeant and head cashier, Mort Dooks. He sat in a teller's cage atop a platform high enough to get him above the crush. He wore a green plastic visor to cut out the glare of the harsh overhead counting light.

"Mort," I called up to him.

He saw me standing there below him, and motioned for me to take the steps that led up to the cage. I moved up. He was counting a large stack of bills, every now and then stopping to lick his thumb. "How's it going, Swain?" he asked loudly. "I thought you'd be dead by now." He put a clip on the stack and stuffed it into a drawer.

"Matter of opinion," I returned.

A young cop with a change machine on his gunbelt came up the steps next to me and handed some more bills to Dooks. "A Mr. Emory gave me this. Says he saw in the vis news that we were running a special on evictions."

"Did he have a coupon?" Dooks asked.

"Un uh."

Dooks handed the money back. "Tell him he can't cash in on the special unless he's clipped the coupon from the bargain sheet we were selling last month."

"Jumpstreet here?" I asked him.

He jerked his thumb, and started counting another pile of money. "He's upstairs . . . but watch out. Your buddy Mack is up there, too."

"Then Fat Mack's the one who'd better watch out."

Two complainants in the assault line began mixing it up as if they really meant business. Four crowd-control uniforms emerged from the shadows armed with twenty-four-inch lead-weighted billy clubs, and began swinging freely into the crowd. There was a pocket of confusion, like a jar full of flies, and the uninvolved part of the crowd moved aside. A knife flashed from somewhere, and one of the cops pulled his service laser and started firing. When everyone had finally settled down, there were five people left lying on the ground. Working in pairs, the cops would drag them across the stone floor by the shoulders and roll them down the big steps outside. As the last body was dragged off, the crowd again filled all the spaces and left no evidence of any altercation. There were a few large spots of blood on the floor, but those would be scuffed away soon enough.

I left the cage and pushed my way to the bare wooden steps with the cracked plastic banister. The steps were exposed to the lobby, and as I neared the ceiling, I got to watch a whole civilization of spiders building their gossamer castles, as if there was nothing else in the world to do.

The second floor had at one time been a number of small rooms, but they had knocked adjoining walls down to make one large place with four entrance doors, all of which said: USE OTHER DOOR above a pointing arrow. The final door had HOMICIDE written on it. I turned the dirty handle and went inside. The room was long and low like a boa constrictor. It looked like a machine forest, with countless odd-shaped whirring and chugging gadgets packing the entire place, leaving only small footpaths and niches for plastic desks. The machines were all painted dull green, like mechanical olives, and pressed in so close that they demanded constant mental attention.

The lighting came from overhead diffusing-panels and spread over the entire room in antiseptic evenness—an artificial sun for growing chlorophylled machinery. People wandered in and out of the conduit jungle, appearing occasionally as heads and upper torsos, feeding the clockwork entities the sustenance of information and removing the excrement of their ruminations. I don't care much for machines; they make it too easy not to think.

It was hot as a kootchie-kootchie dancer in there, and as I wiped my forehead on my sleeve arm, I noticed that the whole front of my one-piece was beginning to darken with dampness.

Captain Jenkins had a walled-off area set in the corner of the room. The opaque glass door that led to the office had PRIVATE written on it in large letters. I moved to the door and tapped lightly, then went in. Jumpstreet Harry was in there, and Fat Mack, and Charles W. stick-it-in-your-ear Beale. Beale was the Commissioner of Police and had been sliding on pad money for so many years that his suits had permanent runners built onto them. He had big, greasy eyebrows that constantly jerked and twitched, and a potato nose that was so pitted he could have started a cherry factory. His flat, expansive face dropped faster than a whore's zipper when he caught sight of me.

"Do you let every bum off the streets in here, Harry?" he asked.

"You took the words right out of my mouth," I said.

Watershed was on his feet, straining that bull neck of his. "Let me take him down to Introg, Captain. I'll teach him some damn manners."

"Down boy," I said, then barked at him.

He moved up close enough for me to feel asphyxiated by his breath.

"Mack, will you sit down," Jenkins said, and his voice sounded like a harmonica with a broken reed.

Mack bulled his head around from one of us to the other. "I've got some things to do downstairs," he said, and turned to the door.

"Don't go away mad," I called after him.

He may have said something clever then, but he closed the door between us and I never got to hear it. Jenkins leaned back in his chair, shaking his head, wanting to smile but looking like he was just too tired.

"You have a way of bringing out the worst in people, Swain," he said.

"I gear myself to the company," I said, and looked at Beale.

Beale gave me a look that he must certainly have reserved for his wife's lovers. "This is a *private* conversation," he said in a voice that probably scared his aides to death.

I parked myself in Fat Mack's chair. "Well, I'll be so quiet you won't even know I'm around."

Beale got out of his chair and began to pace like a stalking mongoose. "How can you tolerate this madman?" he said, and I supposed that he was talking to Harry.

"I think," Jenkins began, and he seemed almost to be forcing himself to finish the sentence, "that Swain is here about the Grover case."

The Commissioner stopped in midstride and turned to glare at me.

What the hell did he have to do with Grover? There was something here that didn't sit right with me.

He returned to his seat, never taking his eyes off me—as if I'd disappear if he blinked. "What do you want?" he asked.

I clasped my hands behind my head and stretched out my legs. "This is a *private* conversation," I told him.

He tightened his lips. I could see the vein in his temple throbbing. He looked over at Jenkins who raised his eyebrows in return. He moved to the door. "I have a luncheon appointment with the Mayor."

"I hope they count the silverware when you leave," I said.

He studiously ignored me. "Call," he told Harry, and took the time to glare at me once more, then was gone.

"What happened to your head?" he asked when we were alone.

"I walked into a door."

He grunted, and tried to smooth that always smooth hair. "You didn't call me yesterday," he said.

"Call you?"

"About that name we discussed."

I nodded slowly. "Oh, *that* call. I must have misprogrammed that case into my files. I just can't seem to locate it."

"A warrant's easy enough to get, Swain."

"Come on, Harry. Why is that name so important to you? Old man Grover said that you're off the case."

He took his eyes from mine, and stared down at the desk top. A small readout screen recessed in the desk was running a never-ending list of police dispatches. He was watching it, but not really looking. "So, you're working for Grover?"

"On your recommendation. What the hell is going on here?"

Sighing, he sat back and played with his lower lip. "We live in a tangled world . . ."

"Let's just skip the build-up and get right on to the punch line."

His face got a little harder. "You don't give an inch, do you?"

"I'm not that clever," I answered.

"Okay. Yesterday, we answered the call for Grover's penthouse. His name was cross-referenced, and he was connected to money . . . so we gave it the first-class treatment. After we talked to his father, we found that he couldn't afford us. So, I threw a little business your way, figuring if nothing else I could recoup part of our loss through your ten percent referral fee."

This sounded like a two-cigarette story. I got out number one and lit it. "I'm with you so far," I said.

He frowned. "Things started to happen after I made that call to Grover. We heard from some . . . people who wanted us to continue the investigation and were willing to pay the price."

"What people?"

"People who want to know everything there is to know about Grover."

"Why?"

Standing up, he walked over and sat in Beale's chair. He was wearing his full-dress captain's toga. "We're paid to do a job, Swain, not to question motivations."

I worked the fag around with my teeth, and tried to think. "So, why don't you call old man Grover and tell him that you're trying to find his son's killer."

"We're not . . . actively trying to do that. It's Phil Grover we're finding out about."

"What about all the work you've done on the case so far?"

He shrugged. "What about it?"

"Can I have it? *I'm* still working on the murder."

"Jesus, you're thick-headed; I thought you understood. The people who purchased this case don't want Grover's killer found. And they sure don't want us turning our prelims over to you.''

''What about the body? You can't keep us from examining that.''

''There's been an unfortunate mix-up,'' he said. ''When the original case cancellation order went out, the morgue destroyed the body.''

The cig turned stale. I put it out and lit number two. ''You might be working for the murderer yourself,'' I said, and didn't want to believe it.

He covered his eyes with a thumb and forefinger. ''Know why it's so hot in here?'' he asked. ''A motor went out on the air conditioning last week, and so far we haven't been able to get the appropriation to get it fixed. It takes money to make things work, Swain. And money is amoral, with a capital A.''

''What? You're protecting a killer so that you can get the air conditioning fixed?''

He stood up and paced the room exactly the way Beale had done. I followed him with my eyes, and he grew old as I watched him. ''We all have our priorities, don't we? Mine is to hold this city and this department together any way I know how. Face up to it, Swain. The world you want doesn't exist any more.''

''Don't give me that bullcrap, Harry. You're the one changing the world. You're doing it right now.''

He turned his back to me and stared at a wall screen that was hypnotically floating a pattern of low intensity lights. He spoke to the wall. ''I want you out of this thing,'' he said.

I got up and went over to him, spinning him around until we were face to face. ''You can go straight to hell,'' I said, and let the smoke from my dangling cig get in his face.

He pulled away from my grasp without losing his composure, and returned to his desk. ''Look, if it's the money . . . .''

''It's not the goddamn money and you know it.'' I followed him back to his desk and stood looking down at him. ''This isn't a ledger sheet where you mark up the debits and the credits and try to show a profit. We're talking human life here.''

60

"It can't be that important to you. Grover was just one man . . . hell, they die by the thousands on those streets."

"Are you a cop or a scorekeeper?" I asked him. "Maybe I *am* thick-headed. I'm just a poor slob trying to earn a living. But it seems to me that *something* has got to matter. Where does it end? Today you sanction murder. What do you do for an encore tomorrow—hire yourself out as an assassin?"

"It's all so simple to you, isn't it?"

"I do what I do because I like people, because deep down inside I feel like I'm helping somehow. That makes me feel good, Harry, helps me sleep at night. Now, if that's a simplistic view of life to you, I offer my sincerest apologies—I guess I'm just a simple guy."

He stared across the desk at me for a long time. When he spoke, it was slow and measured. "I like you, Swain. I don't want anything to happen to you. This is a lot bigger deal than you realize. For your own sake, get out now." He stood, so that we were eye to eye and spoke in a harsh whisper. "You can't stand against this thing alone. It will swallow you whole."

"We all go sometime," I answered, and headed for the door. "Some of us are already gone and don't even know it."

"If you don't give me that name I wanted tomorrow, I'll be over with a warrant." He pointed a crooked finger. "Don't stand in our way, or so help me God, I'll squash you myself."

"Tell it to my insurance man," I said, and walked out the door.

9

I left the squad room feeling I should go home and take a bath. There was another melee going on downstairs. I waited on the fringe while everyone went at it. There was a pay vis on a near wall that wasn't in use, so while I waited I called the garage to tell them I was bringing my hummer in. After that I called George Wesley to tell him that I'd be paying him a visit. Then, almost as an afterthought, I linked a call through to my own vis at the office and used my file code to transfer the Grover file to the Bs, for baloney. I wasn't sure why I did that. Maybe it was just to prick Harry. Maybe it was to protect an innocent woman. If, in fact, she was innocent.

When the furor died down to a whorehouse bellow, I worked my way through the combatants and back out the door. The rain was coming down in sheets now, tinting the atmosphere hazy red. I walked through the water show, and watched the eyes of street animals that stared at me out of dry harbors wondering why I didn't have sense enough to get out of the rain.

The inside of my bullet was soaked when I finally got to it. Unlimbering the door, I slid in and sat on a seat that had soaked up enough water to bathe in. Trying to ignore my predicament, I hummed on and headed for the garage.

After waving the proper green flag in his direction, the guy at the garage told me he could have the bullet ready that evening. I left the dents alone, but had him replace the window and check the coils, just in case I had banged the thing around enough to upset the polarity. He got indignant when I accused him of being a limb stripper for charging me an arm and a leg, but the price didn't go down any.

There was a heli-bus stand at the end of the block. I walked the distance to the towerlike building and, stepping inside, took the tube up to the platform. The platform was smooth and flat, and the rain had left wide puddles that glimmered rust and danced wildly to the tune of a thousand raindrops. Completely round, the platform was the size of a large house. It was described by a chain link all around, and barbed wire on top to discourage suicides and dumpers. A big yellow square was painted in the center point of the platform. Several people were already up there. They were mostly watching the commercial vis that had been placed there to help kill the time. It must have been a humorous show, for everyone occasionally laughed in unison. Things always seem funnier when you're in a crowd. I stood at the opposite side, looking through the holes in the fence, watching the decay that seemed almost physically to creep, deteriorating the dreams of man as easily as it defaced his institutions.

I watched the bus float to the platform. I didn't like to travel this way. It was as if everyone was trying to deny the existence of the decay by traveling above it as if it wasn't there.

It was.

The bus hovered about four meters above the platform for a time, then densified its helipacks and dropped slowly to cover the yellow platform lines. The small crowd queued up in front of the hydraulically opening door, then crushed to enter. Once the shoving was finished, I went in. Slipping my credit blank into the slot provided, I gave my destination to the wall grid. A small screen lit up showing me how close the bus came to my goal. It was near enough to walk the difference without changing transport.

I walked back to the seats. The bus was nearly full of people whose faces all stared above my head. A vis hung at a forty-five-degree angle from the ceiling. I sat next to an old woman whose face was as smooth and slick as a beach ball. I watched her for a moment, but she was too caught up in the screen show to even notice my presence. Looking past her, I watched the crumbling ruins slip by, and wondered what this Grover business was going to come to.

Jenkins said that I was in over my head—the exact same observation I had made about Grover. Organization made sense to me; it explained the punks I tangled with at the old man's place. Those people had been placed there as a control rod, probably to watch for Phil Grover when he was alive, probably to watch for someone like me after he died. That put the police on one side, a large organization that thought nothing of murder on the other, and me in the middle. I felt like I was sitting on a razor blade: No matter which way I slid, I was going to lose my ass. I couldn't help but feel that Mina Goulding was somehow tangled in the middle of all this, but I didn't know how.

The rain stopped as I watched, and I knew the humidity would bottle up again. You couldn't tell inside the bus, we were breathing cold air that tasted as if it had come out of a gleaming metal cylinder somewhere. It was pretend air, something to fool my lungs.

"Mathew Swain."

It was the computer voice, telling me that we had reached my stop. The bus glided down to the depot and I got off, glad to be breathing the real thing again, noxious as it was.

I moved across the platform and down the tube, my own sweat soaking me more than the rain I had walked through earlier. George lived in a nice part of town, nicer, at least, than mine. He had plenty of money, clever gent that he was, and could probably have lived all the way uptown if he'd wanted to; but I think he liked to feel the grit under his nails.

Even here, there were too many Fancy Dans for my taste. As I walked past the stores and apartments of St. Francis, every one of them eyed me suspiciously. I had the strangest feeling that I was being followed, so I stopped at a corner booth and took an oxy-fix and scoped it out. If I was being watched, the street crowd was too large to spot the tail. I went on, soon coming to George's high-rise. The security checkpoints were prepared for my arrival, so I got through easily and tubed up to his place on four and knocked.

"Come in, Swain," a voice called out, and I did.

The room was pitch black when I entered. I came inside

and tripped over an end table, catching myself just before I went head over heels. An amount of well-rehearsed language passed my lips, and the lights came up. George sat in an easy chair within touching distance. He wore a red silk robe with a white obi. His thin, wispy hair was disheveled, leading me to think that he had just gotten up. He was wearing his camglasses, but they were turned off—not glowing. The glasses, which looked like two jeweler's oculars strung together, ran black wires down each side of his neck. The wires were loose, unconnected.

"I'm sorry about the dark," he said, and his grin said he wasn't sorry at all. "I was recharging my batteries, and forgot the lights were off."

I shrugged, then realized it was a wasted gesture. "That's all right, I'll get even with you later," I said, and sat on the bright flowered couch that ran at a ninety-degree angle to George's chair.

He got up, smoothing his robes. "Let me go plug up, and we'll chat," he said. Walking with the precision of a sighted person, he moved to a desk that ran the length of the room, and began fiddling with some stuff on its top.

The apartment was a complete hodgepodge. It contained enough electronic nonsense to fly George to Andromeda if he wanted. Between the vis screen and the holoshows that ran continually, the dancing mobiles and the neon pulsing light sculptures, and the walls that changed colors with the range of sounds from the organ concerto piping gently through unseen speakers, there was hardly enough room to hang your hat. The room itself was a nightmare of color, like a rainbow in a mirrow maze. It looked like an artist's palette, with colors slapdashed everywhere, and the brightest hues imaginable. All of this clashed with the primary day-glo barrage of his furniture, not one piece of which matched any other piece. The place looked like an explosion in a paint store, but it was home to George.

"And what brings you to my humble abode, besides a free drink?" he asked from the desk.

"Should there be anything else?"

"Save it, dear heart, I know you too well. You don't make social calls in the middle of the day."

"I'm liable to turn you into a first-class detective yet."

"I'll bet you tell that to all the Electrex," he said.

"Only the ones who work for percentage," I answered. "I need your help, George."

He returned to his seat with a drink in one hand and a gun-metal gray box in the other. "Those are words I don't hear from the last great individualist very often." He started to set the tumbler on the coffee table in front of me, but stopped just above it. "Is it there, or did you knock that over too?"

"It's there, you bastard."

He set the glass down. Leaning back in his seat, he opened his robe to the navel, and attached the thin box to the retaining belt that ran around his middle. Then he plugged the jacks of the dangling wires into the box, making his stomach muscles his eyes.

"Ah," he said, "that's better. I see that you've been using your head to hammer nails again."

"Nails, hell! They were railroad spikes." I reached out and picked up the drink. Whiskey and water . . . and not much water at that.

"I haven't seen you lately."

"I haven't had any money to lose to you at cards lately." I took a long drink, then set it down. George watched my actions very carefully. It was a habit with him. Since his vision came from his camglasses, he had to continually move his entire head to look at things. "You remember that woman you took those films of a couple of months ago?"

"Mina Goulding? I do indeed." He pursed his lips, then licked them. "Tall young woman, and thin as a mannequin. Her skin was pale, and she dressed as if she were trying to camouflage herself . . . except for that bright green lipstick. That lipstick was all right. I guess that proves that no one is all good or all bad."

"Her boyfriend got himself killed night before last."

"Grover? I hadn't heard."

"Yeah. I guess that's what I wanted to talk to you about."

"I didn't do it," he said.

"Well, that narrows down the field," I answered. "George,

what kind of weapon could chop a body up and leave the pieces intact?''

"Intact how?''

"No burns, no blood, no . . . anything. Half the body wasn't even there, and there wasn't any kind of mess at all. I saw it.''

He touched his fingertips together and began shaking his hands, thus joined, as one. Leaning his head back on the seat cushion, he stared at the moving pattern of stars on his ceiling. "I've never heard of anything like that, I . . .'' He sat upright in his chair. "That girl worked for Bermax Corporation. They do a lot of weapons research there.''

I nodded. We were thinking along the same lines. I told him about the numbers on Grover's vis. Then I told him the rest of the story. He was most disappointed about the lid that Jenkins had put on the investigation.

"I would love to get a look at Jordan's residual wave readings,'' he said. "Do you think you could get us back into Grover's apartment?''

"Why?''

"So I can take some readings myself. If I can develop some theories on my own, it will be easier to know what I'm looking for when we visit Bermax.''

"Who said anything about we?'' I asked. "This is the real rocker, George. There are people out there who want to kill me. I just came in here for advice. The last thing I need is to be worrying about you.''

"Tube it, dear heart,'' he laughed. "You need me on this one. Without me you'd stumble around Bermax like a vacuum tube on a microboard. To find the killer, you're going to have to know what it was that did the killing. I know the risks involved. I was a grown man when you were still shaving without a razor blade, and I can sure as hell look out for myself.'' He leaned up close so that his cams could focus better on me. "Besides, I haven't had a good adrenal rush in months. I can use the excitement.''

"It's your funeral,'' I said, finishing my drink. "Welcome aboard.''

"Georgie,'' a decidedly female voice called from the back of the apartment. "Is this all right?'' A young woman walked into the room. She was naked except for a covering of flourescent paint that made her look like an orange-sherbet sculpture.

"Delicious," I said.

"Oops," she said, and tried to cover herself. "I didn't know we had company."

"He's not company, Janine; he's just Swain."

She walked all the way into the room and extended a hand to me. I shook it. "Pleased to meet you, Swain."

"Do you come in any other flavors?" I wondered aloud.

"Just peach," she replied, and pirouetted like a ballerina. "What do you think?"

George smiled so wide I thought his ears would fall off. "I could be locked up for what I'm thinking."

She giggled. "Don't be long," she called as she ran from the room.

"Housekeeper?" I asked.

He shook his head. "She just fell into my life yesterday night," he said. "She locked herself out of her apartment down the hall, and asked if she could sit in here until the super got back from his sister's and could open it with the pass key. She's been here ever since. I've got enough gear here that I could have opened it myself, but what the hell. Don't look a gift horse in the mouth, right?"

"Tell that to the Trojans."

He bunched up his brows. "We need to go over there as soon as possible," he said. "Wave readings . . ."

"Have to be done quickly," I finished. "Tonight would be the night."

"What time?"

"After dark . . . how about eleven?"

He nodded, and I stood to go. "There's a public vis about a block from the Marmeth. Meet me there." I moved to the door, anxious to leave George to his windfall. "Love those colors, don't you?"

"I lived in the dark for so many years, Swain." He hesitated for just a moment, then said, "Can I ask you a question?"

"As long as it's not about rocket engines."

"Suppose you get the killer? If the police are protecting him, how do you get him arrested . . . or even charged?"

"It's like walking, George. You just take one step at a time. See you."

I left his apartment thinking about orange girls. I'm pretty good with faces; it's part of my job. And Janine's looked awfully familiar. I couldn't connect it with a name, though, so I shook it off.

George was a little strange, but a good, solid friend. He had been blind from birth, and was twenty-five years old before he was able to afford his camglasses. Vision through the specs was more form than detail, which was why he liked the bright colors so much. He had a solid sense of humor and identity, and I liked him just fine.

I still felt I was being followed.

10

I walked for a while. It was early afternoon, and my stomach was asking for a little solid matter to soak up the alcohol. I stopped in a place that looked like a restaurant to get a bite. I didn't recognize anything on the menu, so I ordered whatever looked the most appetizing. What they brought me was a cross between scrambled eggs and a piece of pebble board. They called it health food, and I figured that it was because a person had to be in peak physical condition to choke it down. I tried to get a drink to help smooth it down my throat. They brought me a small glass of something that was reddish pink and the consistency of wet cement. The waitress who served me had a cold, and I knew that it was brought on by eating that junk all the time. I told her to eat burgers and drink booze.

I walked for another few blocks, but had to stop and get a drink to get the taste of that crap out of my mouth. I went into the first place I saw. It turned out to be one of those damned electrobars.

Waves of multicolored smoke blew past me as I stepped into the darkened room. The music hit me, pulsing in and out like a heartbeat. It was loud, but bass low, so that it rumbled through my ears like the afterburners of a space freighter. There was no discernible melody, only that surflike pounding. To my left were booths, each having its own holoshow for the amusement of the customers. To my right was a long bar. I headed for that.

The floor was moving with the music as I walked, and I could begin to understand seasickness. I felt my pebble-board lunch begging for another opportunity at daylight. I got to the bar and sat on the first stool I encountered. The wall behind the bar was made of connecting tetrahedrons that phased through the visible light spectrum at a slow pace. It made me think that if they speeded up that wall they could probably get people to drink faster. The bar was a good fifteen meters long, and as I gazed down its length I saw perhaps ten other occupants, most of whom were wearing alpha rings around their foreheads, stimulating the pleasure centers of their brains.

The bartender was a hard-looking woman with a pig nose and a scar that ran around her neck, as if her throat had been cut. She moved up to me. Her eyes were hydrogen frozen at absolute zero.

"Black Jack, rocks," I said to her before she could ask. Tiny creases appeared at the side of her mouth, and her pig nose snorted. She made the drink silently. I turned around and looked behind me. People were dancing on a large, lighted stage. Their scruffy looks didn't jive with the precision steps that they were performing in unison, as if they had all danced together for years. Then I noticed the contact points on their shoes. The dance had been electrically programmed into the floor, and the dancers were simply standing up there, letting the machine jerk them around.

I turned back to the bar. My drink sat before me on its cracked, polished surface. I left some money, picked up my drink, and looked for a pay vis. There was one by the door where I had come in. I went to it and juggled my Beltel card out of my jacket pocket. When I moved into its steel recesses and the door clanged shut behind, I was mercifully free from the music. I lit a cigarette, and skimmed through the number computer on the wall.

I found the number of the Richmond, Mina Goulding's home base, and called them up. I needed to talk to the girl, and the direct approach seemed as good as any. A man fuzzed in. He was a physical wreck, like the buildings in the decay were a wreck. His clothes didn't fit right, and his long features didn't match his compact, pockmarked face. He had a two-dollar cigar in his maw, and a million-dollar boil on his nose.

"Richmond Hotel," he said, in a voice that sounded like he was recovering from a tracheotomy.

"Could you ring Helen Trent?" I asked.

He simply stared at the screen for several seconds, then crooked a stubby finger around the ugly green thing in his mouth and jerked it out, spitting a small bite of leaf out with it. "No Helen Trent registered here, buddy. Looks like you got the wrong fiber."

"When did she check out?" I asked.

"I been running this board for five years, and we ain't never had no Helen Trent. So tube off and let me get back to work."

He stuck the torpedo back in his face and faded. I finished my drink in the cool recesses of the booth. I didn't like the idea of Mina Goulding dropping out of sight again. It was possible, though, that she was still at the Richmond and just not responding to visitors. I could have gone over there and camped out, but I really didn't have the time. Her parents lived a matter of blocks from the bar. I decided it was time to pay them another visit. Maybe if they thought their daughter was in trouble, they'd be more anxious to talk. Then again, maybe they wouldn't.

Sucking down the last drag of my cig, I dropped it on the ice left in my glass and slipped out of the booth. Setting my homemade ashtray on the nearest table, I suffered through the music and the moving floor just long enough to get out of the place.

I glanced at my watch. It was three-thirty.

By the time I got to March Street, I felt like I needed to wring my clothes out. The Gouldings' place, 1819 March, was a row house in a minimum security neighborhood. It was doubled doored, with view-ports in both doors, and constructed of windowless cinderblock throughout. The entire block was painted aquatint, and reminded me of the federal prison dorms at Gainesville. There were no bullets parked on the semipitted street, so there must have been a security garage close by, underground.

I took the two-step stoop in one jump and pushed the buzzer. There was no response. I pushed it again.

"We don't want any," said a voice through a small speaker grid.

"I'm not selling anything," I called back into the grill. "I have to speak to you about something important."

There was silence for a moment, then I heard the lock click on the first door. The view-port slid open with a clack and a red-rimmed eye was staring out at me. "Let's see some i.d.," said a female voice.

I held up my P.I.'s license, the one with the smiling picture on it.

"We got nothing to say to you," the voice said, and the accent was more syrupy Southern than Texan. Georgia, I figured.

The door-port slid rudely closed, and I began pushing the buzzer again.

"Go away," the speaker voice said.

"I get paid to do this," I returned, "and I can do it for a long time." I sighed, and leaned on the buzzer. A minute later the door opened to admit me. A small woman of begrudging middle age with wispy, tinted hair and a puckered face stood in the entryway as I came through the doors. She was wearing a gaudy pink housecoat that looked like it had been threadbare for ten years. The robe was laced all around with some kind of flourescent red fur. A fat, home-rolled joint dangled from the corner of her mouth, and her eyes told me this wasn't her first of the day.

"Well, you might as well come in," she said.

"Already am," I replied.

She turned and walked into the guts of the house. I followed her. The place was all cracking walls and dying plants stuck on chipped plastic furniture that was probably decrepit when they bought it. Lace doilies hung redundantly on every chair arm and table top, and tiny embroidered pillows lay on the white, sterile furniture, trying unsuccessfully to warm it up. Junk store knickknacks covered every end table and open shelf in the house. The place smelled of dope and cheap cologne.

We went through the living room and kitchen into a downstairs bedroom that had been converted for vis viewing. This room was like the living room only smaller. The vis was working, showing combat scenes from a Central American bush war. A man sat stiffly on one of the plastic chairs, intently watching the show. He was flabby-faced and corpulent, with thick arms that jiggled when he moved. He was dressed only in a pair of boxer shorts. Dirty dishes were piled all around him on the dusty, tattered carpet.

"How do you do," I said to him.

He didn't even blink.

"Harry is pretty hard to talk to when he's watching the vis," Marabeth Goulding said, and her voice trailed off a bit. "He's between jobs, you know."

I sat on a molded plastic sofa next to the woman, and immediately doilies began falling all over me. I'd put them back in their places and they'd fall on the floor. Finally I just left them.

She took a long drag of her smoke and held it out for me. I declined. "Do you remember when I was here before?" I asked her.

"No," she said, and looked me dead in the face. "We've never met. I'd remember a hunk like you."

"I was looking for your daughter, Mina," I said, "and you wouldn't even talk to me about her."

She narrowed her eyes so much I thought the blood would drain out of them. "You know, in this neighborhood all the houses look the same. You're probably on the wrong block. Happens all the time. Isn't he, Harry?"

Harry didn't answer.

"You are Marabeth Goulding, and I'm at the right place," I said.

She shook her head. "Then you belong out on the fruitcake farm, Rocket Ranger, because we don't have any kids—never did. Don't even like them."

There was a roar of mortar fire on the screen, and shells began exploding on a street full of fleeing civilians. The screen switched to a slow-mo and people began blowing apart, pieces flying every which way out of camera range. Harry turned up the control pistol in his hand and it all got very loud. The man began jerking spasmodically in his chair, panting heavily, drool running down his chin.

"There's no reason to play games with me," I said, speaking loudly to get over the roar of the vis. "I found Mina a couple of months ago, but I think she might be in trouble now. I need to locate her again."

She slid back farther on the couch, pulling her bare feet up with her. She dragged on the reef and blew the smoke out through her nose. "You really do have a problem here," she said, and wiggled her purple-nailed toes, "because I don't know what the hell you're talking about."

I pulled a stack of twenties out of my pocket and waved them in her face.

"I'll take your money, mister," she smiled, "but you'll get nothing in return."

I stuck the money away just as she reached for it. "Sorry, no freebies."

Harry, still convulsing, began slipping out of his chair. He got about halfway off, when the weight distribution changed and the chair popped out from under him, sending him crashing to the floor. He lay there for a minute, then raised his head enough to see the screen again. Marabeth kept talking.

"I'd really like to help you, you know. My momma taught me to respect a dollar, but I got nothing for you." She slid off the couch and ran to where her husband lay on the floor. She stuck the cig in his mouth and he took a small puff.

"She could be in real trouble out there," I said. "Don't you understand that."

"I understand trouble real well," she said, and her eyes flashed at me. "And I know that I don't want any. So why don't you just leave decent folks alone and mind your own business. I told you we don't have any children, so just pack it up and take a walk, okay?"

I saw nowhere else to take the discussion, so I left. I talked to the neighbors who had helped me previously. At least I talked with those that were still around. Of the four I spoke with, three had moved away, and the fourth had never spoken with me in her life. Not only that, she backed up Marabeth Goulding's story one hundred percent. And that information cost me twenty bucks. By the time I left there, I was wondering myself whether or not there was such a person as Mina Goulding. If that wasn't bad enough, I stopped at the nearest pay vis and gave one of my friends at the bureau of vital statistics a ring. The Gouldings had lived at 1819 March for twenty-one years, and had never had any children.

I left the vis and walked to the nearest heli-bus stop. It was about time for the bullet to be back in action. I needed to pick it up, needed to feel that I had done something right that day.

11

There wasn't any wind at all, so the smog cover was over-bearing, and the air smelled like the waiting room of the free clinic. Since the cover was so thick, I couldn't even see the moon that had been full the night before. The end of my cig glowed like a throbbing, living thing, and when I pulled it from my lips to deal with the ash, it left an orange streamer in the night air.

Tremaine was dark as a devil's dream as I stood my vigil by the vis—as I waited for a little, fat man who had cameras for eyes and a bag full of tricks that would have made Houdini proud. The stores were deserted and shuttered tight, their steel window slats telling a wanting world that the spoils of war were only for the victors.

The streets belonged to the night people now, the nocturnal creatures who hunted the asphalt pathways in primordial splendor—stalking, prowling, waiting in the shadows for the weaker links in the survival chain. No Fancy Dans in sight now. Even they had better sense. I listened to the night sounds and watched the shadowy night drip down the concrete towers and even now I couldn't shake the feeling that I was being watched. There were occasional police patrols, clanking menace in their riot tanks with riveted walls and moving turrets, but the night creatures could well avoid the lumbering metal beast that preyed on them.

"Swain."

I jumped, startled, and quickly swung around to face a grinning George Wesley, suitcase in hand, yellow white glow where his eyes should have been.

"If I'd have been a monster," he said, "you'd have been eaten up."

"If you'd have been a monster, I wouldn't have been waiting here for you. Got all your gear?"

He patted the suitcase. "And then some."

I dropped my cig and stamped it out. "Let's see what the night sky looks like from the penthouse," I said. We walked toward the Marmeth.

"How do we get in?" he asked. "Overpower the guard, blow the service door?"

I looked him over. He was dressed conservatively in a gray knit one-piece and black jacket. My attire was similar, except in blue. We didn't look like cat burglars or strong arms, so I didn't figure we'd have to play it that way. George tended toward an overactive imagination.

"Take out some of your gear," I said, "something that looks official. Put it around your neck."

We stopped while he did that. He had a miniature version of the readout board that Jordan had used to scan the death scene. It looked real good. We walked on to the Marmeth's big steel door.

The door vis juiced into focus. A Fancy Dan guard's face appeared. "Yeah," he said.

I reached into my jacket pocket and pulled out the wallet that I kept for special occasions. I flipped it open right at the screen, making the police lieutenant's badge stand out. "Watershed," I said, "Homicide. We need to check the Grover apartment."

His eyes glanced down for a second; he was obviously picking Fat Mack's name off a preferred list. "Kind of late for this sort of thing, isn't it?" he asked.

"Your city never sleeps," I answered.

"That's right," George added in spite of my frown in his direction. "Crime doesn't punch a time clock, neither can we."

I liked George, but sometimes he got carried away. The Fancy Dan buzzed the door, it swung open, and we went in. I hoped that Mrs. Rodriguez wasn't anywhere around.

We tubed up to the penthouse and George used his wiles to get us through Grover's door. He must have been a frustrated second-story man, because he really enjoyed breaking into things. The electricity had already been shut off, but George had a small generator in his suitcase that had a dome light attached to the top. He set it up in the bedroom and went to work with his wave scanner. I stumbled into the kitchen to check it out. Jordan had said that the killer went to the kitchen after the murder. That's not an unusual situation considering the physical/sexual implications of the crime, but I looked anyway, just in case there was something in that room that had nothing to do with food.

I ignited my lighter, and in the pale flickering glow tried to examine the molded plastic cabinets and fixtures in the room. It was an exercise in futility in the semidarkness. I did detect an odd odor. I followed my nose to the mike. When I opened it, there was a half-cooked soy casserole inside. The recipe on Grover's vis. Did the killer go to the kitchen to shut off Grover's dinner?

"Come here, quick!"

It was George calling from the bedroom. I hurried through the house more by memory than sight and found him standing in the middle of the bedroom, turning his head from side to side.

"Find something?"

"Not exactly . . . wait." He unzipped his one-piece down to the navel. Reaching inside the open place he fiddled with the power pack for his eyes. The small running light went out. He stood there, blind now, and began moving his head from side to side again.

"George, I . . ."

"Shhh."

He seemed to be sniffing the air, like a bloodhound, crinkling his nose and twisting his hairy brows. "Yes," he hissed, and his voice had an edge to it. "It's smoke, Swain. I smell smoke. There's a fire somewhere in the building."

I stared. He was deadly serious and I knew better than to question his instinct on this. I felt my own mind begin to race. "Let's get the hell out of here," I said.

"My gear, I . . ."

"Let's go," I said. "Now!"

He turned his eyes back on and we dashed for the front

door. The foyer was empty. I bent and touched the floor; it was hot. George was shaking, near panic. The game was over. He punched the tube button. When the door slid open, thick gray smoke billowed out. We gagged and I moved blindly into the smoke to button the door closed.

"Back in the apartment," I said.

"Are there stairs?"

"Not up here. Come on."

We got back inside the apartment and shut the door. We didn't have much time. Smoke was beginning to seep through the cracks in the walls and floor. George was still coughing from his dose at the tube.

I ran to the big overlook window in the bedroom. It was sealed tight, not designed to be opened. Knocking a lamp off a heavy-looking night stand, I hefted the whitened monstrosity up to shoulder level and made a grunting run at the window. I pushed it away from me and it shattered the glass with an almost explosive sound, then plummeted to the street below. Jumping, I jerked the big curtain, letting my weight pull it down. The rod came with it.

Using the rod to clean the fragments of glass out of the window frame, I stuck my head out the open place and looked down. My window was the only one in the Marmeth. I was staring at a thirty-story drop of straight concrete. Since there were no windows, there was no fire escape.

There was an explosion behind me. I ran to the bedroom door and saw Grover's front door shattered in pieces on the carpet. Huge tongues of red and orange flame shot through the open place, and I felt panic rising in my throat. George was hugging the wall by the bedroom, petrified, staring in horror at the flames.

"Anything explosive in your case?" I yelled above the crackling roar.

He kept jerking his head back and forth between me and the fire. "No, I don't think so, I . . ."

"Think, damn it! Unless you want to burn to death."

He stared straight at me, his glowing headlamps betraying no emotion behind them. "My wave scanner," he said. "It passes electrons through a chamber to react with the atmosphere. If we could block off the chamber and turn the machine on, it would build up a hell of a lot of pressure in there.''

"Get it ready," I said, and ran back in the bedroom. Small pennants of flame were already licking the bedroom walls. The heat and smoke were overpowering. Pulling out a handkerchief, I used it to cover my nose and mouth, but it didn't help much. Sweat rolled freely from every part of my body, and I could feel a hot glow searing my face.

I fought through the smoke to the linen closet. I was afraid that because he owned a stasis bed, Grover wouldn't have any sheets. But he did. Grabbing an armload, I stumbled through the smoke-choked room and back to George.

The living room was a solid sheet of flame. I held my arm up in front of me just to try and relieve the heat pressure on my face. George was no more than a meter from the fire. He was holding his wave scanner by its semicircular display board and banging the business-end of the thing against a corner of the wall, trying to jam the outtake vent.

"In here!" I yelled, waving him into the bedroom.

He just kept banging that damn machine. I had to grab him by the arm and physically pull him into the bedroom with me. I ran to the window and stuck my head out, gagging for air. My face felt as if it were on fire. A holocaust was raging inside the building, yet outside everything looked calm and peaceful. The fire was building pressure, just like George's electron chamber. It was feeding on ventilator-supplied air and was looking for a place to escape. When it could contain itself no longer, there'd be the devil to pay.

I pulled George to the window and forced his head out. As he choked on the smoke, I began tying the corners of the sheets together, knotting them as best I could. There were ten sheets, a good thirty meters' worth. The curtain rod that I had used on the glass was solid brass. I tied one end of the sheet rope around the rod's middle.

George pulled his head back in, shaking it. He looked at me and held up the scanner. "I think I've got it!" he yelled, louder than he needed to. The flames had completely engulfed the room. We were boxed in, there was nowhere else for us to go.

"Anything in your suitcase that could go up?"

"Probably."

I tied wave scanner and suitcase to the end of the sheets. George turned on the machine, and I lowered everything out the window just as a section of the floor collapsed around us. With barely enough room to stand, we stared down into a fiery pit. Hell on earth.

I got the case lowered to the end of the sheet rope. I turned to George. The glass of his cams was reflecting the room, making it look as if his eyes were burning.

"How long . . ." I began, but was cut off by the sound of an explosion below. Jerking around, I stuck my head out the window. The sheet was swinging freely, no weight holding it down. There was no sign of George's equipment, but smoke was pouring out of a large hole in the side of the building.

"Come on," I told him.

He edged over to the window and looked. "What?"

"Down the rope," I yelled.

He hoisted one leg over the sill, hesitated, then turned to me, his face looking like a baked apple. "I'm afraid of heights, Swain."

"Get your ass down there!" I began pushing him, just as the flames were nipping my shoe leather.

He took one more look at the fire, which was all that could be seen of Grover's apartment, took a deep breath, and pulled his other leg over the sill. Grunting, he started hand-over-handing down the rope, his weight pulling the brass rod tight up against the window frame.

I stuck my head out and watched him go down. The fire crept closer; I was forced to sit on the sill. People were beginning to fill the streets by this time. Displaced from their homes, they lined the boulevard in their night clothes, keeping one eye on the fire and the other on the night-creatured streets.

As George neared the end of the tether, I took my place. The zipper on my one-piece had heated up so that it was burning my chest. I unzipped the thing part way and started down. My eyes were burning, and I realized just how much I was gagging. As I descended painfully, one hand at a time

82

carrying my entire weight, I began feeling lightheaded, dizzy. I drew in large gulps of fresh air, and threw up, and still kept moving.

The penthouse window got farther away, but it was all like a dream. I went down farther, farther than I thought the rope would reach, and then I smelled smoke again.

A voice was calling to me, calling my name. I looked below me: George was leaning out of a jagged hole in the side of the building. One hand held a piece of cloth up to his nose and mouth, the other was reaching out to me. I looked up. The fire had climbed out the window and was dancing on my lifeline. The line tugged, and I went down a bit.

Shaking my head to clear the smoke-dream demons that had control there, I slithered down the last meter of distance to the hole in the wall and swung in with George's help. A second after my feet landed on solid ground, my sheet rope floated by the window—floated because 220 pounds weren't on the end to hurry it along.

I swung around. We were in a smoke-filled apartment. Lights were on, but it was gray, like the light of morning before the sun rises.

"I think it's above us," George said.

"There should be stairs in this part of the building."

We made for the door. There were people out in the hall. They were running around like shorted andies, seemingly without destination, their faces looking much more animal than human. They filled the hall; they screamed; they carried inconsequential items as if the whole world depended on the safety of those items.

George and I pushed into the flow. They went in every direction, so we had to take pot luck. Moving to our left, we pushed along with a large group heading around a corner. I hoped they were going for the stairs. They weren't. The tubes were the immediate transport that came to everyone's mind. As soon as I saw them crowding around the tube area, we turned and headed back where we had just been.

The ceiling collapsed behind us, burying the unfortunates who waited for a tube that would never come. Now the screaming got louder. I was coughing again, and practically blind. I ran into something on the ground and fell, George right on top of me. I looked, and was staring into the face of Mrs. Rodriguez, her flesh-encased eyes staring wide and unseeing.

Others fell on us. I grabbed George, calling his name and pulling. The air was better closer to the floor, so I moved us to the wall and we crept, crablike, along that route. More of the ceiling went behind us.

The hallways were built on a square. We rounded another corner, and saw the mob clustered around a plain metal door. The door was open and they fought their way inside. I knew that it had EXIT written on the other side.

We stood up and were swept along with the crush, all of us sensing freedom; the urge for self-preservation became all-consuming, like the fire. It was instinct—move or die. There was incredible pushing, and I found myself doing it too. We were careful of the floor; there were obstacles beneath our feet, obstacles that had once lived and breathed and thought themselves immortal.

We made the door. I turned to make sure George was still with me. The smoke was thick, but I could see his eyeglow through the fog.

More of the ceiling fell, and one of the inside walls crumbled. We got through the door frame, and everything behind us was gone. I looked back once to see people caught in the rubble, screaming as their hair and clothes burned, their flesh charring with a sickening stench. My stomach heaved, even though I had emptied it on the climb down the ladder.

The steps were treacherous. They wound back and forth, with landings for each floor. The farther we descended, the more people jammed in through the doors from each floor. A metal rail acted as a blockage on the open-ended side of the stairs, but so many people crushed against it that a whole section gave way, taking five or six screamers down the remaining flights the fast way.

"Hug the wall, George," I called, but he was already doing it. Walls rumbled, then fell, and a whole section of the stairs disappeared behind us. As the mob moved from the higher elevations, those on the edge of the missing landing were systematically pushed off the edge.

We kept going. It was a long way down. The smoke cleared a bit the farther down we went, but strewn rubble and bodies jammed the steps, making the going tough. Finally we reached ground level and stumbled through an emergency exit that was twisted off its hinges, out into the night air. We ran, coughing, across the street, and let ourselves fall on the sidewalk.

The building was collapsing in earnest now, large tongues of flame climbing upward like flowers reaching for the heavens. Nearby buildings were beginning to go, ignited by burning debris spewed from the guts of the inferno. There wasn't a fire engine to be seen. This was less of a priority area than I had realized.

We lay there, panting and checking our wounds for a time. I wanted more than anything to just lie there and go to sleep, but there was something that I had to do. Things were beginning to come together in my mind.

I staggered, still light-headed, to my feet.

George stared at me. "Where are you going?"

"Playing a hunch," I said, and spit on the ground to get the cinders out of my throat. "Take it easy."

"Okay," he said, and stretched out flat on the pavement. "But if I get mugged while you're gone, it'll be your fault."

The crowd in the streets had grown large. I moved toward it, then into it. It was a sea of flickering fire and upturned faces, like sunnyside eggs frying in a pan. I was looking for one, but they were all the same to me. I frantically shoved my way through the throng, but it was useless. Finally I gave up and returned to George.

"Let's go," I said.

He stood, and we walked through the sparse fringe crowd on Tremaine, toward my bullet.

"What was that all about?" he asked, and cocked his head toward the mob that I had just come out of.

"It was about arson, George."

"Arson?"

"Yeah, most arsonists like to stick around to see the results of their labors."

"What makes you think that someone deliberately set the fire?"

85

I didn't answer him. He wouldn't have liked the answer anyway. The watchers had dwindled to small clustered groups as we neared my bullet. I happened to glance at the pay vis where I had met George as we passed it, and in the dull attraction light of the booth, I saw it. Peach ice cream that had once been orange sherbet. George's gift horse stood watching her handiwork, the corners of her mouth upturned in an obscene smile.

George saw her too. His mouth worked uncontrollably. I clamped my hand over it before he could speak. "Let's go," I whispered.

We slid quietly past the booth, and made our way back to my bullet. Climbing inside, I felt the weight of my body sink gratefully against the seat cushions. I juiced the hum, and we took off.

We drove in silence for a few blocks. When I looked over at George, he was staring at me. "Janine," he said softly.

"I remember her now," I said. "The last time I saw her, though, she was an insurance torch for Maria Hidalgo's bunch. This kind of thing isn't Maria's style. It doesn't jibe."

"I don't understand," George said.

"Janine's real name is Martha Johns," I said. "And I could kick myself for not remembering her sooner. She does this sort of thing for a living."

"Someone paid her to set that fire? Why?"

"Two reasons. To kill us, and to destroy any evidence in the apartment."

"But all those people . . ."

"I know," I replied. "I know."

He rolled down his window and sank back into the seat, rubbing his char-blackened cheeks with equally dirty palms. I wondered if I looked as bad as he did. "Why didn't we nab her, Swain?"

"We've been followed on this every step of the way," I answered. "We need a little breathing room. The damage has been done. We can get her later. Right now, I think it would be better if whoever is behind all this thinks we *are* dead for a while."

We went a few more blocks, and I tried to concentrate on

my driving to wash away the image of what we had lived through, and what a lot of others didn't live through—just to make my death look like an accident.

I turned back to George. "I think I could use a drink," I said.

12

I let George do all the talking. It made him feel like a big shot. Besides, I didn't know beans about it anyway.

The big man in the permapress checkered toga waddled toward us on feet that should have been corrected when he was a child. He flashed us the universal salesman's smile and jutted his smooth, manicured hand into our paths. "Name's Stalher," he said, and studied us with his dull brown eyes. "I run herd over the new accounts here. Guess you could say that I put the nails in the sales." He laughed at his own joke. At least I assumed it was a joke.

George shook Stalher's monstrous hand. "I'm Parker," he said, "and this is Merkle." He pushed a thumb in my direction.

Stalher moved to me. I shook his hand as he sized me up. His grip was firm, but not overpowering. This was a man who knew better than to intimidate the customer.

"How are you?" he asked.

"Well done," I answered.

He smiled. "Fine, fine. The compusec tells me that you gentlemen are interested in security systems."

"Foolproof security systems," George said, "for a manufacturing plant."

"And what price range were you considering?"

"Money is no object."

Stalher raised his eyebrows, and I swear that his eyes twinkled. "Money is always the object," he said, "or else you wouldn't be so interested in protecting your business. Follow me and I'll show you what we have to offer."

He led us from a waiting room of total acrylic, like a room carved from ice, through a set of double doors that plunged into the heart of the Bermax Building. The lighting immediately became as dim as my chances of living past forty, and until I irised in, everything was just lumpy shadows.

He hand-printed us through two more sets of heavily guarded security doors until we were looking down the gullet of a long narrow hallway that angled continually downward. The end of the tunnel couldn't be seen.

"Here at the Bermax Corporation," he said, falling into his spiel, "we have employed the finest scientific and engineering brains in the world to design and construct new technological systems and products with you, the discerning buyer, in mind. In the twenty years of our existence, we have received over ten thousand patents—a thousand of those in the last year alone. Our manufacturing techniques are, as you will soon see, without peer. And I think that I can safely say, without fear of contradiction, that the goods we produce are the finest in the world."

He led us to a line of electric cars and we boarded the first one. Stalher plucked a small plastic disc out of his toga and slipped it into a comparably sized slot in the small vehicle. He sat in a single seat in the front of the car, while George and I huddled on a benchlike seat in the back.

We were searching for the link between Bermax and the murder weapon. George knew his stuff. Me, I was just a strong arm who was keeping an eye out for a girl who everyone said did not exist. I had asked for her at the reception desk, and, of course, no one by that name had ever worked there.

We drove the streets all night after the fire, not knowing to what extent we were being watched. What I did know was that I had been played for a sucker from the word go, and if they wanted me now they were going to have to catch me. It was really kind of flattering actually, having someone trying to send me to detective heaven for the important information I was carrying around. I only wish I knew what it was that made me so high on the expendability list. Maybe I could get excited about it too. In the morning we bought new clothes rather than return to our flats. If anyone was watching for it, they could identify us through our credit purchases, but that was a chance we had to take. I was beginning to understand just how small a world it was.

The case itself made absolutely no sense to me, and was getting more complicated all the time. The Bermax Building covered an area the size of a small state, and was powerful enough to be sovereign if it wanted to be. I suppose that it could have eaten up Grover, but I just couldn't see what a man like him could have meant to a machine like Bermax. And why go to so much trouble to get rid of me? I tried, in all the jumble, to find a place for Mina Goulding in the jigsaw, but that was worse than futile. The more rocks I uncovered, the more worms I found staring back at me.

"We're approaching fabrication, gentlemen," Stalher said. He donned a clear, bubbled hard hat emblazoned with the Bermax insignia—a bold B with a lighting bolt bisecting it—and motioned for us to do the same.

We rapidly approached an area of bright lights. In the long, redundant stretch, it was difficult to accurately judge distance, and it took us longer to reach the tunnel's terminus than I figured. When we finally did, I couldn't believe what I was looking at. We came out into a huge room of such volume that, standing at the north wall, you'd need binocs to see the south. There were people in there, thousands of them, all wearing hard hats and moving around like army ants on a food foray. There was heavy construction going on, with beams and girders floating through the room's upper strata on grav conveyors. Huge gas feed lines and fusion turbines occupied part of the room, like the basement plumbing in an apartment house, and the walls were filled with scoreboards that continually displayed running totals and lines of language written in some secret engineers' dialect that I had never seen before. Blueprints for mammoth, multi-story machines were projected lifesized in holo on the site of the various constructions, so that all the workers had to do was place the genuine article over the air occupied by the projection. There were a myriad of tall, stone towers, set in pegboard symmetry across the length of the entire room. Each tower contained two uniformed guards and a small laser cannon. I wondered about that.

"This is Fab 7," Stalher said. "One of our smaller construction areas."

If he was trying to impress us, he was doing a fine job of it.

"What are those things for?" I asked, pointing to one of the towers.

"Security," he said, and turned to stare at me. "We do a lot of top secret government stuff here. It pays to be careful."

I didn't believe him, but that could just have been my natural cynicism. I began looking at the machines. "How do you get those things out of here after you've got them put together?"

His eyes widened and he had the look of an alley cat in the kitchen of a seafood restaurant.

A group of workmen carrying a piece of lightweight metal that was twisted like a pretzel passed in front of the car. They all looked the same—I mean exactly the same. My first thought was that they were andies, but industrial robots were never as sophisticatedly human-looking as these seemed to be. Their faces were all just alike, and their hands were all covered with mechanical grippers that connected to simple exoskeletons just beneath their blue coveralls. On closer scrutiny, they were different sizes and builds, so I had to assume that they were wearing masks to hide the way they really looked. I started to ask Stalher about that, but he just glared at me, so I shut up.

A corridor cut through the center of the room. We drove on, right through the midst of the activity. I glanced over at George. He was staring, open-mouthed at the incredible things going on around us. I think, for the first time, that he was beginning to understand what we were up against.

When we passed through Fab 7, we entered a central receiving area from which a number of hallways branched off. They were each marked with neon script. We turned down a corridor that was marked, among other things, as security displays.

"Now, we'll take a look at the fall line," Stalher said, "and couple it with what you feel you need in the way of security. I'm sure that we'll be more than able to accommodate your needs."

We sped through the darkened corridor, and I hoped that we'd be able to get out as easily as we got in. Occasionally we'd pass a hallway that branched off in other directions, each branch marked with its particular function. After several of those, we turned down the security display corridor. We drove a short distance until we came to a set of double sliding-glass doors. The car stopped. Stalher called out a series of numbers, and the doors moved to open. We pulled in and stopped again.

"This is our stop," Stalher said, and grinned like a jack-o'-lantern. "Everybody out."

We stepped onto the stone floor. I was happy to be on my feet again. George looked a little apprehensive. I hoped that he would hold together okay.

"I'd hate to have to sweep the floors in here," I said. Stalher laughed; he was more of a customer-pleaser than I'd thought.

"This way, gentlemen," he said, and led us off to the side, into a series of alcoves. The first was totally empty, except for a typer-sized table that supported a small computer. Two folding chairs were placed in front of the machine.

"Sit down," the little com said when we got close to it.

We sat on the folding chairs, while Stalher hovered in the background like a prison-yard supervisor.

"Welcome to the security systems display lab," the machine said through a ceiling speaker that gave it a certain omniscience. "We hope that we can be of service to your company. If you would be so kind as to answer a few simple questions, Mr. Stalher will be better able to serve your needs."

"Fire," I said, and George grimaced.

"What's the name of your company?"

"Acme Grommet," George answered.

"We don't seem to have any . . ."

"We're a new company," I said.

". . . file on you," the computer finished. "What about a D and B?"

"No," I said. "We're strictly cash and carry."

"Then you would pay your bills with us in cash?"

"Absolutely."

"What price range were you considering?"

"We want the best you have."

"What size are the grounds?"

"Five acres."

"Do you want outside or inside security?"

"Outside," George said.

"Do you have any moral or ethical ideals concerning the value of human life?"

I looked at George. "No," I said.

"Thank you." The machine increased its volume. "Mister Stalher, will you please show these gentlemen section C?"

Stalher smiled. "Right away," he answered, as if he were talking to his boss. He walked immediately out of the alcove, bidding us to follow.

"Nice chatting with you," I told the machine. "We'll have lunch sometime."

We moved past other alcoves that housed shelfloads of strange-looking electronic apparatus, all of them different, none bigger than a small microwave. These were hand-held Fancy Dan weapon prototypes, the kind that were sold through the retail outlets.

We passed two storerooms filled with larger machines of various designs that suited some purpose I would probably never know. As we walked, Stalher flicked us a quick look.

"You saved yourselves some money by choosing a lethal defense system," he said. "It's a lot easier and cheaper to design a system that eliminates rather than incapacitates."

I stuck a cig in my mouth. "Yeah. We think that the punks should get what they've got coming."

"I'm sorry," Stalher glared, then returned to his smile immediately, "there's no smoking allowed anywhere in the building. Here at Bermax, we don't believe in the propagation of negative habits. Mr. Charon believes . . ."

"Mr. Charon?"

"Our owner and general manager. He believes that negative habits are symptomatic of deep-rooted problems, and as such, should be eliminated so that the real problems can be attacked."

"Like with the punks," I replied, and stuck the cig back into my waistcoat.

"Exactly. Until the source of the social sickness can be removed, the body of society can never be healed."

"Charon sounds like he'd be great fun at a party," I said, wishing that my negative habit was lit and in my mouth.

We stopped in front of an entry door marked: SECTION C—RESTRICTED. Stalher went through some security procedures to get us inside that one.

"Do you know what you're looking for?" I whispered to George as we walked into the machine-filled room.

"Yeah," he answered, "a polite way of killing you for getting me into this place."

"In this section, we house our wide-area security devices." Stalher had moved to a stainless steal sphere roughly the size of a medicine ball. It sat on a single stem, like a chrome dandelion. He patted the light-reflecting surface. "This baby is one of the prettiest models in our line, but don't let its looks fool you . . . it's a real workhorse. Plug this little jewel into your sub station, and stand back. She gets to rotating," he started twisting cupped hands to describe the rotation of an invisible ball within, "like this, and starts putting out some volts . . . about half a million."

Stalher's eyes were gleaming like ball bearings; his voice had fallen to a melodious banter. "We call her the Juice Queen, and she'll fry anything within a two-acre area. Why, three of these babies could cover your plant grounds with enough spare juice to have a barbecue. And they're a real bargain at fifty-eight thousand each."

I looked at George; he was shaking his head.

"Too messy," I said. "What else have you got?"

He rubbed his large hands together and gazed around. "Well," he said, as if wrestling in his mind as to just what would be right for us. He clapped his hands with a loud slap. "How about this."

He led us to a rectangular box about the size of a coffin. It sprouted nozzles in porcupinelike profusion. "We call this the Armageddon III," he said. "This is a deadly adversary, and doesn't use a lot of electricity. What it does is spray a fine aluminum silicate into the atmosphere around your building. The mist is barely visible and tends to lure prospective felons, unsuspecting, on to your grounds. They go about twenty paces and—bingo! They can't breathe. The stuff coats their lungs and they suffocate, leaving a recognizable corpse and one less cul-de-sac on the avenue of society.''

He looked at me expectantly. I shook my head.

"No?" he said, and seemed disappointed.

"What about that one over there?" George asked, pointing to a flat black mat that occupied a corner. It was roped off by a red velvet cord attached to steel posts.

Stalher raised his eyebrows, knotting his broad forehead. "That, gentlemen, is the top of the line, the crème de la crème, as it were. And it's brand new this fall. Its technical name is Positive Charge Motivator for Molecular Displacement. But we like to call it the Electron Dump."

George seemed interested. He turned his head to face Stalher, then turned it back to stare at the machine. "How does it work?" he asked.

"I'll show you," he said, then walked over to flip a wall switch. A low, moaning hum emanated from the mat, and the slightest odor of ammonia touched my nose like the smell of a house when you walk into it. Other than that, the machine showed no evidence of being operational.

"In essence," Stalher said, "the dump charges the electrons in the air . . . makes them move very fast. As you can see, the barrier resulting is not visible to the eye. But then, neither is radiation."

He took a pen from an inside pocket of his toga and walked very carefully up to the velvet divider. He slowly stuck the pen past the rope, holding it gingerly by the tip and moving the thing into the air. It looked pretty foolish.

"They don't like me doing this . . ." he started to say, but before he could get the words out, an electric crackle cut him off. There were no sparks, nothing visual. In fact, nothing to show that anything had happened, except for the fact that the end of the pen was completely gone—as if it had never existed.

"Where is it?" I asked stupidly.

"It's all still here," he said. "The molecules got caught in the flux and literally came apart, mixing with the electrons of the air around us."

Stalher was still holding the pen out. "Do you mind?"

George asked, and smiled. He took the pen from Stalher's fingers and looked at the end. Grunting once, he handed it to me. The end where the pen had been sheared off was cut clean and left totally intact, as if the pen were made to be that way. I saw Phil Grover's body lying on his bedroom floor, bloodless and tidy.

Stalher nodded knowingly. "The edge of the field tends to leave things that way," he said. "The movement of the electrons just kind of packs the molecules tightly together as it moves past. Here, I'll give you another example."

He moved to a recessed water dispenser in a near wall. Pushing the release, a paper cup dropped into his hand. He filled it from the thumb spout. Coming back, he held it with thumb and index finger on the rim, and pushed it into the field the same way he had done with the pen. There was the same crackle, and when he pulled the cup away, it was sliced in two . . . and still holding water. It was crazy, as if a glass partition had been shoved in to hold the water. I reached out and touched the open place. The hard water had a cold, slick feel.

"Do you have these in hand-held models?" George asked.

If Stalher flinched, I didn't notice it.

"Not that I know of, Mr. Parker. I thought that it was wide-area security systems you were interested in."

"We are," I said. "Mr. Parker has a fascination for handguns, don't you, George?"

George swung his cams to each of us in turn. "Yes. First things first, I suppose. How much for this unit?"

Stalher unbelted his pocketcom. "Seven acres?" he asked.

"Five," I answered.

He read the figures into his machine, while George and I stared across the open expanse at each other. Until we found the Electron Dump, I didn't know how badly I had hoped that our search would end somewhere besides here.

"That'll be . . . approximately a million, one fifty. I think they would probably let me round it off to a million even for you."

"We'll have to think about it," I told him, ready to get out of there and breathe in some good old stale air. "Can we sleep on it?"

Stalher's eyes narrowed slightly. "Certainly," he said and pulled a business card out of his toga. "When you make up your mind, use my name if you would."

"Sure," I said, and took the card from him. "Friendly Ed Stalher," it read.

Stalher wasn't nearly as friendly on the ride back up. I guess he thought that losing a sale was something of a negative habit. Well, we had a line on the murder weapon, but that was a far cry from motive. The connection was there; I had leads to follow, but where those leads would take me was anybody's guess. When we drove through Fab 7, I carefully watched the workers in that area. I saw nothing to change my opinion that they were humans wearing masks. Interesting.

We returned to the acrylic sales office, where Stalher grudgingly bid us adieu. It was while we were being escorted out of the building by one of their security men that I saw her.

Sheila Grover.

She was talking with a tall, gray man down one of the aisles that branched off the exit corridor. Just when I thought things couldn't get any more complicated.

I could have buttered our rails and got us out of enemy territory as we originally intended, but this was just too sweet a nut to leave in the shell.

Poor George. He was relaxing noticeably with every step we took that brought us closer to the front door. "Hold onto your hat," I whispered to him. Sheila was perhaps fifteen paces from us. "Miss Grover!" I called out. She turned to the sound of her name. "Hello," I said, waving.

A look crossed her face such as I hadn't seen since the last time George beat me at gin. She waved back to me. The man standing next to her had turned also and was watching us in perplexity. I could tell that he didn't like surprises at his expense.

Sheila pulled his head down to mouth level and said something in his ear. His expression changed very little, but his eyes did widen just a touch. I had made an impression.

"What in the name of Freznel are you doing, Swain?" George growled.

"Shaking the beehive," I replied.

The tall man motioned for us to join him. The security man started to come along, but he was waved away. I closed the distance between us, with George following reluctantly behind, four-lettering me under his breath.

I walked up next to Grover. She tiptoed and quickly kissed me on the cheek, letting her body rest heavily against mine. It was a show designed for an audience of one. Her almond eyes were clicking like a roulette ball when she straightened up again. She looked good, done up like a veteran on flag day in a latex body-suit covered with spangles. "What brings you to Bermax, Marco Polo?" she asked in her little girl, inquisitive voice.

"I was about to ask you the same question," I returned.

She pursed her lips to keep from smiling broadly. "I'm having lunch with my fiancé," she replied, drifting her eyes in the tall man's direction.

"Rick Charon," the man said and his hand was in front of me. I shook it. He was tall—I had to look up to meet his eyes—and lean, like a praying mantis. His hair was as white as sun-bleached bones, and his pale gray eyes as direct as armour-piercing shells. He looked at me, or rather through me, and I could tell that he was mean the way a lot of people think they're mean.

"Swain," I said. "Nice little set-up you've got here."

"It pays the rent," he said.

I nodded. "And the rent for the rest of Texas too."

"What does bring you to Bermax?" he asked, and took me apart with those eyes.

'I'm here with my friend, Mr. Parker," I answered. George nodded grimly. "He wanted me to look at security systems with him for his new plant."

"I see," he said. "I hope that we are able to take care of you." His face was smooth, unlined, as if it had never known a smile or grimace before. That made it impossible to determine his age. His lips remained continually set in a thin slash. His gray three-piece was silk, but simply cut, not at all flashy, except that it fit him as if those little worms had all had Rick Charon in mind.

Sheila looped her arm through mine and pressed herself up

against me again. Charon tightened his jaw muscles, but his expression remained rock solid. "Swain is supposed to be working for my father right now," she said. "Shame on you for playing hooky."

I shrugged. "I'll work overtime tomorrow," I said.

"We were just about to go to my offices for a drink before lunch," Charon said. "Would you care to join us?"

George spoke up. "Well, I don't think that we . . ."

"We'd be delighted," I said.

We went down the hall in the direction they were headed in before I had stopped them. Sheila was still all over me. She was playing me off Charon, which may have been a lot like giving a baby a cobra to cuddle in his crib.

We arrived at Charon's office in short order. His door was guarded both electronically and by Fancy Dans. We entered a palatial suite of rooms that resembled an office in much the same way the sun resembles a bright light. The place was a warehouselike room, wide open, that had been carved in levels. The levels sat like platforms at various heights within the truly incredible chamber. They were all connected by wide, sweeping steps. The whole place was marble-pillared, looking like the twenty-first century's dream of what ancient Greek or Roman splendor must have been but really wasn't. On the lowest level, a large, tiled pool waited invitingly. The office was clean to a fault, like a restaurant bathroom when the health department comes to visit. The cold, metallic air fairly reeked of frankincense. It was so idyllic that it made me want to take a grease pencil and scribble graffiti all over those white clean walls to humanize the place a little. I guess I'm just uncultured.

We descended a broad staircase, then climbed another, then another, until we were on the highest platform of a very high room. From there, the whole place spread out before us like a Christmas garden. This top level really was done up like an office, with desks and computers and a 3-D vis on the wall. The vis was turned on; it was showing scenes of the fire the night before. It was a long shot, encompassing a wide area . . . all of it on fire. Buildings burned like candles on an octogenarian's birthday cake, and meat machines filled the skies, dropping into the excitement like metal vultures smelling death on an asphalt desert.

"Quite a tragedy last night," Charon said, when he saw me watching the picture.

"I wouldn't know," I answered.

"Twenty-three buildings destroyed in a five-block area."

"How many dead?" George asked him.

Charon blinked a couple of times, then went and sat behind his big marble desk. "Of course, they haven't sifted through all the rubble yet," he answered, "but it looks like the toll may climb to over four hundred. Drink?"

"Bourbon," I said. "Rocks. What caused the fire? Do they know?"

"They think it may have been arson," he replied, and his lips wanted to smile but they didn't. "They say a man pretending to be a policeman got into the building where the fire began just before it happened."

"I'll have some sherry, Rick darling," Sheila said, and she kittened herself on a swivel chair facing away from the screen. "Do you want to hear a coincidence, Swain? The fire started in the building where my brother Phil used to live."

"Small world."

She nodded. "So he gets diced on Monday instead of french-fried on Wednesday. I guess his goose would have been cooked either way." She chuckled at her own joke. "Did you know the police accidentally sent his body down the dumper?"

"I heard," I replied.

"Drink, Mr. . . . ah, Parker?" Charon asked George, who had elected to sit on a hard-backed chair close to the steps.

George pointed to his stomach. "No, thanks. Alcohol impairs my vision."

"Very wise," Charon nodded. "Drinking is an extremely negative habit." He looked up at me. "It dulls the senses, slows our reactions and awareness, causes us to make . . . fatal mistakes."

There was a portable bar next to the desk. He fixed my drink and Sheila's, and then poured himself a glass of distilled water. "A toast," he said.

"To negative habits," Sheila responded.

"And to coincidence," I added and drained my glass in one gulp.

I set my empty glass down on his desk and walked to the edge of the platform to look down at the pool. It almost seemed as if I could jump and hit it from way up there.

"Another drink?" Charon asked.

"No, thanks," I said, turning my back to him.

"Sheila tells me that you're looking for the person who killed her brother Phil."

"Sheila says a lot of things," I answered.

"Don't be tacky, street person," she smiled from her chair.

"Oh, I get it," he said. "You're protecting your client's confidence, right?"

"Something like that."

"That's a very professional attitude."

"I take my work very seriously." I walked back to the desk and sat on the edge. "Why the interest? Was Phil a friend of yours?"

Charon sipped his water in tiny gulps, like a bird. "Never met the man," he said, "but he was to be my brother-in-law."

"A dubious honor, darling," Sheila said from over her glass. She finished it and gave it back to Charon to pour another. He gave her a stern look, which she returned with more than equal vehemence. Shaking his head slowly, he refilled the glass and handed it back to her.

Charon folded his hands on the desk top and gave me that X-ray look again. "Suppose that you *are* investigating Phil Grover's death . . ."

"Ricky, please," Sheila said. "I'm in mourning."

"Okay," I said. "Just hypothetically."

"What makes you think that you could find out more than the police could about it?"

"Never said I could," I answered, and leaned down a little closer to him. "Tell you one thing though, I'd make a horse race out of it. I'd give old man Grover his money's worth, because that's the kind of guy I am. And I'd follow up every lead, no matter where it took me."

"Even to the gates of hell, Mr. Swain?"

"And back again, Mr. Charon."

He leaned back and folded his arms across his chest. "You're an extraordinary man," he said. "I didn't think they made them like you anymore—tough, principled, tenacious, fearless . . ."

"Not so fearless," I replied.

Charon looked around slowly, then stared at me. "I think you underestimate yourself. Don't you agree, Mr. Parker?"

George gulped once and nodded.

"I'm just a worn-out pavement pounder trying to do a job," I said.

"You're much more than that," Charon replied. "You're a first-class game player."

"Game?"

"The life game, Swain. To me, life is a never-ending contest, a tournament. Every move we make puts us into conflict with others, the opposition. The job of life is to try to ascertain exactly what it is we want, and then to move toward that goal in the most expeditious manner possible. We must illuminate our positive attributes and curtail our negative habits. We must understand the opposition and the threat they pose to us. We must study the strengths and weaknesses of our opposition, then do whatever is necessary to clear the obstacles that they place in our path to success."

"What if we figure the opposition wrong?" I asked.

He put his hands down flat on the table. "Exactly," he said. "That sometimes happens. When it does, we must reevaluate the contest, putting the opposition in proper perspective. I've always felt that if you can't demolish a house with a velvet-covered hammer, you use dynamite."

Sheila stood up, yawning. "I'm hungry," she said. "Let's eat."

"Would you gentlemen care to join us?" Charon asked.

I shook my head, and I could hear George sigh with relief. "Me and Mr. Parker have some things we have to do. We'll take a rain check."

"A man with as many negative habits as you seem to have may not have time to claim too many rain checks."

"You'd be surprised," I answered. "I'm like the India

rubber man: stretch me all out of shape and I always manage to snap back.''

"I'm hungry," Sheila pouted and began stamping her feet like a little kid.

Charon let his eyes drift toward the girl without changing his relative position. In a second he was looking at me again. "I like you," he said. "You're not afraid of me. That's good." He nodded slowly up and down. "I've enjoyed our little talk. It's been a nice . . . break. But alas," he stood up and everyone else did the same, "all good things must come to an end, and it's time to return to the games. Eh, Swain?"

"I don't play games," I answered.

He shrugged with his eyes. "Pity. You'd make anyone a worthy opponent. I hope you enjoyed your sightseeing tour."

"It was very informative," I said.

"Clever fellow," he responded. "Mr. Parker. Good day."

George was already moving down the steps. "Good day," he called over his shoulder.

"See you again," I said, hurrying to catch up with George.

"I seriously doubt it, Mr. Swain," Charon called back to me.

We got out of there while the getting was good. I had confronted the "opposition" and come away in one piece, even if it was because Charon thought it was cute. He was playing with me, cat-and-mouse fashion, with me as the gray one with the big ears.

As I hummed my bullet across the grounds, George kept mumbling and looking over his shoulder. At least now I knew who I was up against. The big question, of course, was why?

13

I decided to take a chance and stopped at my apartment since they knew I was alive now anyway. Matilda hadn't been fed for a while, and I didn't care much for hiding in alleyways. Everything looked natural out on the street, so I left George out in the bullet with instructions to get to Ginny's if anything happened to me, and went inside.

I keyed open the door. The street-view shutters were drawn, so it was black as the water in Lake Michigan in there. I no sooner got all the way in the door than I knew I should be someplace else.

"Who's in here?"

I reached for the light switch and my arms were roughly grabbed from behind. I struggled until I felt the barrel of the laser jamming me rudely under the chin. The lights came up and I was face to face with Fat Mack's diseased meatball of a face. He was chuckling low, almost a groan. Two of his bully boys had me by the arms.

"Have I waited for this," he said and ground the gun a little farther into my breathing. "I've wanted to get you in my ballpark for a long time."

"You're too fat," I choked out. "I could never fit."

"Shuddup," he squealed, and pulling the gun away from my neck, slammed it into my gut with his full weight and his full anger. My knees turned to quicksilver and I sank, supported only by the arms of the guys holding me. I closed my eyes and felt the nausea rifle through my body. I hoped I wouldn't give Mack the satisfaction of seeing me throw up.

"Do you heah me, Swain," his voice drifted through the pain. I tried to speak—couldn't.

He grabbed me by the hair, jerking my head up to meet his. "I said, do you heah me!"

I nodded, gritting my teeth.

"Good," he said, straightening up. "I've got me a warrant for your arrest, and I'd purely hate to have you miss the reading of your rights."

"When did you learn how to read?" I mumbled, and he hit me again.

And again.

14

I woke up on the chair, with Jumpstreet Harry staring sullenly at me. I hurt all over. Fat Mack and his buddies had apparently had a good time. I really didn't remember too much of it.

"Damn you, Swain. I told you this would happen if you weren't careful." His face puttied into something of a frown, like brown bread dough sagging off the rolling board. It struck me that he was getting fleshier as the years went by. "You can't imagine the trouble you're causing me and the whole department."

"Someday, Harry. Someday, I'm going to see you looking as if you had a full night's sleep."

He hitched his hands onto his hips and shook his head. "Maybe some day I'll get a full night's sleep. Sorry about Mack, but you know how you antagonize him. Anything broken?"

I was strapped down by the wrists and ankles, with an alpha band holding my head in check. "Don't think so, but can't you get this crap off me?"

"I will, just as soon as you give me the name of the person you investigated for Phil Grover."

"Check my files," I said.

"Come on. We already did. You've programmed that info out of there, or hidden it someplace. What difference could it possibly make if you give us that name?"

"If I reveal professional confidences, I may as well close down shop."

"Your client is dead, blown to pieces. He can't possibly

care. I don't know what this is all about, but I'm under incredible pressure right now. Will you please give me that name?''

I twisted my head as much as the ring would allow. Introg was a bare, black room occupied only by the Truth Chair. A small window was set near the top of the cinderblock chamber, where technicians in the booth beyond could view the proceedings. It was cold in there, and damp like the D.T.'s.

''What happens if I tell you what you want to know?''

''Right now, your life isn't worth a heli-bus token. I swear to you, Swain. Help me now and I'll try to keep you alive.'' He put his mouth close to my ear and whispered. ''I'll put you in protective custody, look out for you for a month or so until this blows over. And that's about the only chance you've got.''

I couldn't help but laugh. ''You're going to help me out by putting me in jail. Now that's an interesting twist.''

He stood up straight, his face harder. ''You know,'' he said, ''the descriptions of the two police impersonators at the Marmeth last night sounded embarrassingly like you and your friend Wesley. If you want, I can bring that guard down here to identify you.''

''An identification would mean a trial. I'm not so sure that your . . . benefactor would want all this brought out in open court.''

''And what do you know about my benefactor?''

''I met Mr. Charon this morning.''

Harry started. If there was doubt in my mind about the mysterious controller of the Grover investigation, Harry cleared it up with a glance.

He got right up in my face. ''Your nobility is touching, Swain, but it's going to get you killed. You're playing Don Quixote to an empty house. Don't you see,'' he rasped, ''nobody cares. Give me that name and save yourself.''

''Use your machines, Harry. Sell yourself out. Just don't ask me to make it easy for you.''

''Damn you,'' he said through clenched teeth. Stepping back, he nodded in the direction of the window.

I felt it coming up indolently, seeping slowly into my brain like a cat stalking a bird—slowly, slowly. I could feel it

107

slipping into me, wrapping my brain with tentacles, sucking away my private thoughts, leaving me naked and exposed. I felt ashamed; I felt dirty. I looked through a haze of dull red at Harry, whose face was etched with inner pain. He didn't like the Truth Chair any more than I did.

"What's your name?" he asked me.

"Mathew Swain," I heard my voice say.

"What's your age?"

"Thirty-three."

"Did you ever work for Philip Grover?"

I tried to lie, tried to say no. There was pain, like an ice pick, that went straight down my spinal cord. I saw myself straining against the straps that held me, but felt nothing but the ice-cold agony in my neck and back.

"Stop fighting it, you idiot," Harry was saying. "You can't beat the machine."

"Go to hell," I managed, and the pain got worse.

"The name, Swain. The name of the person you investigated for Grover."

The name flashed out in my head, first in neon, then in flaming letters. I bit down hard, gnashing my teeth to keep from letting the name out. The letters began to grow, to push against the inside of my skull, trying to force their way out.

"Damn it Swain!"

The letters grew; my head grew. The tentacles tightened and forced the pain farther down my back. I heard a retching sound from far away, but couldn't connect it with myself.

"The name!" Harry was screaming, grabbing my lapels. "For God's sake, stop torturing yourself."

The letters were stretching my skull, trying to pop my head like a balloon. I wanted to pass out—couldn't.

"The name, the name."

The letters forced themselves into my throat, up my tongue, into my mouth. When they came out, somebody else was saying them in a voice that couldn't have belonged to me.

"Mi-n-a Goul-d-ing."

The pressure stopped immediately. My body, tensed like a taut bow, suddenly relaxed. I felt as if I were melting into the chair. Harry's face was twisted with anguish. He was drenched with sweat and his eyes were afraid . . . of what I didn't know.

He turned silently and started to leave the room.

"Harry," I called to him, and my voice was weak.

He hesitated slightly before walking back to me. He bent down low so he could hear my muffled, slurring speech. "You give Charon that name," I said. "If she dies, you killed her just as surely as if you'd strangled her with your own hands. Think about it."

He stood over me, as if trying to think of something to say. Finally he sighed. "You'll sleep for a while," he said, and walked from the room.

I wanted to stay awake, but couldn't see any point to it. They had taken my mind and my dignity, and maybe a little sleep would help me forget for a while. As I drifted away, I saw Mina Goulding running down a long dark street. She was calling for help, but no one could hear her.

15

Harry had me released after I came around. That was the biggest surprise I'd had since I didn't get a pony for my tenth birthday. I left headquarters feeling sore all over and toting around the granddaddy of all hangovers. After my arrest, I didn't see George. I hoped that he made it to Ginny's all right. Her place was the most secured I'd ever seen, and I figured he'd be as safe there as anyplace else I could think of.

I took a heli-bus to her place, taking a circuitous route just in case. When I let myself in, George was on the sofa watching naked women doing exercises on the vis. He had worked some sort of feedback pattern on the screen, and the women were coming through as well-angled blotches of bright, distorted color. Ginny was sitting at her formica counter, head in hands, apparently thinking of more ways to get rich.

"I didn't expect a brass band," I said, "but this is ridiculous."

They both jerked to my voice. Ginny was on her feet and in my arms before I finished talking. She held on to me for a minute, shaking. George had gotten off the sofa and walked toward us, grinning with his mouth and glowing with his eyes.

"You don't seem too much the worse for wear," he said, and patted me lightly on the shoulder.

Ginny pulled away from me. "You had me worried sick, you louse. Now I remember why I had to go to California and get away from you." She scolded with her voice, but her eyes were happy.

I turned and headed back out the door. "If it'll make you

guys happy," I said, "I'll go out and come back in with a broken arm."

Ginny pulled me back. "You'll do no such thing," she said, and was in my arms again, making obscene suggestions in my ear.

It was good to be back in friendly territory again. My pain and humiliation were beginning to fade, like the memory of winter after the first warmth of spring. I remembered that I hadn't eaten all day.

"You got anything to eat around here besides stock market quotations?" I asked.

Ginny made another whispered suggestion. I slapped her on her chair warmer.

"Good," I said, "but not very filling."

George got a kick out of that.

Ginny walked to the vis and juiced it to the kitchen computer, which made a quick inventory of edibles and flashed them on the screen, along with possible nutritious combinations. Nutrition was something I'd always been suspicious of, like ladies' pistols and months with twenty-eight days. I had a bologna sandwich and a carton of beer.

They sat around the table watching me wolf down my food. Between gulps, I told them about what happened at the station house. I finished the sandwich; and wanted another. Ginny offered to fix it. George waited until she was out of the room before speaking.

"So what do we do now?" he asked. "We're getting it from both ends. I can't go on living here the rest of my life."

"What would the neighbors say," I replied.

"This is serious, Swain. Ginny's probability computer wouldn't even give me odds against our survival chances."

I took a drink of beer directly from its waxed container. "I'm sorry, George. I really am. I dragged you into this thing before I realized just how . . ."

He waved me to silence, then stood up. He was nervous. "That's not the point. I wanted in . . . hell, I forced my way in. My problem now is how to get out. I feel like a fisherman with a whale on the end of his hook: I've got a whopper, but it's going to eat me."

"What do you want from me, George?"

111

"I guess I want you to tell me that we've got a chance."

George looked up quickly. Ginny had reentered the room.

"Answer him, Matt," she said, and set the sandwich down on my plate. "I'm in this as much as you are."

I frowned. She was probably right. So far they had been a step ahead of me most of the way. It had been my own fault. I should have understood what I was up against when that punk guard decked me at the Grover place. Now we were all standing on our tiptoes with the water up to our noses and rising. But Ginny's building was secure . . . and fireproof.

"A chance," I said. They were both standing over me, staring, waiting for me to tell them something that would make it all easier. I couldn't think of anything. "We're still alive. We know what to look out for. Sure, we've got a chance. Charon's flesh and blood the same as we are. At least, I think he is."

"What would happen if you just gave it up?" Ginny asked.

"Can't do that," I answered. "Not until I'm convinced that I can't do the job. Besides, at this juncture I don't think it would matter."

George sat again and focused his cams on me from across the table. "Is it the job?" he asked. "Or is it some sort of perverted contest between you and Charon?"

"I'm a reacter, George, not a philosopher. But Charon has already covered up one murder with hundreds. He's got the money, the organization, the power . . . he's even got the law. I don't know about you, but I couldn't live with myself if I turned my back on this now."

He leaned back and smiled. "What do you want me to do?"

"Keep looking for Mina Goulding, although I'm afraid that may be a blank wall now. Shadow the Richmond like we did before."

"What if I find her?"

"Grab her, kidnap her, hit her on the head . . . just get her back here so I can talk to her."

"Sounds like fun," he said, his eyebrows jerking up and down above his black-bulging, silent eyes. "What about you?"

"I've got to visit some new friends," I said, and looked at Ginny, "and some old ones."

Ginny narrowed her eyes and looked at me sideways. "I hope you're not talking about the old friend that I think you're talking about."

I dug into the second sandwich. "At this point in time, we need all the help we can get."

She took a seat right next to me. Reaching out, she rested her hand on my knee. "Rick Charon's not a man who accepts failure," she said.

I turned and stared at her. There was concern straining her features. "You know Charon?"

She smiled an automatic, unhappy smile. "Money travels in the same circles, my love. I even dated the man for a while . . . a long time ago."

"What do you make of him?" I asked, not wanting to dwell on a relationship between Ginny and the man who was trying to kill me. George was watching her intently.

She giggled nervously and stared straight ahead, at no one. Her fingers continually played with her lower lip, as if tugging it could help her pull the words out.

"I've never talked about Charon," she began, and glanced quickly at me, just touching me with her eyes. "I don't like to think about him. There's not a whole lot—he's a very private person. Started the business himself, with money he got from heaven knows where. He hired some very bright people to invent things, mostly military-type things, and then was able to back up his inventions with low-cost manufacturing techniques. He succeeded from the first because nobody was able to put together systems nearly as cheaply as Rick Charon. He runs his business himself, talks to no one about it. It's his baby all the way down the line. I suppose you could say, in his field, that he's a genius. His techniques have never been duplicated."

"How old is he?" I asked, just to relieve the question that had bothered me ever since I had seen his unfeatured face.

Ginny slowly shook her head. "Don't know. Don't think anybody does. He confides in nobody, mostly because he doesn't have a very high opinion of the human race. He believes that the majority of humanity doesn't understand the game-playing nature of life, and are consequently unfit to live it."

"That part I've heard about," I said.

"The only thing he likes about people is their boundless desire to be manipulated. He likes to control. He's got everything else. Personal power over people is the thing that gives him pleasure in life. It's all a big game to him . . . the manipulation. I think he's consciously trying to work it out so that he can manipulate the whole world."

She looked at me again, and this time her eyes held mine. "I'm not so sure he can't do it either."

George leaned back and put his hands behind his head. "When you pick an enemy," he said, "you don't screw around."

"What about him and Sheila Grover?"

"It's got to be another game. He senses a weakness in her that he feels is worth exploiting for one reason or another. Somewhere down the line, this fiancé business has got to clobber little Sheila right between the eyes. Watch out, though. He's very possessive about his women. Once he's made his conquest . . . staked his claim, his women belong to him alone. Even when he's through with them, they're still his property."

Ginny saw me staring at her. "No, I never," she said. "He scared me too much. He's inhuman, Matt. This thing with you is no more than a trifle to him."

I left the second sandwich half-finished. I wasn't very hungry anymore. "It wasn't a trifle to Phil Grover," I said standing up, "or to all the people who died in that fire. Mind if I use your shower?"

16

There was a good wind from the south, and it had managed to clear the smog cover enough to let some late afternoon sunshine in. The Grovers' house reflected the bright light like a dull mirror, making it glow hotly—controlled fire. I saw only two guards on the grounds this time, the two I had accosted last time. They treated me with understandable trepidation. I thought that they were probably all right, but I dealt with them carefully because at this point all I trusted was the reflection I saw in my own looking glass, and even that had a certain wavy quality.

I showed up without notice, and by a route probably used last by the Spanish looking for El Dorado. Mr. Barnett ushered me in, and said that old man Grover was asleep. That was okay with me; I was there to see Sheila anyway. I was directed to her rooms on the second floor. I went up by myself and knocked lightly on the door. No response. I knocked again, then let myself in. The room was round and gauzy, like being on the inside of a cocoon. A gentle light filtered through all around and pulsed with a heartbeat rhythm. It was very compelling. I felt like a dog lying in a sunspot on a cold day. There was a big stasis bed to my right, and the cream-colored, fuzzy floor pulsed the same light as the rest of the place.

The room was full of Sheilas. They were everywhere—dancing and miming and curling up in little balls all over the room. Some of them were dressed like clowns, some like Parisian streetwalkers of the fondly remembered, early twentieth century, some like oriental maidens of antiquity, some like Eve before the Fall. All of them were phonies. I went to each in turn, calling to them like a damn fool and putting my hand through the projection. They kept moving and that confused me. Finally, I saw the genuine article.

She was sitting in a secluded section of the room, dressed in the same gown that she had worn the first time I met her. She sat on the floor, her knees drawn up so that she could rest her chin on them. Her arms were curled tightly around her legs. She was staring at what passed for the wall.

I called her name without result. I moved closer and saw that she was staring at a cobweb-infested area that stood in marked contrast to the spotlessness of the rest of the room.

I came right next to her and hunched down.

"This is their place," she said, without turning to me. "When I first put them here, they'd go off and try to build their houses in other parts of the room. But I wouldn't let them. I'd always bring them back and bring them food to this place, and after a while they learned to stay here."

"Let's talk about Charon," I said.

"Look," she said, and pointed to a large, hairy spider that was feeding off a slick black cockroach that had gotten caught in its web. "I call him Porthos."

"Porthos?"

"I read a book one time—just to see what it felt like—and it had a character in it who liked to eat all the time. His name was Porthos. Have you ever seen a book?"

"Seen a couple. I tried to read one once, but I couldn't get all the way through. It *was* pretty long."

She looked at me and smiled a little-girl smile. "I caught that bug for Porthos this morning, but he'll be hungry again before the day is over. I wonder what a bug tastes like? How do you think it tastes to the spider . . . like steak maybe, or soyburger?"

"I don't think it tastes like anything."

"Oh, pooh," she said with a frown. "You don't have any imagination. Rick's going to kill you, you know."

"Not if I have anything to say about it. What do you know about this?"

"About what?"

"Charon and your brother." My knees were beginning to

116

stiffen up; I had to stand. Sheila looked up at me, then extended a bare arm. I helped her to her feet.

"I don't know what you're talking about," she answered. "Rick's going to kill you because of the way you were shamelessly throwing yourself at me in his office. He's very jealous." She ran across the room and threw herself on the stasis. "That was really impulsive of you. I think he suspects all about us now."

I walked over to the bed and looked down at her floating form. "Stop it, Sheila," I said angrily. "This isn't some rich girl fun. Charon's up to his ears in your brother's murder, and I want to know what you've got to do with him."

She sat up. Her eyes flared like industrial lasers. "You're crazy," she said. "What a freak show."

"What did Phil talk to you about the day he died?" I asked.

She looked surprised, but only for a second. "What did Phil always talk about?" she said. "Money. He said he was into a big deal and wanted me to put the touch on the old bones."

"Why didn't he do it himself?"

"He didn't want to have to earn it, if you know what I mean. Figured I had paid my family dues and could get it easier."

"What could you get in return?"

"It never got that far," she said. "I wouldn't cross the street for my brother. I let him ramble on for a few minutes, then blanked him. He didn't call back."

"What was his connection with Charon?"

"Stop inventing games," she said, and her voice was low and guttural. "I know what you really want here." She ran her hands along her upper thighs. "And you'd do anything to get it. Wouldn't you, street person?"

I wanted to hit her, but didn't. "I wouldn't dirty my hands on you," I told her.

She sprang from the bed, nails bared like claws, and hit me full force. We struggled through the projections as if we were waltzing in a ballroom full of dancing ghosts. I tried to hold her off at first, but she fought like a banshee, and when she drew blood from my face, I tapped her a pretty good one on the jaw to save my eyes. She crumpled to the floor, where her spectres danced all over her. She sat there for a minute in shock.

When she looked at me, her eyes were glazed. "Get out of here," she growled, "before I scream rape."

I smiled and shook my head. "Who in this house would believe that?" I replied.

"Get out!" she yelled, and she was shaking all over. "Get out!"

I pulled her up and threw her on the bed. "Listen, little girl," I said. "I'm working for your daddy, but when it all comes down that's not going to protect you. You can't keep playing both ends against the middle and not get burned. If you're in this when I bump your boyfriend, I'm sure as shooting going to bump you too."

She rolled, facing away from me. "Go screw yourself," she hissed. "You'll be lucky to see the sun rise tomorrow."

I watched her back for a moment, watched the rise and fall of her labored, hysterical breathing, then walked quickly from the room. Closing the door behind me, I moved to the edge of the balcony and looked down. Mr. Barnett was nowhere to be seen. I decided it was time to take a private tour of the premises.

Moving slowly around the curve of the exposed hallway, I listened at each door I came to, then opened it. There were two bathrooms, and several vacant bedrooms, furnished and kept in meticulous order. Finding nothing of consequence on the second floor, I climbed the stairs to the third.

Up there were more bathrooms and a few totally empty chambers. I kept going until I heard noise from behind one of the doors. I opened it a crack. Mr. Grover was lying, apparently asleep, on a black-cushioned table with a fringed canopy over it, like a four poster. The table was surrounded by push-up machines that had wires connecting into Grover's inert form. The machines hummed and clicked, as if the old man were getting recharged like a wet-cell battery.

I closed the door and moved on.

Music drifted from behind the next door. It was gentle music—formless, but pleasant. I stood close to the door for a time, straining for other sounds.

"Don't stand out there in the cold," a female voice said. "Come in."

I turned the knob and entered.

"Please, close it behind you," the voice said. "I get so few visitors . . . I don't want to lose you just yet."

The voice came from a young woman who sat on a plain wooden chair in the center of the room. The room was bare, except for a small bed (a real one) in the corner, and the music computer, which was mathematically creating the random melody that drew me to the chamber. The entire ceiling was a skylight that windowed the smog cover. Its glass was cerulean, forcing the light that entered to bathe the entire room in hazy blue, like the inside of an opal.

"I can barely feel you," she said. "Come closer."

I walked up to her. She was dressed in white cotton that the air made blue. Her hair was black velvet, like Sheila's only longer—much longer. This could only be Angela. Her resemblance to Sheila was striking, except that her aspect was much calmer and more controlled, which made her beauty far more appealing.

"You're a man of violence," she said, and shuddered.

I leaned closer, studying her face. "Only when pushed to it," I answered. Her eyes were smoky, unfocused. She was blind.

"I see better this way," she said as if knowing my thoughts. "I see the inner light."

"I've come to talk to you about your brother, Phil."

"Brother?" she asked, and her brows bunched in concern. "What is a brother?"

"Your father's son," I answered in confusion. "Your brother."

"Father," she said, and I could see that she didn't understand.

I tried again. "Tell me about your life."

She smiled. "There's nothing to know. My life is dreams. My life is shadows that slip past me to leave marks on my inside eyes." She pointed to her head. "There is food, and, I think, sleep sometimes. But sleep is dreams too. Things get large in me sometimes, and sometimes small, and voices call to me about things I don't understand."

I straightened, staring down at her. "What sort of things?"

"Things I tell people who come to me. Things that make them glow bright and fuzzy." She clenched her fists and began shaking convulsively. The music suddenly became hard and angry. It wrapped us in a package of blue and floated me down a river of twisted estuaries running to a dying sea. I shook my head; she was somehow affecting me. I spoke just to break the spell.

"Tell me about the things you tell people."

She stopped shaking and looked at me with unseeing eyes. "I tell them about ripe rotted fruit and the links we share with death and decay. I tell them about the leech within, the bloodsucking worm. I tell them, and they grow fuzzy and angry, and that frightens me."

"Mr. Swain."

I turned to the sound. Barnett was standing at the door, scowling at me.

"Took a wrong turn," I said.

The man accosted me with his eyes, trying to rip me with a glance. "I think you'd better go now," he said simply, though I could tell he wanted to say much more.

"Sure," I answered, and looked back to the girl. "Goodbye, Angie."

"Touch my face," she said.

I looked at Barnett. He nodded. Reaching out, I let my fingertips brush her cheeks. She grabbed my hand in both of hers and pressed the palm firmly against her face. She smiled broadly, and the music became gentle again. "You flow warm," she said. "Nice."

"You're not so bad yourself," I answered.

I started to move off, but she held my hand firmly. I turned back to her.

"You search for currents in a stagnant pond," she said sadly. "Don't drown."

She released my hand and I left with Mr. Barnett.

"I hope you didn't upset her too much," the old man said as we walked down the hall. "Her fits of depression are . . . indescribable."

"What exactly is wrong with her?" I asked, as we rounded the corridor and started down the steps.

He shook his head. "She's always been like that. There's apparently nothing that can be done for her, but Mr. Grover doesn't have the heart to have her institutionalized."

"But surely with all the . . ."

"Mr. Grover has tried everything, done everything. Angela is a hopeless case."

"I'm sorry," I said, because I couldn't think of anything else to say.

Barnett dead-eyed me. "Yes."

He walked me all the way to the door, and hummed the pitch to open it.

"What about Phil's time in the asylum?" I asked him. "What do you know about that?"

"Philip Grover had no tolerance for alcohol or drugs," he said. "When he used them to excess, they would have an . . . unsettling effect on his mind. He went to a sanitarium several times to pull himself back together."

"Why weren't the doctor's reports included in the official police records?"

"Mr. Grover believes in keeping family matters within the family. Good evening, Mr. Swain."

He watched me all the way down the steps before closing the door. As I was crunching down the drive, I saw Sheila out in the yard, examining a hedge in great detail. She waved when she saw me, as if we were the best of friends.

"Porthos is hungry," she called, and held up a jar full of bugs.

I waved back and climbed into the bullet, humming it down the drive and through the gate, which had been dragged out of the way but never replaced. Things were falling apart everywhere.

17

I left my bullet at the last safe parking spot and walked into no man's land. It was already getting dark as I moved into the building forest that secluded every kind of four- and two-legged animal. The setting sun filtered through the oxide-rich atmosphere, turning the sky into a blue-black, rainbow-veined, carnival dream. Dark, colorless buildings loomed hundreds of meters straight up, casting shadows that were long, like a pimp's yellow sheet, and darker than the darkness that surrounded them.

I walked quickly, listening to my shoe leather slap the cracked and broken sidewalks beneath me, occasionally catching the strain of other sounds from deep within the guts of the electricless towers. They were human sounds and not human. They were the sounds of the street animals, the scrabblers and hangers-on, the survivors who sharpened their carnivorous claws on brick and set their traps near drain-gutter water pools. They hunted by night; they hunted each other; they hunted in packs; they hunted alone; they hunted warm blood and cold cash.

This was the beginning of the concrete DMZ, the point of debarkation into the complete decay. This was the place where civilization dare not enter, lest it be ripped to bloody shreds in the jaws of survival. This was the pretty place where the monthly drug-and-food welfare handouts were dropped from never-landing helium machines to salve the conscience of a guilt-ridden world. This was where the police never ventured, where every doorway held the promise of death, where Maria Hidalgo ruled like a feudal baroness.

And all I could think about was bloodsucking worms.

I was still on Tremaine, but it was unrecognizable as a major thoroughfare. Weeds with big leaves that dripped thick, gooey sap pushed through every crack in the streets and sidewalks. Incredibly, mesquite trees grew also, punching through asphalt, their twisted, gnarled roots ripping the street cover off in huge shards and pushing it aside like the scab on a healed place. Everything was in crumble. The buildings were falling, littering the ground with rocky rubbish. Light poles, traffic poles, sign poles, once proudly erect, now rested impotently on their sides, blocking streets that had long since spurned traffic.

A half-block ahead of me, a figure stepped out of an alleyway. He was young, and black as the descending night. He was lean and streamlined and tensed tight, arms dangling at his sides. I moved closer. He was shoeless and clad only in bulky trousers that were tied around his middle with a length of rope. A red bandanna was tied around his forehead to hold his shoulder-length matted hair in place. And I could tell by his bearing that he had friends waiting close by. I walked right up to him.

"Hey, rich white," he said, and his eyes caught mine and never wavered. His eyes were bottomless pits; they were unyielding finality; they had me dead and gutted. "Got spend?"

I knew better than to bring money into the decay. "No spend," I answered, and tried to move around him.

He shifted to block my path. "Got clothes," he replied, touching my suit. "Got trade," he smiled through devastated teeth, and held up my wristwatched arm. He continued to smile and without moving his lips said, "Got sell-meat." He already had me divided up to the bootleg organ people.

I turned to my right, and there was another one standing there, and another behind me, then more poured out of the alley. They stood around me, jabbering excitedly, moving up and down to amphetamine rhythms. Their eyes were glazed and hollow, their faces lit with childlike happiness. They were savoring the kill.

The human circle around me began to close in. The leader's hand slowly reached for my face. I began laughing. Loud laughter. Hysterical laughter. The hand jerked away from me and the circle loosened somewhat.

I started jumping up and down, skipping imaginary rope. "Chinka, chinka, Chinaman, sittin' on a fence." I hopped and chanted, watching the ragged faces around me slacken in concern. "Trying to make a dollar out of fifty-nine cents."

They were looking at each other, fear mirrored in their sunken eyes. The leader, suspicious, took a step toward me. A naked white female with dirt-stringy hair and large, swaying breasts grabbed him by the arm.

"Zerk'r," she said. "Zerk'r."

He turned to stare at her, then back to me.

I bowed deeply.

He took a step toward me.

"Once there was an elephone who tried to use the telephone."

He stopped, narrowing his eyes.

"No, no, I mean an elephant who tried to use the telephant."

I began moving toward my assailants.

"Dear me I am not certain quite, that even now I've got it right."

They shrank from my touch, backpeddling to avoid my grasp. The word zerk'r drifted through their midst. I moved right up to the leader, folding my hands in front of him. "Here is the church, and here is the steeple."

His eyes grew wide.

"Open it up, and see all the people." I turned my hands palms up and began wiggling my fingers, all the while giggling like a madman. He stepped back and protectively put an arm around the woman.

"Zerk'r," he said, and as a man, the group broke and ran.

All except one.

A meticulously groomed black man wearing a cement-grey latex body-suit stood looking at me. A large meerschaum pipe was clamped firmly in his lips, which were curled into a tight smile. *He* wouldn't believe that I was a berserker from Ground Zero. A napalm rifle was slung over his shoulder, and his hands held the biggest frump gun I'd ever seen. It was pointed at my gut.

"Very good," he said, and his voice was like a foghorn with a cold.

"My friends tell me I'm a frustrated actor," I replied.

"I don't think your friends are going to see you anymore," he answered. "We have a . . . private party here. RSVP, you understand. Gate-crashing is frowned upon."

"I'm Swain," I said.

"So?"

"So Hermanita would be very upset if she found out that anything happened to me."

He removed his pipe and, turning it upside down, tapped it lightly against the side of the frump. Twilight was rapidly turning into night and with every second, the man blended more and more with the buildings.

"Anyone can know a name," he said.

"Yeah, and anyone can make a mistake."

He grunted from out of the darkness and unbelted a pocketcom. He worked with quick fingers, the terminal beep the only sound in the thick air. "Hmmm," he said. "I guess you're invited after all."

"See, now that wasn't so hard."

"Come on."

I followed him into the darkness. "No hard feelings," he said over his shoulder. "I'm just trying to do my job."

"No hard feelings," I answered, glad for the protection. We walked for about two blocks until we came to a transom in the middle of the sidewalk. My guide bent down and banged on it with the butt of his gun. It swung open from the middle in two sections. Another man, dressed like the first, poked his head up through the opening.

"Take him to the Keep," my bodyguard said.

The man in the hole nodded and motioned me down with him. I walked to the opening and saw a dimly lit metal ladder leading down. I sat on the edge, then slid around and started climbing.

"Distinguished visitor," the pipe-smoker said, and the other grunted in return.

I scaled the fifteen or so steps down and stepped off into the main trunk of what was once the sewer system. Small red lights illuminated the tunnel in a dim, bloody haze. The smell was musty, like wet plaster, but not overpowering. I felt for the wall; it was cold, but not damp as I had expected.

The man who had preceded me down the ladder was talking on a small black gadget that could only function as a voice communicator. He finished talking and put the thing away.

"It'll be a few minutes," he said.

I leaned against the cold wall and lit a fag, puffing it out in billows of red smoke. I had been a fool to come into the decay the way I did, but I couldn't think of any faster way of getting in touch with Maria. She wasn't an easy person to see. The street people were superstitious about the crazy people in Old Town, a fact which saved my life. I'd like to think that my friend with the pipe wouldn't have let them do anything to me, but then I always pick the long shot at the race track, too.

A light appeared way off in the distance. I finished my cig while watching it move in on me. It was a wheeled car, an electric one. It was traveling at a pretty good clip and skidded to a halt right next to me with a tire screech that echoed through the manmade cavern the same way bats must sound in a natural one.

"Ha'dya do?" the driver said. He was a little white guy with a beak nose and darting eyes. He looked at home in his beat-up leatherette short coat and peaked cap. He patted the seat next to him. I climbed in.

Immediately the car lurched backward with another squeal that threw me forward against the dash. We went back like that until we reached a branch of the tunnel, which he backed into at full speed, almost turning us over.

"Take it easy," I said. "My doctor told me to avoid excitement."

He threw his head back and laughed. "That's rich," he answered, and screeched the car forward again to head us down the main tunnel. "Doctor's orders," he said, and shook his head. "Wadda'ya think about the weather, Mac?"

"I think I'd like to live to see some more of it."

He laughed some more. "You're a real comedian, ain't you?"

"People always tell me I'm in the wrong business."

We sped through the tunnel at an incredible pace. The small side-lights were zipping past in streaks. I had my hands and feet braced on the front of the car, waiting for the inevitable crash. I spent the rest of the ride suffering through a never-ending monologue from my driver, as he took corners on two wheels and missed obstacles by millimeters. It was all I could do to keep my heart out of *my* mouth, and my fist out of *his*. By the time we finally screeched to a stop by the main guard station, I had decided that I preferred the company of the street animals.

The Keep entry was well lighted, and made up of a series of long tables that were each manned by two gray-suited guards. I was made to walk up to one of the tables and empty my pockets. After that, I was passed through a metal detector and X-ray machine to check for hidden weapons. Then finally, I was given a thorough going-over by one of the guards, just in case. My personal belongings were returned to me, all except for my wristwatch, which was kept as "tribute."

When I was back in order, one of the guards silently led me up a series of steps and into the interior of a building. It was a nice place, sturdy stone, with a wide staircase that led up to a mezzanine. It had been a public library during the time when people had use for such things; so it was a large open room with a two-story ceiling. All the walls had been reinforced with heavily riveted steel, then every book in the place had been piled against the walls for extra protection and insulation. The shelves that had housed the books were piled against them. There was electricity in there, so we had light and circulating air from large fans stuck up in the corners.

The room was full of people. Some were of the general category of the ones with whom I had done business earlier. Some were of indeterminate status. Many were, quite obviously, rich boys. Armed guards stood along the walls.

Everyone was waiting for an audience. According to the length of time each had been waiting, he or she was taken up the steps after the last had been dealt with. Maria Hidalgo sat on a large, high-backed chair at the top of the steps. She was dressed in khaki: shirt and belted trousers that ballooned out of the top of her knee-high jackboots. A class-1, gleaming gold laser was strapped on her hip in a black leather holster.

A bandolier full of extra power packs was slung across her shoulder. A white Stetson sat atop jet black hair that she wore trussed up behind her in a ponytail.

She was as beautiful as I had remembered, but it was a beauty born of alienness. Her cheekbones were extremely high, giving her face a long, angular appearance. Her black eyes, set wide apart, shone from under sleek, tilted eyebrows. Her mouth was large, the lips full and red enough to stand out in marked contrast to the shoe-polish brown of her complexion.

I moved to take my place in line, but she caught sight of me and waved me up. The guards watched me indifferently as I climbed the steps. The second floor was wide and open, and stretched back into darkness. On either side of Maria's place were manned, wide-beam laser cannons—the kind that people like her weren't supposed to be able to get hold of.

"Como estas?" I said when I was within reach of her.

She grabbed my sleeves and pulled me to her, kissing me hungrily on the mouth. *"Mi novio,"* she whispered in my ear, then kissed me again.

"You've stayed away from me for a long time," she said when I finally straightened up.

"Five years," I answered. "They've been good ones for you."

She pouted out that full lower lip, and I remembered what it was that I liked about her so much. "We do what we can," she said.

I grinned. "And what we want."

She opened her mouth and let out a throaty laugh. "You haven't changed, Swain. Damn, I've missed you."

"I've missed you, too," I said, and meant it. Five years before I'd been working for the D.A.'s office as a liaison man to try and keep the struggle for control in the DMZ from spilling over into police-protected areas. Maria was leading one of the opposing factions. There had been chemistry between us and we made sparks for a while—but the ball has to keep rolling. Now, she had succeeded as the undisputed leader of the city's underworld junta, and I was still chasing after a buck.

"Much as I'd like to believe it," she said, "I have the feeling that you're not here to rekindle past memories."

I shook my head. "No."

She nodded and smiled sadly. "Give me fifteen minutes."

One of the street animals, a short black man, was brought up to complain that one of his neighbor tribes was horning in on his family's food ration. Maria dispatched one of her people to take care of it. One of the well-to-do's offered her a great deal of money to assassinate his business partner and the man's family. She refused, saying that she dealt in retribution, not cold-blooded murder. After the man had been sent away, she arranged to have a message sent to the partner, warning him of the plot against his life and asking if he wanted, for a price, to strike first. There were numbers problems, and prostitutes' union problems, and small-boss territorial problems, all of which Maria handled with her usual intelligence and élan.

Finally, she motioned to a man with a ledgercom, who stood at the top of the stairs and took everything down. He announced to the crowd that the audience was completed for the evening and that everyone would have to come back tomorrow. A small groan rose from those that were left waiting, but they all filed out in orderly fashion.

We watched them leave, then Maria stood and silently led me away from the meeting area, farther back into the mezzanine's darkness. A steel chamber had been erected in the far corner. We gained entry through a wheel-lock that led us into an anteroom where another steel door awaited. Maria turned the wheel and we entered.

"Solitary confinement?" I asked.

"I'm not very good at sleeping with one eye open," she answered. "Security is the best barbiturate in the world."

We were in a small but elegantly furnished room, hung in rich tapestries with real wood and cushioned furniture. There was electronic apparatus available, but it was small, functional, and kept to a minimum.

Two boys, no older than fourteen or fifteen, lounged on an oversized couch. They were wrapped, like spaghetti on a fork, in long-flowing saffron robes. Maria looked at them and smiled, then tilted her head toward the door.

"Out," she said.

They looked disappointed, but rose silently and left the room.

"I see you still like the young ones," I said, and plopped myself on a large chair that looked comfortable and was even better than it appeared.

Maria went to a portable bar next to the large couch and began fixing us drinks. "What they lack stylistically," she said over her shoulder, "they more than make up for in exuberance."

She brought me the drink, still remembering what I liked. "I've been hearing some things about you," she said, and pulled the twin to my chair directly across from me.

"What sort of things?"

She sipped her Black Jack (she always drank what her guests were having), and looked at me over the top of the glass. "Well, for starters, you tried to give your kidneys to some of my people out on the streets."

"That's not the half of it. Can't you change things out there?"

"Why should I? I keep everyone fed, and give opportunities to those who want them, but you have to understand that the great majority of street people enjoy their lives."

"What?"

"Sure. The hunting life is a simple one. I hesitate to use the word pastoral. Simplicity seems to be the key to happiness. The hunters are happy with what they're doing. It's not much by your standards, but it has its own degree of fulfillment."

I smiled at her politics. "And it does help keep unwanted visitors off your back," I said.

She raised her glass in salute. "I've been hearing other things about you, too."

"I'm a regular celebrity."

"My friends at the police department tell me that you're hotter than a laser with a short circuit right now. My friends on the street tell me that anyone who rockets around with you better have his life insurance paid up. Who're you taking on, Swain, the Virgin of Guadalupe?"

"Rick Charon," I answered.

She stood up and wheeled the inner office door shut,

clicked it until the bolt slid through, and locked it tight. She returned to her seat. "Tell me about it."

I told her the story. She listened attentively, every now and then grunting in response to something I said, but keeping her mouth shut tight until I was finished. When I mentioned the part about her torcher, Martha Johns, burning down the Marmeth, her jaw tightened noticeably, but she kept her peace.

When I was through, she removed her cowboy hat and laid it beside her on the floor. Then she undid the ponytail so that her hair could flow loose over her shoulders.

"What do you think, Hermanita?" I asked her when she hesitated in speaking up. She looked unsure of herself, a state of mind I had never detected in her before.

"Do you know," she began, "that the DMZ has grown by a third since I took control five years ago? I'm sitting here in my armored bedroom, dressed in my war-lord outfit and drinking whisky with an old lover . . ."

"Watch who you're calling old."

". . . while out in that dark, dead city nearly sixty thousand people depend on me for their existence. I'm talking power, Swain. The addiction to power. I don't know that it's possible to understand that unless you've experienced it."

"I don't know that I . . ."

She waved me to silence. "Let me make my point while it's in my mind. I have my own government here. It has its own commerce, its own laws, its own . . . taxes. I employ as many of my people as I can and try to feed the rest. And it's all under my control. It's a rush. The flush of power is an incredible thing. It's like a drug, except a million times more intense. Now let's apply this to Rick Charon. Charon is a lot like me, except on a far larger scale. He controls the commerce of the 'straight' government and, consequently, its activities. His rule extends to millions, and its purpose is the perpetuation of his own personal power. He's crazy for power in a way that is even difficult for me to understand. He wants to do with money what Alexander the Great did with armies. The only amazing thing about this entire situation is the fact that you're still alive right now."

I took a long drink. "He wanted to explain the game to me," I said.

She sat back. Holding her glass out in front of her, she stared into its murky interior. "Charon is a man unhampered by any conventional morality or ethics. He's consequently able to sustain an overview of life, a larger picture. I think the game has changed for him, mutated into something else. He's crazy, Swain, anything can happen."

"It's called megalomania," I said. "What about Martha Johns?"

Her jaw tightened again. "Charon's taken my people before. He offers them a lot of money to do things for him. One day, when the DMZ gets too large for him, he'll hire my people to kill me." She stood up and walked to the small desk that sat unobtrusively off to the side and juiced her tiny vis. A black face appeared on the screen. "Martha Johns," Maria said. "Is she out tonight?"

The man blanked for a moment, then reappeared. "She's in the dorms," he said.

"I want her here right now," she said evenly, business-like. "Don't lose her."

The man nodded grimly and blanked.

She walked up behind me and began massaging my neck. It felt good; I hadn't realized how tight I was getting. "Do you remember that night on Bomar Street?" she asked.

I smiled. "You couldn't wait until we got back to secure territory, so we had to make it in the back of my bullet."

"Then those four street punks jumped us."

"I was trying to defend myself and get into my clothes at the same time."

"And every time you threw a punch, your one-piece dropped to your ankles."

"It seems like a long time ago," I said. "You know, I still have a knot on the back of my head where I banged it on the top of the bullet when they surprised us."

"I could probably hide you," she said.

"I didn't come here for that."

"I know." She moved around my chair and sat back in hers. "Another drink?"

I looked at the floor where I had left my glass. I hadn't even finished my first one. "No thanks," I said.

She let her head fall back on the chair cushion. "You want to know what I know."

"Something like that. This has gotten bigger than me."

"At least you understand that much," she sighed. "I think the answer to your question may lie in Old Town."

I narrowed my eyes and sat up straight. "You do know something."

"Yes and no." She looked at me with that same uncertainty. "If I thought it would do any good, I would tell you to get the hell out of here and forget the whole thing . . . but I know you too well. I didn't know Phil Grover, but I've done a lot of transactions with Michael Grover."

"His brother?"

She showed me empty palms. "You tell me."

"What sort of transactions?"

"He lives in Old Town. He has a sort of underground railroad to help the crazies get out of there."

"You mean, he smuggles mutants into the city?"

"Interesting world, isn't it?"

"How?"

"The ones who look . . . normal. The ones who can pass. He gets them new identities, or pays people to raise the children as their own. We help on the transportation end sometimes."

"Why does he do it?"

"Now there's a question. He seems very altruistic about the whole affair, but I can't help feeling that there's a great deal of money involved in this somewhere. I know that he spends a lot, but where it comes from I couldn't begin to imagine."

"What's this got to do with Charon?"

"Here's where the plot thickens. Charon has been importing illegal berserkers for years to work in his factory. He takes the ones who are mutated physically and uses them as slave labor in his manufacturing processes."

I thought about all those people wearing the human masks. "That's how he's able to produce his equipment so cheaply."

"It was one of the key links to his success. In fact, the

133

name of his company: Bermax, meaning berserker maximizing, is his little joke on the world.''

She stood up and went over to fix herself another drink. ''Sure I can't get you one?'' she asked. And when I didn't respond, she came over with the one for herself. ''The name has another meaning, too,'' she said seriously. ''Bermax also stands for Bergson's Maxim.'' She watched me knit my brows in confusion. ''Bergson was a Frenchman who believed that the world represented a process of creative evolution in which the novelty of the successive phenomena was the only significant fact. Life means nothing to Charon. The progress of the game is all that matters to him.''

''Does Michael Grover know that Charon uses the berserkers as slave labor?''

She sat back and put a finger to her lips. ''I don't know,'' she said at last. ''I make it a point never to interfere in other people's affairs, so I never told him. I just assumed . . . why do you ask?''

''You've given me a link,'' I said. ''I'm trying to stretch it into motivation.''

''Why don't you ask him about it yourself?''

''Can you get in contact with him?''

''Not through any conventional channels. Old Town is a different world from anything you've ever seen. It moves under its own set of principles, its own internal logic. There is border contact, of course. That's how we have always gotten in contact previously. His people tell my people, or vice versa. Then we arrange a meeting. Have you ever been to Ground Zero?''

I shook my head.

''I was there once, for just a little while.'' She shivered, hugging herself. ''I'll never go again.''

There was a tapping on the door that sounded far away. Maria swiveled her chair around to face it. ''Would you get that?'' she asked me.

I stood up and moved across the smooth stone floor. Pushing in the catch that released the bolt, I turned the wheel-lock and opened the door so that I was hidden behind it when it swung. Martha Johns stepped in. She wasn't painted orange.

She moved into the room without seeing me, and right up to Maria. "I took care of the Lawson thing over in the industrial district this morning," she said. "Made it look like the wiring went."

"Anybody hurt?" Maria asked.

"No, of course not, I . . ."

I let the door slam shut and wheeled the lock. Johns turned with the sound, and when she saw me her eyes grew as big as coconuts. "Hi," I said. "Remember me?"

"But you're . . ."

"Supposed to be dead," I finished. "Sloppy work, Martha." I walked back to my seat and stared at her, wondering how somebody so nice-looking could be so ugly.

Maria turned to me. I nodded.

"Margin for error?"

I shook my head.

Maria turned back to the woman. "I'm really disappointed in you, Martha. You've been with me from the first. How could you betray me this way?"

Johns's eyes darted from one of us to the other, as if looking for something she could say that would smooth things over. Then she gave that up and tried another tact. "I—I'm sorry. I don't know what came over me. It wasn't like going against you; it was just another job—like moonlighting. He offered me so much money, I couldn't turn it down."

"Who offered?"

"The man who set up the deal about torching the electrosex parlor."

Maria grunted. "It was a messenger from a man who owned a chain of those places," she told me. "I accepted the terms of the deal and sent it over to the dorms for whoever was next on rotation. Charon's got his fingers in more pies than I suspected."

"Where did you set up your arrangement?" I asked her.

"He had a room at the Richmond Hotel," she said, looking at the floor. She was playing babe in the woods right to the hilt.

"Is that all?" Maria asked her. She unholstered her laser and hummed on the primary charge. "Or was there more? Maybe . . . something else that you'd do for them later."

"No, Maria. I swear on my life that there was nothing else." The girl's face widened in horror, and she backed up until she bumped into the door behind her.

"Right now, your life is a worthless commodity," Maria said, and pointed the gun at the girl's chest.

"Maria . . ." I began.

"Stay out of this, Swain," she snapped. "I maintain control here by being strong. This has nothing to do with you."

Johns fell to her knees, tears washing her cheeks. "Please," she sobbed. "I didn't think . . . I won't ever . . ."

"I've always treated you like a sister, Martha. And this was my repayment. I'm sorry, but I could never trust you again."

She fingered the silent trigger, and a pink-hot band of light slid out of the gun's muzzle easily, pencil-thin and beautifully symmetrical. I didn't much like lasers. Machines of death should be as ugly and vicious-sounding as the deeds they perform. The beam caught Martha Johns on the chest and went straight through, bloodlessly, cauterizing her heart in the process. Her face looked sad as she bent forward ever so slowly until her forehead was touching the ground and I could see the tiny burn mark on her back. She stayed that way for a few seconds, then rolled onto her side, all folded up, like a switchblade.

Maria reholstered her shooter and swiveled back to face me. "We'll never talk of this again," she said, and her face was drained of color. Getting up, she moved to her desk and pressed a button. Directly thereafter, there was a knocking on the door.

"Would you give me a hand?" she asked. I moved over and helped her drag Martha's body out of the way of the door. Then I unlocked it and let her people inside. They picked up the body and carried it away without a word. Maria locked the door behind them. She moved slowly back to her seat to stare intently at me. She looked uneasy.

"Tell me about the Richmond," I said.

"That's where Charon keeps his women," she said, but her mind was someplace else. "He keeps them there under guard, so that no other man can get to them. Charon's women are his for life."

Something was bothering her. "What is it?" I asked.

"Charon," she said. "The whole thing. I'm sure he's studied you. That means he knows about me." She suddenly jumped up and ran to her vis. The same face from before appeared. "Jarsen," she said, and she was breathing heavily, her chest rising and falling as if she had just run the kilo. "I want all the troops out on the streets. Everybody out of the dorms and on perimeter watch! Get it rolling, then get back to me for instr—"

The building shook with the force of a severe blast that knocked Maria up against her desk and me out of my chair. Muffled sounds drifted through the steel walls, sounds that had to be loud to be heard at all in there. The lights flickered, but stayed on.

"What's that?!" I yelled, and as I tried to get to my feet, another blast knocked me down again.

Maria was up, staggering for the wheel-lock. "Charon!" she screamed, and it could have been a battle cry. "That son of a bitch is kicking me in the ass because you're here."

She wheeled open the door, as another blast rocked the chamber. The lights flickered again, and this time they stayed off. We felt our way to the anteroom door and I could hear Maria cursing gutturally as she fumbled with the wheel-lock. I added my hands to hers. The lock didn't want to turn. We worked it with all our strength until we finally got it going. When it was loosened, we pulled on the door. It was jammed tight, but we were able to get it open just a crack. We were greeted by a billow of gray smoke and yellow-orange light. We shoved the door until it made an opening large enough for us to squeeze through. On the outside, the mezzanine was shadow-jumping from the flickering light of a dozen small fires. Debris choked the floor, making movement nearly impossible. We were forced to climb over a fallen I-beam that had crushed the door guard.

"Bastard!" she yelled, and shook her fist at the sky. We scooted through the burning rubble as quickly as we could, making for the steps. She was going for the cannons; I knew that without asking. We made the stairway, and I looked down. A section of the wall had been punched through on the ground floor and a small army of Charon's punks in full dress regalia was pouring through, fighting it out with the gray-suits. It was a tangle of confusion as frumps and lasers and lead spewers ripped through the scream-infested air.

A section of the mezzanine had been blown away, leaving one of the cannons lying on ground level, a twisted hunk of useless garbage. The other seemed operational. Maria turned to me, her face smeared with black soot. She leered, seeming to change complexion in the throbbing light. Her eyes glowed brighter than the fire. "Let's kick back," she grinned.

"Just like old times," I answered.

"Just like old times."

Working quickly, she slipped off her bandolier and slung it across my arm. Then she handed me her laser. "Keep them off me!"

There were rumbling noises, deep and painful, and the air smelled like a diseased thing as I watched Maria mount the metal beast that waited patiently for her. She climbed onto the cannon platform, juicing the turret motor and the primary charge. Her troops, outnumbered and unprepared, were doing badly on the floor as Charon's punks moved through the wall gash at will. They saw us at the top of the steps and began flowing our way.

I waited until I had clear targets, then hammered away, aiming at head-level so that any hit would be fatal. I tried to keep them off the steps, as frumps exploded around me. My vision was coming in flashes. The candy-pink line of my laser zipped through the smoky darkness like a tiny spotlight that ate what it lit.

Maria jerked the pistol grips on either side of her. The motor worked through foot pedals. With a loud hum, the machine arced downward. Her face was hard against the sighting screen. She screamed and opened it up with a frightening electronic hum, stentorian and gut-clutching horrible.

The room lit to daylight as a beam the width of an aqueduct poured from the cannon's mammoth barrel. It cut a swath through the mob pouring into the open place, cutting people in half or thirds. The ones who were left scattered, and I went to work on those, humming my power-packs to exhaustion, then reloading from the bandolier.

Maria worked the beam slowly upwards, going for the hole

already there, then up still farther. Sections of the wall disappeared before the light as if they had never been there at all, and we were all at once looking out at the open street. The streets were full of punks and police-type street-clankers. Maria bore down on them unmercifully and unstoppably, burning through street and buildings. I watched in horrified fascination as massive buildings collapsed under the relentless eye of the light that burned and buried the streets in mountainous piles of rubble.

So much of the Keep's wall went that the front section of the roof fell in, burying any of those left alive on the first floor, and leaving us standing in open air. When fire stopped returning, she shut down the machine, and slumped back in the turret seat. Small bands of the invaders were scurrying off down side streets like cockroaches running from the light.

Maria noted their movement and said in a low voice, "They won't get far." And I had the feeling that their fate when caught would be far worse than the conflagration they were deserting.

I walked up to her. She was pushing her hair back out of her face. Her right side was bleeding from a profusion of small frump-shrapnel cuts.

"You okay?"

She looked at me without understanding. Then her gaze fell to her bloody khakis. "I get worse than that from a good roll in the sack," she said.

I handed back her pistol and bandolier. "I don't know what to say, Maria, I . . ."

She reached out and put a finger to my lips, silencing me. "Let me say it. Charon came for me tonight, not you. You were the catalyst, but not the cause. I'm sorry that I couldn't provide a safer harbor for you, *novio*."

Large numbers of Maria's people began moving into the ruins of the Keep, looking for survivors. *"Hombres,"* she called to them, waving and patting her cannon. A cheer rose from the ranks and they hoisted their weapons in salute.

"Maybe we needed this," she told me. "Fighters get flabby when they're not in training."

I walked to the edge of the steps and looked down. The

rubble from the roof was covering the bodies of the men I had killed coming up. "I don't understand any of this," I said.

"You think small, Swain. You always have."

"Can't help it," I answered, and searched through my waist-coat pockets until I found a crumpled pack of cigs. "That's the only way I know to get through this insanity."

"Where do you go from here?"

"Old Town," I answered and pulled a bent fag out of the pack and lit it on a glowing cinder that lay nearby. I offered Maria a smoke.

"Bad for your health," she said, and smiled. "This is my fight now."

"Not yet," I said. "Let me have my shot first. There are people lying dead all over this town because I wanted to give an old man a dose of happiness on the way to the graveyard. From here on out, I work alone on this—risk nobody but myself. If I don't make it in the next couple of days, then you can take over."

"What will you do even if you find what you're looking for?"

"I'll worry about that when the time comes."

I smoked while Maria thought. Some of her people had picked their way through the mess and were moving up the steps to join us. Below, amid the crackling of burning timber, I could hear the mourning wails of those who had lost loved ones in the fighting.

Several of the latexed troops pushed past me to Maria. She embraced them each in turn, then gave them orders in a low voice. They moved off, back down the steps.

"I'll respect your wishes," she said to me. "But only for three days. And I'm going to keep you under close watch."

"Not too close," I said. "I've got to be able to move around."

She nodded, pulling paper and pen out of her breast pocket. She wrote on the paper and handed it to me. "Memorize this number, then destroy the paper. When you need me, this is where I'll be. It's my war bunker."

"Thanks," I replied. "I'll be needing guidance through Old Town."

"It's yours. Would you like to spend the rest of the night with me, then move into Old Town in the daylight?"

"Thank you, Hermanita," I answered as I read the number on the paper, "but I've got to get back uptown tonight. I'll be back in the morning." I walked over to the nearest fire and dropped the paper in the hungry flames.

"She's a lucky woman," Maria said.

"Who?"

"Whoever you're going back for."

I closed the distance between us, dropping my cig on the way. Pulling her close, I wished that life wasn't so complicated. I kissed her on the lips, then the neck. "I've got to go," I whispered in her ear.

"I know," she said, and I felt moisture on my face.

18

There weren't any meat machines for Maria's part of town; they had to bury their own dead. She had me vac'ed out of there on a heli-sled as the bodies were being ritualistically carried away in torchlight procession. My watch was gone, lost as tribute, but I made it to be already three or four in the morning. Soon, the smog cover would light with yellow-pinks and Rick Charon would be another sun closer to finding out that all of us have to dance a jig that's ultimately played to an unfamiliar tune, to a tune that drags us down into a muck-pit of dark, twisted harmonies, a funeral dirge of unending dissonance. I hoped that Charon's song would be played sooner rather than later.

When I got back to the safe-park and my bullet, there was a weight on my brain that I was afraid would crush me. Part of it was lack of sleep; part of it was melancholy brought on by the proximity of death; part of it was an intuitive gut fear. As I began to understand the possibilities of Charon's warped mind, I thought about two people who cared enough about me to help me chase my windmills. I hummed through the decay without regard for legal or physical safety. I was calling myself a fool, and all the while knowing I wasn't.

By the time I got to Ginny's parking garage, I felt as if my insides were deciding all at once to look for a new body. I parked and voice-printed in. There were small groups milling around in the lobby, and I wanted to believe that maybe there had been a party that lasted late. I tubed up and off at Ginny's floor. There were more people in the hall. I shoved my way past them. Some were crowded around her open door, looking in, but not entering.

I moved into their midst. A fat, bald man tried to hold me up by officiously telling me that the police were supposed to go in first. I remember shoving; I think he fell down. It's not very clear.

The living room was a shambles. Frumps had been fired in there. I called Ginny's name. Over and over. The vis had been busted through, black smoke seeped through a crackling rend in the screen, and I wondered what could be burning to make smoke so dark. Walls were scarred black and broken through. All the tables had been overturned and crippled. The hanging sofa, ripped from the ceiling, lay on the floor.

Something was sticking out from under the wreck of the couch. I moved toward it.

It was a hand.

Taking a deep breath, I pulled up the bulk of the sofa and tossed it aside. What lay beneath was barely recognizable as a human being. Barely. A pair of lightless camglasses was stuck to the limpid flesh that puddled around my feet.

George.

I heard words tearing from my throat. I raced through the rest of the flat. In the hall in front of Ginny's bedroom lay a man I had never seen before. He was face up on the carpet, legs twisted beneath him, a frump clutched in his hand. A long, jagged burn mark snaked across his chest—a laser shot from a shaking hand.

"Ginny!"

I walked quickly into the bedroom. The bed was half gone, the remains singed black. The black extended to the wall, which had an obscene hole blown through it. Another body lay, face down, in the middle of the floor, an ice cube-sized burn hole in the ceiling directly above the body. The man was covered with a thin, snowlike blanket of powdered sheetrock and splinters.

Where was Ginny? I circled the room, then began opening closet doors. My hand turned the latch on the third, when a laser slash bored through the metal at head level, just next to my right ear.

I hit the deck.

"Ginny?" I called and another beam flared through. I rolled away from the door and reached up to handle it from a distance. Turning the knob, I swung the door out without occupying the space.

"Ginny, it's Matt . . . Matt."

"Matt?" came a weak, confused voice from inside the depths of the closet. I wanted to run in to her, but knew better than to jump into that dark room in the condition she was in.

"It's all over," I said. "Put down the gun and come on out."

"Matt?"

"I'm here. Come out. It's all over."

There was silence for a few seconds, then the rustling of clothes. Ginny came crawling out on her hands and knees, her face far away. I moved to her, down there on the floor, and took her in my arms.

She was quiet for a moment, then the floodgates opened. "It was awful," she choked from deep down. "George was just going out to . . . to . . ."

"I know, I know."

"And they were there and they . . ."

"Don't think about it," I said, and stroked her hair. "Just cry it out." I cradled her in my arms and rocked her, letting her sob out the horror that had built up in her. All the while I sat there and thought about things that were dark and twisted as swampland pathways.

"Well, ain't that a sight."

I looked. Fat Mack was leering down at me.

"If you've got one decent bone in your body," I said, with as much control as I could muster, "you'll turn around and walk out of here right now."

He laughed, clutching his immense belly. "Why, Swain, I'm surprised at you. I'm a public servant trying to do his job."

I stood, helping Ginny to her feet. I held her against me so that she wouldn't see the bodies on the floor. I wanted to throttle Watershed. I wanted it so bad I was quaking. But the last thing that anyone needed right then was more trouble. "Mack, no one's going to pay for any investigation here.

Why don't you just take your boys and go someplace where you can make the city a little money."

"Not that simple," he said, and rolled the dough of his face around with his stubby hands. "Y'see, Jumpstreet Harry got in a shitload of trouble for letting you go yesterday. Now, I'm just like an andy; they don't tell me nothing but orders. I'm smart enough to figure that someone wants you real bad, though. There's an APB out on you, son. And a big reward for the flatfoot who brings you in."

I looked at Fat Mack, then past him down the hall at the swarming investigative team that was mulling around the living room, waiting for the go-ahead. I couldn't fight my way out.

"So what happens now?" I asked.

"So now, you give me a big reason why Fat Mack shouldn't collect on those bucks."

I studied his bloated face and decided that he wasn't just stringing me along. "Maybe you'll let me walk out of here because you're a simple guy just like me and you think that maybe there ought to be something right in this world, something more important than a few bucks. Or maybe you'll let me go because this set-up stinks to you and you think the city deserves better than the gospel according to Rick Charon."

"Naw," he said, and frowned with his lower lip. "I'm a lot of things, but a do-gooder ain't one of them. And I wouldn't know what's right if I ate it for dinner. I figure it this way, though: If I run you in, you'll be dead before another day passes. And if they burn you, who in the hell will I have to fuck with?" He shook his head and winked at me. "My life's boring enough already, you heah? They woke me up to bring me out heah this morning. If I hurry, I can still catch a couple of hours sack time before my shift starts. If you're smart, you'll put some pavement between me and you in the meantime."

With that, he turned from me and jellied out of the room, walking right across the corpse in the hallway. He grumbled around in the living room for a minute, then left with all his men.

Ginny was beginning to get a measure of control over herself. I walked her out of her room and past the dead man.

In the living room, the meat-machine people had bored a hole right through Ginny's wall. The machine hovered outside, its chute leading into the hole, a hole which its reconstruction people would later repair and bill to Ginny. Two attendants were scooping up what was left of George onto a stainless steel pallet, preparing to dump him into the acid pit.

I wished that there was someone I could call who would cry and be upset over George's death, but there was no one.

Ginny was shaking again when I got her into the hall. There was still a small crowd around the door. "Show's over," I growled at them. "Get the hell out of here." I guess they could see that I meant business, because the hall cleared faster than an amnesty prison.

The anger was building up in me. I was working to replace it with clear-headed persistence, but it wasn't working very well. We stood in the now-empty hall for a minute, and all the angles and planes looked harder to me, the shadows deeper and more clearly defined.

"Wait here for just a second," I said, and went back into the apartment. George was just sliding down the chute. I went into the hallway and pried the frump out of the dead punk's grasp. I didn't like guns at all, but I held this one gently, cradled it as one would a lover. I tugged the punk out of his short coat and relieved him of his shoulder holster. Shoving the frump in its place, I looped the thing over my arm. I went through his pockets, found a couple of extra clips for the frump and kept them also. I left just as the black-garbed meat people were loading the punk's carcass onto their pallet.

I moved quickly out of the apartment, closing the door behind me. Ignoring the tube, Ginny and I walked the eight floors down to the lobby. I put on the holster as we climbed the stairs. Once on ground level, we took the service lift to the parking garage.

The garage was deserted when we got down there, and for once, I was glad that it was so brightly lit. Pushing my token into the meter, I hoped that no one had had time to tamper with my bullet. I was through taking chances with anyone else's life. We boarded the platform and began our ascent to level seven, where I was parked.

She leaned against me, still needing the support. "How did they get in?" she asked.

"Are you kidding?" I returned. "Charon probably owns the building. He seems to own everything else."

"Where are we going?"

"*We're* not going anywhere. *You* are going on a nice, long trip."

She looked at me, but didn't put up an argument.

The platform eased us up to the bullet, and I made Ginny move way off down the aisle while I started the thing. My fears were unfounded, and in a matter of minutes we were out of the garage and moving into the decay.

"Where am I going?" she asked after a time.

"Do you still have that orbiting chateau you're always trying to drag me off to?"

"Sure."

"Well, you're going to hop a lift with the next shuttle and take yourself a nice vacation."

She reached over and took my arm. "Come with me. We can sneak away and forget about all this."

"You know I get airsick," I said, and my face told her not to ask any more.

19

I drove silently and watched Ginny out of the corner of my eye. It was dim, fuzzy daylight. She leaned her head against the window and watched the still-piled garbage and the human refuse that slept in it. She was distant, off in a world where frump guns didn't blow her best friends to pieces and people didn't make garbage to collect. Occasionally, she would reach over and squeeze my arm to reassure herself that I was there.

I didn't want to make things any worse for her, but I had to ask some questions that couldn't wait until she was back in circulation. It looked to me that she would hold up all right.

"Can you tell me what happened?" I asked quietly.

"Nothing to tell. George was going out to get cigarettes, and they were standing there."

"Cigarettes in the middle of the night?"

"He was trying to wait up for you. When he went and watched that hotel . . ."

"The Richmond?"

"That's it. He stayed around there until pretty late. When he came in he was all excited. Said that he saw two men taking that girl away, Mina what's-her-face, and she wasn't very happy about going with them."

I turned off down Molner and headed away from town on the interchange. Life was just beginning to stir. The early birds were out looking for worms in the fuzzy glow. "Did he try to follow them?"

"Tried, but lost them after a few blocks." She wound down the window and let the morning coolness blow past her face. Ginny was strong; she would be okay.

"Were there just two of them at the apartment?"

"I don't think so, but I can't be sure. I had just gone to my room to turn down the bed and get ready for sleep, when I heard yelling in the living room. I could see George fighting with some men. It was all a jumble. I stood there for a second, then their guns were out and there was noise . . . and fire . . ." She closed her eyes for an instant then continued. "I somehow moved back to the bedroom and got my gun out of the dresser. When they came for me I guess I just started pulling the trigger. I don't even remember going into the closet."

We finished the drive to the shuttleport mostly in silence. I wasn't very good company, I guess; I kept looking in the rear-view mirror and trying to stay awake. It had been a long time since I'd had anything resembling real sleep, and it was beginning to show. Once, I thought we were being followed, and I jerked us off the road to hide, almost smashing us up in the process. It turned out that I was being "followed" by an old woman and her grandchildren.

I didn't trust anything, and my own paranoia was beginning to scare me. Something would soon have to give one way or the other.

The shuttleport was one of three in the country, and it flew twice a day. It catered mostly to engineers and contract spacers who would jump off at Beltel's big orbit wheel, then take smaller flights to various of the thousands of labs and construction balls that filled the ether like gnats around a swamp. I guess space people were okay, but I just couldn't see the point of moving our mistakes someplace else.

By the time we got there, the smog was bright and the heat was up. The semi-oval ship loomed large in the morning sky, squatting on its concrete launching dock like a giant frog waiting to leap off a lily pad. Ginny didn't have any of her credit slats, but she was well known around there and was cleared through soon enough, her flight expenses being deducted through the bank directly over the vis.

We had to wait for an hour or so, and I spent the whole time checking out the looks of the other passengers. Finally, satisfied with their authenticity, I saw her on to the unwieldy-looking machine and waited until it jumped, leaving behind a cloud of orange-red smoke dust that hung in the air like dirty fog. I went back out to my bullet and watched Ginny disappear into the smog bank. She would take the shuttle to the big wheel, then transfer to a flight that would drop her at her orbiting vacation home. I hoped that everything would work out all right.

I climbed in the bullet and nosed it back toward the decay. Ginny had given me a simple hug as she was boarding the shuttle and nothing more. We were both moving mechanically, knowing what we had to do and doing it without a great deal of thought. I felt like a four-string banjo in a five-string world.

I wanted to sleep, but there wasn't time. By the time I got back to town I was flagging badly. I stopped in a drugstore and got something that would keep me going for a while. The man told me to take one every six hours. I threw three in my mouth and hit the streets again. In a few minutes I felt my mind grind into gear, making everything seem a lot clearer than it was. With the clearness came the anger again. Charon had played with me—just for fun. The bastard had dared me to try and get something on him, then slapped me down just to show me he could do it.

I wasn't much: a mouth that didn't know when to shut up, a little muscle, and shoes that weren't afraid to do a bit of walking. But, by God, Rick Charon was going to hear from me.

I headed for the Richmond, the place where Charon kept his harem, where his women went in . . . and stayed. Charon wanted control, but he couldn't control me. He couldn't even control Fat Mack. He was going to learn what it was to face life on someone else's terms.

I was still in Fancy Dan territory on Beaumont. At the end of the block stood the Richmond, namesake of another sovereignty in a time gone by. I pulled directly across from it and waited until I had a clear shot. When the street was empty, I turned the bullet in a direct line with the double-glass front doors and opened it up full.

The two outside punks reacted slowly, not believing that I was going to crash through the doors. Their faces got longer and more comical the closer I got. Finally, at the last second, they dove aside and ate pavement.

I was submarining for the floorboards myself about then.

The doors shattered like an icicle explosion when my bullet pounded through. There was a center post that cracked in the middle and plunged—along with large shards of glass—through my windshield, demolishing my steering wheel—and me if I'd been sitting there. The bullet buckled and careened once it hit the door, and I braced myself for whatever it would be that would stop us in the lobby. I hit something broadside and stopped dead. It was a tooth-cracking jolt, but left me unhurt. I reached out for the passenger-side door handle and pushed out quickly.

I fell out head-first and landed gracelessly on the tile floor. Taking a quick glance around, I saw people standing like statues, still in shock, unmoving. My body felt like it was in one piece. I tried jumping to my feet just to make sure. It worked.

The frump was out and in my hand. Everyone in the large, comfortable lobby—women mostly—stepped back a few paces, as if they were in a chorus line, when they saw the frump. I swung in the other direction. My bullet was demolished; it had crashed into the sign-in desk. I hurried around the wreck and saw the desk man who had been so unhelpful to me on the vis when I was looking for Mina Goulding. I looked at him and smiled. His mouth dropped like the cord had been cut, and his ugly green cigar jumped for the ground.

I was over the desk and pushing the barrel of the gun in his neck before he knew what was happening. "I've got a message for your boss," I said.

He nodded dumbly, as if he knew that already.

"Tell Charon that I know where he gets his factory help. Tell him I'm piling up evidence against him that even his money won't get him out of. And tell him that if he touches so much as one hair of Mina Goulding's head, I'll have his in return. Got it?"

He nodded again. A man of few words.

"Is your bullet outside?"

Another nod.

"Then you and I are going to take a little walk." I grabbed

151

him by the scruff of his tunic and put the gun in his ear. We moved around what was left of the desk. The bullet's exposed magnets were pulling metallic objects onto the car. Paper clips, hop bells, small tables. The punks from outside were inside now, and they had dangerous-looking things in their hands. I nodded to them and wiggled my gun around. The people in the lobby were big-eyed snowmen, trying to move their eyebrows up to their hairlines.

"Run!" I shouted, and I think I got an idea of what a buffalo stampede must have been like.

Removing the frump from my mute friend's ear, I pumped four or five into the room. Ornate lamps and Ming vases and potted palms all went to hell, along with a huge stuffed sofa that filled the room with goose-down snow.

We left through the busted-out front door, and I kept the Fancy Dans at bay with my nasty scowl alone. My friend was shaking badly and smelled like scared sweat, but he was able to direct me to his bullet, which was parked around the side of the building. He fumbled around and got me his keys.

"It's been real," I said, and butted him once in his belly. He groaned to the pavement, as I jumped in his wagon and took off.

I watched the rear-view as a score of angry punks rounded the building like long-shotters to the two-dollar window. I laughed, deep and hard. I had done something entirely useless and crazy, and it felt good.

It felt real good.

20

Maria Hidalgo had the heel of each hand embedded in a corresponding eye. She rubbed them around for a moment, then slid her hands down her face as if trying to mold her features into human form. "Don't you ever sleep?" she asked, with a voice that came from the bottom of a bale of cotton.

"Good morning," I said to her image on the pay vis. "How're you doing?"

"I'm horny," she pouted, and used her hands to pull her loose hair back. She looked good even in the morning. "Just a minute," she said. Getting up, she moved away from the screen, tying the sash of her robe as she did so. The background was plain concrete, very cold-looking and unadorned. A small section of what looked to be a wall map was visible just on the screen's edge.

Maria came back with a huge cup of coffee in her hand, and a joint stuck solidly in her mouth. When she sat, I started talking again, but she held up a hand to silence me. We sat there looking at each other while she took four or five puffs of the joint and a gulp of coffee that would have made Rabelais proud. She sat very still then, looking around as if to gauge her grasp of reality. Finally she took a deep breath. "Okay," she said. "I'm awake."

Taking the joint out of her lips, she laid it out of camera range, although the smoke kept sliding into the line of vision. I searched through my own pockets for cigarettes and found that I didn't have any more. My lighter had been missing since the incident at the Keep. "I'm ready to go to Old Town," I told her.

"When?"

"The sooner the better."

She sat lost in thought for a time, then looked down, away from my face, as if maybe my fly was open. Her face began to split in a big grin, like a plaster crack in an earthquake area.

"The Richmond?" she said. There must have been a read-out on the bottom of her screen.

"I thought it was about time for a futile gesture."

Maria's face suddenly got harder. "They've got a fix on the bullet that you're humming. You'd better get the hell out of there right now."

"But, what about . . ."

"Now, Swain!" she said, and blanked just to make the point.

"Damn!" I turned and began sliding the door open. The bullet was parked about a half-block away on my side of the street. Through the door crack I could see it, along with a group of riot-suited cops and Charon punks. There was a bunch of them, and black-and-whites, and even a clanker. I suppose that was a compliment to me.

I took out the frump and made sure I had a fresh clip locked inside. I didn't want a shoot-out with the police, but I knew that I was finished for sure if I let them take me.

The men had been grouped around the bullet, but now they were beginning to spread out and do a quick search of the area. I gently eased the steel door shut and used the butt of my frump to bust out the light inside the booth.

I kept the gun in my hand and tensed. Inching against the side wall, I hugged it with my back so that whoever opened that door would have to slide it all the way open to see me.

The waiting seemed interminable. I kept wanting to go to the door and take a peek. I was just beginning to loosen up when the door latch clicked from the touch of a credit disc. Bringing the frump up, I was a time bomb with a second left on the ticker; I was a reactor that had reached critical mass; I was poised on the gallows with the trap door dropping below my feet.

The door opened a crack, admitting a shaft of light like a tiny, luminous wall. It stayed that way for a long second, then it banged open to a nova of light. I jumped, blinded, and swung my frump at what I hoped was head-level.

Flesh met flesh, and a pained grunt escaped from the connecting end of my swing. We went down hard on the pavement, and my shot must have put him out, because he fell like a bag of wet cement. I rolled, squinting, almost seeing, and jumped to my feet. There were voices from down the street, so I turned the other way and ran like cheap paint on a tile wall. After a few steps, the world was discernible again.

I looked behind me; they were all over the streets and they all knew where I was. I ran hard, looking for a building that would let me in. Running past the holowindows of a department store, I turned to go in there. A Fancy Dan challenged me at the door, but I knocked him over without breaking stride.

The store was half-full of people, women mostly, who were rummaging through the tables full of clothes and gadgets. The place was wall-crawling with lights and displays that were all geared subliminally to appeal to certain personality types. Merchandise overflowed the display tables like food from a horn of plenty.

As I shoved my way through the aisles, I looked back to see cops and punks pouring into the store, shouting and pointing.

It was a circus in there, with smells and colors and thrills for all ages; it was the stockyards in there with people moving cattlelike through the checkout stands to be relieved of the lifeblood of their wallets. And when the first frump blast exploded a glass counter full of jewelry to oblivion, the place became a madhouse of screaming, writhing insanity.

There were two more explosions, but I didn't turn to see where they connected. People went running in every direction, and, to my good fortune, they held up the progress of the punk-brigade. I kept pushing toward the back of the store, through the lines of interference, hoping that I could exit on that side.

There was a doorway, but it was jammed with people.

I ran toward the line of display windows and ripped plywood backing from hinges to find myself looking into a holodisplay in which an enticing woman was opening up the transparent robe of a black lace peignoir to reveal the nightgown beneath, only to close it modestly again. I jumped into the display, my form interfering with the image. A toothless old street bum was watching the young lady and me from street level with a look of perplexity across his ancient face.

A frump hit where I had just been, rocking the display cabinet. I looked around frantically. The projector was set on the floor of the booth. I bent and picked it up. It was heavy, but not hernia stuff. The sexy woman was doing her tricks for the ceiling, and the bum outside looked horrified, pleading with me with his hands and with words that I couldn't hear through the thick glass. I motioned him aside and, raising the projector over my head, chucked it through the window.

I was right behind the machine, through the window even before all the glass stopped falling. I hit the pavement running and was off down the street, leaving the bum on his hands and knees, fondling the broken projector.

I got halfway down the block when some of them rounded the building at the street's end. I couldn't go back the way I had come, so I cut into the street itself just as black-and-whites came siren-screaming from both directions.

There was an alleyway between two long rows of concrete towers. I had nowhere else to go. It was long and strewn with garbage that smelled of death and compost rot. Rats as large as dogs scurried as I charged, full speed, through their rentless housing. I pulled boxes and garbage cans down behind me as I ran, hoping to slow the going of those following me.

I moved, still up mentally but feeling my body tiring despite the reassurances my brain was giving it. I was nearly through the long stretch of alley when I heard banging cans behind me. I turned. One of the black-and-whites had pulled into the narrow lane and was driving toward me, knocking metal and cardboard barricades aside with wrenching echoes.

I kept going, no more than fifty steps from daylight. Then there was a bullet from out of nowhere, blocking the mouth of the alley diagonally. I tried to stop, but my momentum carried me right up to it. I went into my jacket for my frump, but one was already sticking out of the bullet's back window. "Don't," a voice said.

Turning the way I had come, I saw the cop-hummer bearing down ever closer. I swung around again, and the back door of the big, black bullet was open.

"Get in," the voice said.

I had played out all my options.

21

I'd never seen a bullet move so fast. Not only did it tear through traffic like a paper shredder with a thyroid condition, but someone had souped-up the magnets so that it could hum up to and over other things in the streets. I sat huddled in a corner of the back seat, wanting nothing more than a cigarette as my last request. The black man who was holding me in his unwavering gaze smiled continually with a Cheshire-cat grin that seemed to glow in the dark of the window-tinted hummer.

"Got a fag," I asked laughing boy, "or won't I have time to finish it?"

He smiled even wider and a thick, beefsteak tongue came out to lick his dry, cracked lips. "Put your hands behind your head," he said.

I thought that was a pretty silly way to smoke a cig, but I'm one of those guys who would walk a mile. I interlocked my fingers at the base of my neck, and tried to figure the odds of getting out of this one.

My friend slowly reached the distance between us and plucked the frump out of its resting place. He knocked on a small partition that separated the front and back seats, and a trapdoor slid open. He handed the gun through, and the door snapped shut.

"Whew," he said, and took a deep breath. "Am I glad that you didn't try anything." He replaced his own gun.

"Can I, uh . . ."

"Yeah, yeah," he laughed. "Put them down."

I brought down my hands.

He reached into a side pocket of his short coat and pulled

out a package of smokers. "If anything would have happened to you, Hermanita would have used my head to play kick ball." He handed me the whole package.

I fumbled one out and stuck it in my mouth. "You mean you're from Maria?"

"Who else?"

"Why the hell didn't you tell me?" I asked and tried to hand the remaining cigs back to him.

"Keep them," he returned. "Brother, the way you were wound up back there, I wasn't about to try to tell you nothing."

I shrugged. That seemed logical. I patted my pockets all around, looking for the lighter that I knew wasn't there. "Got a match?"

He pulled out a solar lighter and handed it across. I lit the fag on its glowing coils and made to give it back. He waved that away also. "So where to?"

"DMZ," he responded, and, pulling a stick of lip balm out of his jacket, began applying it to his lower lip. He shook his head. "I have this problem with dry lips," he said. "And I've got this other problem—I'd guess you'd call it a defense mechanism—with smiling when I'm nervous." He smiled. "The one aggravates the other." He shook his head again.

"Stop smiling so much."

"I told you, I can't help it. Nerves, remember?"

"Stop getting nervous."

He smiled, then grimaced. "It comes with the territory."

"Find a new line of work."

"This is all I know."

"Then stop complaining."

We moved through the safe areas, then the semi-safe areas, then the initial decay, then the serious decay, then into the DMZ. Later on, I'd be going all the way down to Ground Zero—Old Town. If the city were a target, Ground Zero would be the bull's-eye. I wasn't looking forward to the trip to Old Town. People in the city were conditioned to hate and fear the rad-hot mutants, in much the same way that people living in the Middle Ages had probably been conditioned to react to lepers or plague-carriers.

We traveled deep into the DMZ, deeper than I'd ever been.

The inhabitants of that section of the city were totally survival-minded. Bound mostly into small tribes, usually family-sized, they took their existence where they could find it. Whichever organization—Maria's in this case—controlled the DMZ also tried to look out for the welfare of the inhabitants. It was a symbiotic relationship, for the citizens of the DMZ repaid Maria's kindness by being sixty thousand sets of eyes and ears, keeping a continual check on the comings and goings in their little section of the universe.

As we drove, I realized why the bullet was designed the way it was. The streets, or what was left of them, would have been impassable for a close-to-the-ground vehicle. As we bumped our way over the obstacle course, I could occasionally see groups of naked children playing hunting games. They laughed and ran in and out of the decay like sunlight peeking through the smog bank. I wondered how many of them would make it to adulthood.

We stopped next to what appeared to be a demolished skyscraper. Its remains were piled like dung, uselessly mountainlike, on the ground.

"This is where we get off," laughing boy said, and swung his door open.

"Can I have my gun back?"

He licked his lips. "I guess we understand each other now." He started to smile, but held back. Then he knocked on the partition again, and my frump was soon nestled back in its leather bed, safe and sound.

We climbed out of the bullet and walked up to the rubble. "Open the door, Richard," my companion sang in a rich baritone, and a whole section of the concrete junk swung outward, creaking on rusted hinges.

I was led through the opening to find myself in a cramped, dark chamber. A small dry-cell light hung on the wall, but provided no more illumination than was necessary to keep me from running into things.

There was a hole in the center of the floor and another ladder than led straight down. We climbed.

And climbed.

We went down a long way, maybe a hundred meters, long

enough for me to realize how out of shape my legs were. By the time I got my feet on solid ground, my knees felt like they needed a lube job.

We were standing in a large hallway. The corridor was well lit and new-looking. Maria must have had it built special. Gray-latexed men with nasty-looking shooters lined the length of the hallway. We began walking. Every twenty paces or so was a heavy iron door that could close to unwanted visitors.

After a while, the hallway curved and we lost the line of guards. It branched off into a labyrinth of sections, all of which looked about the same.

"Where do those go?" I asked my companion.

"Direct to hell," he answered, and this time he wasn't smiling. "There's only one safe road under here. The rest . . ." He rolled his eyes to emphasize the danger of getting off the proper path. I hoped he knew where he was going, for I couldn't tell any difference.

As we walked, I felt fatigue creeping up my neck like ivy up a wall. I pulled out the bottle of pills and took several more. My mind kept returning to Angela Grover. She talked about ripe, rotted fruit and made people angry. Angry how? They said that she was crazy. If that was true, why would the things she said get everyone so upset? Old Grover sat there dying before my eyes, wanting nothing more in this world than to know that his son's killer had been brought to justice; yet he kept things from me. He kept Angela from me; they all did. Ripe, rotted fruit and inner leeches and a girl who lived in shadows, knowing people from their vibrations rather than from their looks.

We came finally to a large door with a regulation vis set next to it. My friend stood before the screen, and after we had been checked visually, we were allowed inside. We came into a room that was like a small army barrack. Cots lined the walls in triple tiers. There was a shower room off to my left and a small kitchen to the right. There was ample walk-around space, but no surplus. Every available millimeter was jammed with weapons and ammo. The place smelled like sweat, and the voices of the twenty or so men who lived there clamored in locker-room resonance. This was the war bunker.

161

My guide pointed to a door at the far end of the room. I started forward, then realized that he wasn't coming with me. I turned to thank him for saving my bacon back in the safe zone, but he had already turned on his heels and left.

The door opened before I got to it, and Maria, a business-like smile on her face, stood in the open space and beckoned me in. She was wearing the same grays as her men, except that hers was an armored exoskeleton. Her suit looked uncomfortable, but would protect her from frump shrapnel. It wouldn't be of much use against a laser, though.

I moved past her and into the room beyond. It was the one I had seen on the vis and was every bit as cold and lifeless as my small glimpse had told me earlier. She closed and locked the door behind us. Coming up to me, she kissed me. It was a dry-lipped, old-friend kiss. Moving back, she stared at my eyes.

"You're speeding," she said.

"I'm surviving."

There was one desk in the room with a chair behind it. The desk was literally covered with electronic gear. A long, one-piece bench wound around three of the four walls, allowing large briefings. Three walls were covered from floor to ceiling with vis screens, the fourth with the map that I had partially seen in my earlier conversation. It was a map of the city, gridded off into coordinates. Maria sat at her desk. I parked on the bench.

"You had a close one back there."

I raised my eyebrows and let air hiss between my lips. "Your men did a good job," I answered. "I appreciate it."

She shook her head. Hard as nails she was, befitting an absolute autocrat. The years of command had put an edge on her. She was tough because she had to be, tough because it was the only way to maintain herself and her people.

"It's too dangerous for you out on the streets," she said coldly. "Half the damn city wants your ass."

I stood and began pacing. The speed was working my body like a marionette. My brain told me to rest, but I had to move. "Just get me to Old Town and back," I said, "and then we'll talk about it."

"This isn't just you anymore."

"You promised me a couple of days."

"My advisors want me to go against Charon. They say that if I don't, I'll be showing a weakness to my people and to Charon that will prove fatal."

"Fatal to whom?"

She stood up. Anger flashed through her eyes. "Fatal to everything that I've worked so hard to build up. I believe in what I'm doing here." She rapped on the exo with her knuckles. "You think I want to wear this? I'm not afraid to die . . . never have been. But life in the DMZ flows through me. I am the DMZ, and if I die the DMZ, pitiful as it may be, dies also. I'm not ready for that to happen."

I looked at the floor and thought about priorities and about Jumpstreet Harry and about bloodsucking worms. "I'm sorry," I said. "I guess I'm not too good at keeping more than one thing at a time in my head. I think, though, that I can work this out for both of us. You're going to have to let me get to Old Town first."

She sat down, her face set in a frown. Her eyes were staring into empty space, and I could almost see the wheels turning behind them. "You know too much about this operation," she said. "If you were to get caught . . ."

"Give me a break," I said. "I swear I won't make a move without you."

"At this moment, Swain, letting you stay alive may be the best break I can offer you."

I just stared at her.

She returned my gaze. "What about George Wesley?"

"You tell me."

"All right," she answered. "A vendetta can be a fool-hardy venture when dealing with a man like Charon. My advisors are beginning to have serious doubts about your reliability."

It was my turn to get mad. "I can do my job, lady. You just worry about yourself. What is your little military retaliation if not a vendetta?"

"Business," she said. She looked at me for a long time, then sighed. Reaching a hand to a toggle on her desk, she juiced a wall vis. When the face came up she started talking. "Mr. Swain is going to Old Town," she said. "Get everything ready." She looked up at me and smiled. "To hell with my advisors."

Maria toggled off and, standing up, moved around the desk to where I stood. She put her arms around me and held me close. I returned the embrace, feeling the smooth hardness of the exo. I lost my face in her hair, and that, at least, felt real. She smelled of sweet honeysuckle that wrapped me in faraway dreams.

"I'm sorry," she whispered. "I had to ask you those things."

"I know."

"I'm sorry about George, too. I really am."

"Yeah," I answered. "So am I."

22

There wasn't any barbed wire.

There weren't any electron fields, or high walls, or armed guards to separate the DMZ from Old Town. All there was was a big red swath the color of blood that ran down the middle of Jefferson Street in either direction. Signs were posted, for those who could read, on every pole that was left standing. All the signs said the same thing:

APPROACHING GROUND ZERO
GO BACK!

For the nonreaders, a skull and crossbones occupied the lower half of the sign.

There were six of us, standing like tulips in a ragweed patch, looking down at that red line and wondering what the hell could be so different on the other side of that streak of paint. There were buildings over there, that much I could see. And the buildings looked like . . . buildings.

"So now what?" I asked laughing boy, who was standing next to me and looking like the winner of the smiling contest. His name was Corman (but I didn't know if that was a first or last), and he had done such a fine job of rescuing me that he was rewarded by having to go to Ground Zero with me. He couldn't stop grinning, so I knew he must have been as scared as a pickpocket at the policemen's ball.

He shrugged and pulled out his lip balm. His lower lip looked as if he had used it to repave a road, and it was bleeding slightly from a myriad of small cuts. "I guess we go in," he said, and his eyes were saying, no-no.

The four other men remained silent. They all wore the grays that were reserved for Maria's elite guard. I knew they weren't happy about this excursion, but I also knew they wouldn't let me down if it came to a fight. They had left their long guns back at the war bunker, but each had a laser strapped to his belt.

I walked across the line. It didn't hurt a bit. Corman followed me over, and the rest came shortly after. It was a regular follow-the-leader.

"Isn't someone supposed to meet us?" I asked, as I watched the bullets that delivered us hum quickly away.

"Supposed to," Corman replied through tight, sore lips. "But the only thing certain about Old Town is the smog."

We walked through the intersection on Brockhurst into thickening underbrush. "You ever been here?"

"A couple of times."

"What's it like?"

He looked at me, wide-eyed, and, shaking his head, made a snorting sound. That was the only reply I got.

We walked for several more blocks without seeing any signs of life. The decay was complete here. The streets were tangles of gnarled trees and Johnson grass that could hide a man by the time summer was over. The buildings were like so much rock to the wiles of Nature; large growths of ivy and twisted vines climbed their sides, hiding their stark, unpleasant nakedness. Flowers grew in profusion. Strange flowers with blossoms big as stop signs and colors that throbbed like beating hearts.

"Mutation," Corman said. "It gets worse."

We moved through the mess as best we could. Mosquitoes as large as my hand buzzed us continually, fearlessly, and it was all we could do to keep them from draining our blood a pint at a time. It was as hot as an unserialed frump out there; the smog pressed in on us, terrariumlike. I wanted to take off my jacket, but didn't dare expose any more of my arms to the mosquitoes.

Every now and then I'd turn and barely glimpse something

out of the corner of my eye that quickly faded back into the swollen shadows. We were being watched, but not approached.

We went farther, and the covered sun played pat-a-cake on my head and my insides wanted a drink and the speed jerked me around and made all the world seem like a cellophane package that wouldn't open and everything moved in and out and my teeth clenched together and stayed that way as I swam through my own sweat, wondering not so much if I could trust my senses, but exactly how far—and then I saw him.

He was perched on a mesquite limb, legs dangling, rubbing his hands over the bark and examining the texture. He had seen us a long time before we had seen him, and he giggled when I finally noticed his posture. He was dressed in polka-dot knee-pants and cowboy boots. He wore a long-sleeved, long-tailed coat with a matching vest and black and white striped ascot. A top hat, brushed smooth, sat tilted slightly atop his totally hairless head.

One of the latexed black men began easing a laser out of its home.

"Don't," Corman snapped. "That's our connection."

We walked right up to the tree. The man jumped off his limb, tumbling to the ground. He jumped back to his feet, dusting off his dirty knees. He had large ears. He had very large ears.

He smiled, then tightened his face, gazing past us into the shadows beyond through eyes reduced to focusing slits. "This is real important stuff, isn't it?" he whispered, while nodding his head vigorously. His eyes darted, dancing from one of us to the other. "Something big on the outside."

Corman opened his mouth to say something, but the man stopped. "Not here," he said, and there was real urgency in his tone. "There are spies everywhere. You just follow old Billy Ding." He winked five or six times. "I'll get you to safety."

The man stooped into a crouch and swung his head slowly back and forth. He half-hopped about ten paces, did the bit with his head again, then motioned with his arm for us to follow.

I looked at Corman, who smiled painfully in return.

We followed Ding into the underbrush for about a block while he bunny-hopped with all the stealth of a wrecking ball. Suddenly, he jumped to his feet and dashed off the path and into an alleyway. We followed. The alley got no sun, so all that grew there was thick, damp moss. We slipped and slid over the moss cover and caught up to Ding about halfway down the length of the buildings. He was breathing hard and hugging the slimy wall.

"Did you see them?" he asked. "Did you *see them*?" He craned his neck and looked past us down the way we had come. "God, that was close." He wiped a sweaty forehead with the back of his arm, and made a strange hand sign.

I looked back; there was no one.

"Okay," he gasped, his breathing still labored. "I think we're safe now, at least for a while. Give me the story. Don't hold anything back. You can trust me."

"We want you to take us to Michael Grover," I said, as I watched a six-legged chameleon scurry under a pile of fuzzy green bricks.

"OOOH!" he yelled, jerking his head around and making exaggerated theatrical gestures. "Is that all? You just want me to waltz you right in to see Michael Grover as if this were a goddamn cotillion." His voice had taken on a strained, high timbre. He grabbed me by the lapels and got right up in my face. "Well, let me tell you something," he snarled. "I've got principles. I don't just take any outsider I meet to Michael Grover. No sir, not me. You know what I think? I think you people are spies, that's what I think. What do you have to say about that?"

He let me go and started strutting around like a peacock, coming up to each of us in turn and saying, "Spy!" to every face he encountered.

"We're from Hermanita," Corman said.

His eyes widened and he began gazing around suspiciously again. "This really is big, isn't it?" he asked. "You can tell me. You can trust me."

"It's big," I said.

He pounded a fist into an open palm. "I *knew* it," he said, looking heavenward. "You came to me with the big stuff, because you knew you could trust me, right?"

"Right," I answered.

He looked back over his shoulder. "Come on, you can tell me. It's war, isn't it? You can trust me."

I nodded, and he knowingly returned my nod.

Walking up to me, Ding put his arm around my shoulder and drew me away from the rest. "I'm going to tell you this because I know that you're trustworthy," he said, and turned to glare at my companions. "I think I recognize some of them other fellas. I think they might be spies."

"Well, I . . ."

"Can you read? I don't trust people who can read. They're always keeping secrets."

"I can't read," I said. "Neither can my friends."

He thought about that for a minute. "Maybe they're okay then. Maybe they just look like somebody who'd be a spy." He nodded and thought some more. "All right then, I'll take you to Grover, but he lives right near Ground Zero, and I think it's only fair to warn you . . ." He put his mouth right up to my ear. ". . . the people there are crazy."

"Go on," I said.

He winked again and nodded his head slowly up and down.

"I guess we'll just have to take our chances."

"That's the spirit that made this country great!" he bellowed. "Do your duty. Never say die. Oh God, this is going to be an adventure." He let me go and paced around nervously for a minute, then he came back up to me. "Are you *sure* you can trust those guys?"

I lowered my voice. "Listen," I said, conspiratorial as hell, "if any of those bozos give us trouble . . ." I opened my jacket and showed him my frump.

"Say no more." He smiled. "Say no more." And he nudged me with his elbow.

We moved back to the others. I was glad to get away from Ding. He had a strange odor—not sweat, not even filth (although those smells were there); it was something . . . different. "Our very dear friend, Mr. Ding," I announced, "has kindly consented to guide us to our destination."

Ding stepped to the fore and took a deep bow, holding the bowing position. He turned his head upward, looking at us, waiting. I began to applaud and the others followed suit. Ding grinned broadly and then straightened.

"Thank you," he said modestly. "And now my friends . . . into the breach!"

He suddenly took off, running at full speed, only to skid to a halt at alley's end. We jogged until we caught up with him. When I got beside him, he grabbed my arm.

"This is the tricky part," he whispered. "We'll have to go for it one at a time. You see that color pole?"

I nodded. He was pointing to a traffic light that leaned at a forty-five-degree angle about a block away.

"I'll make a dash for it. If I make it, send your men one at a time."

I agreed. We needed Ding to get us to Grover, and I wasn't about to antagonize him.

He peered around the corner of the building, then looked back at me. "Well, this is it," he philosophized. "If I don't see you again . . ." he gave me a quick hug. ". . . keep 'em flying." He shot me the thumbs-up sign and took off running.

I watched him as he cut a zigzag pattern through the tall brush, the tails of his formal coat flapping behind him like twin pennants in a stiff wind. He lost his hat once, and had to go back for it. He made the remainder of his run holding it squarely on his head. When he reached the traffic light, he jumped up and down, waving his arms frenetically.

"Send somebody before he has a fit," Corman said.

I nodded to one of the grays, a short man with a bushy moustache, and he followed Ding's route. "Can we trust him to get us there?" I asked Corman.

"We can't trust him to get us down the block," he answered, smiling. "But what else are we going to do?"

I agreed, and started another man running. My head was knocking like a bullet motor with out-of-sync polarity. I didn't even know what I was doing there. It was a checkerboard on which all the squares were the same color. I was pinning all my hopes on a man I'd never met, expecting answers from a person who, more than likely, didn't have any answers to give me. George had called it a contest between me and Charon. If that was true, I was playing

David to his Goliath, and I was hoping that Michael Grover would be the stone that would knock him down.

I sent them all to Ding, then went myself. As I ran, I noticed just how altered my mental state was, for my feet seemed to be moving as a separate entity altogether. I watched them go, but couldn't connect them up with any motivation in my mind. That bothered me.

Ding greeted me like a long lost brother when I reached him. He was excited as hell that we all made that one-block trip in safety. He announced at that point that it would be all right to travel together for a while, a fact that improved my disposition considerably.

We were still on Brockhurst and moved along that way for a time. Ding talked incessantly about Old Town politics, which seemed to be a kind of benign anarchy. The citizens of Old Town, so the story went, were held together by their mutual hatred and distrust of outsiders, whom they called food-droppers because of the monthly welfare rationing. They were extremely broad-minded when it came to the habits of actions of their fellows, and extremely bitter toward those who they felt kept them prisoner in their decay.

The government called it a permanent quarantine, with immediate execution the penalty for noncompliance. That made it all neat and legal.

We turned off Brockhurst onto I don't know what street. The undergrowth had gotten tedious. Thick, knotty vines scrabbled snakelike on the black ground, tangling ankles, tripping. Maybe I was just too used to walking on concrete. We were seeing people now—gross, misshapen heads poking through window spaces, watching us with eyes that had seen hell and knew that what they had was worse.

The buildings were painted bright colors, at least for a couple of stories. Strange insignias were meticulously painted on every doorway, perhaps as a means of warding off evil spirits, perhaps as a simple familial shield. I never thought to ask. Portions of the streets were used as farmland, and we made our way through several fields of grotesque-looking vegetables that could almost have been recognizable foods, but not quite. There were totems everywhere, monstrous things with bulging eyes and screaming mouths, things that could only have come from minds that traveled roads mine had never taken.

The berserkers watched us intently as we made our way through their fields. Some were naked, some dressed in fashions not seen for a hundred years. The rotted carcasses of ancient automobiles were scattered here and there, and I finally realized that this end of town had lived in a total cultural vacuum for nearly a century.

There were some children playing a game. Some of them looked almost normal, some looked like half-formed lumps of clay with missing limbs and large heads with drooling toothless mouths and running eyes and noses slapped across their faces like mudballs on a window. Most had no hair.

As near as I could understand it, this was their game: the most horribly mutated child in the group was picked by general consensus and appointed leader. The leader then had to assign tasks to the others to perform in a certain length of time. The tasks were geared to encompass the physical or mental limitations of the participants. So a boy with one leg was told to run around the block. A skeletal, hollow-eyed little girl with obvious digestive deficiencies was made to eat ten banana-like pieces of fruit. And so on. The winner was an armless girl who was able to knock herself unconscious by running up against a brick wall. Her reward was a handful of powdered milk—one of the commodities included in the welfare drops, which the Old Towners apparently burned as incense.

There weren't any old people at all. I could only suppose that their internal complications were just too overpowering to keep them alive for very many years. "Where do you bury your dead?" I asked Ding.

He looked surprised. "Well, right here," he said, and pointed to a building as if I were totally ignorant.

"In there?"

"In all these," he said, and I could tell by his tone that he was wondering if I was a spy again. "When someone dies, we take them up and give them their own room, nice and peaceful. Then we stick all those canned things that the food-droppers bring in there in case they wake up and get hungry. There's plenty of rooms. Plenty."

"Do they ever?"

"What?"

"Wake up and get hungry."

"Not very often."

We moved on. The way was full of people by this time. They called to us or jeered, keeping their distance because of our weapons. I watched them as they watched me, and I thought about Bergson's maxim. I wondered if Mr. Bergson could have considered the novelty of this particular evolutionary jump. They were humans, a fact my brain found difficult to accept. In many of them, the resemblance to humanity was barely circumstantial. The thing that struck me the most, however, was the undeniable fact that here, in this world, I was the one out of place. My actions, my mannerisms, my thought patterns, even my ethics were as alien to these people as knives and forks to a Chinaman. It was like a freak show, with me as the geek.

Maria's people were as uneasy as I was and kept their hands resting on their equalizers. We moved single-file, and I could hear Corman behind me continually talking to his men, trying to keep them calm. Ding was still prattling on, but I was no longer able to pay attention to him, so filled was my mind with double images.

A man came up and started walking next to me. He had a large, bald head, and hideous boils all over his face. He was dressed in overalls covering flannel underwear. He had only three fingers on each hand, like a cartoon character.

"You look like an intelligent man," he said, and his voice was a slur. "Maybe you can make them understand."

I didn't say anything, but instead reached into my pocket and took a couple more pills.

"Say you've got a full moon, right?" He put his cartoon hands together in a full-moon shape.

"Okay," I answered.

"Well, have you noticed that with every passing night the moon gets smaller?"

"I've noticed."

Ding turned to the man and was glaring at him.

173

"It gets all the way down to nothing, then starts building back up again."

Ding walked up to the man and half-shoved his shoulder. "What's your name? I've never seen you before."

The man ignored him and kept talking. "They try to hide it with that smoke cover, but I've been watching the moon for years and feel that I'm qualified to speak as an expert in this area." The man's head was vibrating steadily, his fat tongue lolling through swollen lips. "I've got documentation to prove that I'm right."

"Let's see some identification," Ding said, walking backwards so that he could face the man, and half-falling with every step.

"If what I say is true," the man continued, "then that means there is an intelligence . . . a guiding force out there that is performing miracles with the moon right before our eyes. Think of it . . ."

"How long have you lived here?" Ding asked. Then he raised his voice to the crowd: "DOES ANYBODY KNOW THIS FELLA?"

"He's my sister," someone called.

"IS HE A SPY?"

". . . a divine force out there that can destroy and reshape the moon every month. Why are they trying to keep it from us?"

"He spies on me when I'm taking a bath," someone else said.

That was all Ding needed. "Ah ha! That's what I . . ." He tripped over a vine and crashed to the ground.

"Why don't they want us to know the master plan?"

There was a moan behind me, almost orgasmic. The sound pulled me around. One of the gray-suited men stood staring at a large, shafted arrow that protruded from his chest. Then he looked up, puzzled, and started walking towards me. Grabbing the shaft with both hands, he tried to pull it out, buckling his body with every tug. He got right up to me and the thing came out, followed by a rush of black heart-blood. Reaching out, he handed the arrow to me, the bewilderment never leaving his face. He opened his mouth to speak, but

174

blood came instead of words. He dropped to his knees as if he were praying, then fell on his face in a way that left no doubt he was dead.

"Put em up!" a hard drawl commanded. "You're all under arrest."

23

There were a bunch of them, and not very many of us. They all wore white Stetsons, blue- and white-checkered shirts tucked into blue jeans turned up at the cuff, and string ties. Their boots ran up under their pants, and they all had crudely fashioned stars pinned prominently to their chests. Their bows and arrows were obviously home-fashioned, but had been constructed well enough—as the guy who was eating dirt by my feet would most certainly have admitted if he were able.

We probably could have gone for our guns, but it would have been the last movement from any of us. I voted to stay alive for a while longer and raised my hands over my head to let them know my desires. I looked behind me to see what my little company was doing, and found that their decision had come even before my own. Amazing how the survival instinct will have its way.

The crowd moved in on us, with hands extended and frowning, growling mouths. I frantically jerked my head around, looking for Ding to make an explanation, but he had apparently decided that, in his case, discretion was the better part of valor. Our guide was gone, nowhere to be seen.

Hands grabbed me—rough hands, hands bloated and ill-proportioned and smelling the way Ding did. They buffeted me back and forth, knocked me around like a piñata filled with liquid-red candy. I talked to them, but the words were formed in some primal center of my brain that had nothing to do with my conscious mind, and I don't remember what I told them. I was pushed to my knees, then to my stomach on top of the man who had died in such confusion. Fists pounded me, and God knows what else. I began to envy the dead man beneath me.

I heard loud voices barking commands, and looked up to see white hats pushing my attackers off me. "We'll kill him later," they were saying, "after the trial. After the trial we'll kill him."

I never thought that I'd be glad to hear someone say they were going to kill me.

I was pulled to my feet, an act that I don't think I could have accomplished on my own. I hurt all over, especially in my ribs, but I didn't think anything was broken. My face was covered with dust and with blood from the cut on my temple, which had reopened. One of the white hats reached into my jacket and pulled the frump out of its home. He smiled at me with his huge, round, billiard-ball face, and his lipless mouth was a cavernous maw of red, diseased gums. There was a cancerous hole where his nose should have been and he snorted through the place. Slinging the bow over his shoulder, he held the gun on me.

He motioned with the gun for me to raise my hands again.

"Can I wipe my face off first?" I asked.

He shook his head, and I stayed dirty.

Two of the others didn't get up, reducing our forces by fifty percent. Corman was on his feet, but in pretty bad shape. One of his eyes was swollen shut and an arm dangled uselessly at his side. They tried to make him raise it, but when he couldn't, he was allowed to raise only his good arm.

A man with a lower lip the size of a piece of raw liver was speaking to the crowd, which had quieted to listen to him. His lip wiggled back and forth with every word.

"Now folks, I know how y'all feel about these varmints, 'cause I feel the same way too. And I guarandamnteeya that after the judge has a little set-to with these fellas, we'll have a necktie party that will make even Missus Mercantile's quilting bees look tame."

A big cheer went up from the crowd. Missus Mercantile's quilting bees must have really been something.

"Who is that?" I asked the man with my frump.

His eyes shifted around a bit, until he decided that there was no harm in talking to me. "That's Sheriff Nat Bank," he said proudly, "and we're the all-volunteer vigilante committee."

"Now what I want you to do," Bank was saying, "is to go on back to your bunkhouses and get some rest, 'cause it's gonna be a long night ."

I didn't like the sound of that; I had always preferred to stay in the background. Being the center of attention made me nervous. Bank motioned for us with his arm, and we were walking again. After we had moved on, the crowd descended like carrion crows on the corpses left behind. I didn't want to think about that very much.

We moved along, hands in the air, past a lot more of the same. The mobs were thick along the way and kept up a constant racket that made it almost impossible to think. I tried to key my mind on Ginny: Ginny quietly orbiting the insanity in her own personal universe that I would never let her take me to. I made a promise to myself that if I ever got out of Old Town, I'd take that trip into the sky, just to see what it was all about.

A few things were coming clear to me. As I drowned in the insanity around me, I began to understand about inner leeches. Was Angela Grover's family rooted in Old Town? Could Grover blood be tainted by mutation? It would certainly explain a lot of things about that family.

I edged my way up to the head of the delegation until I was walking next to the leader. "Sheriff Bank . . ."

"Call me Nat, son."

"What's this all about, Nat?"

He turned to me, and the sight of that purple-red tumor where his lower lip should have been made my skin crawl. "I may be just a small-time lawman, son, but that don't mean I just fell out the cottonwood tree. This here's about rustling, and you damn well know it."

I tried to focus on his puffy squint-eyes, so as to block out that lip. I suppose that I shouldn't have expected more than the answer he gave me. I tried again. "I think you must have us mixed up with someone else," I said. "We're here trying to find somebody."

He eased his hat back farther on his cue-ball head and wiped a line of sweat off his brow with a nailless thumb.

"Yep. You're here to rustle our town's leading citizen. You food-droppers figger you can just meander on in here whenever you've a mind to, and then sashay out with the goods. Well, he warned us that you'd be coming, and we've been waiting."

"But I'm trying to help Grover, I . . ."

"You'd best take your place in line, son."

"You don't understand . . ."

"Fall back in line. Do I have to knock out all those pretty teeth to make my point?"

I moved back into formation. Grover must have been afraid that whoever killed his brother would be coming for him. That made a definite connection between the two. Maybe a connection named Mina Goulding. Michael Grover illegally placed quarantined Old Towners in straight society, at least the ones who could get away with it physically. Mina Goulding had no records, which told me she had no past. Harry and Marabeth Goulding refused to claim her as a daughter because she wasn't. Even if they had wanted to help her, they couldn't, because the penalty for harboring mutants was as severe as the penalty for being a mutant. Charon wanted the woman's past covered, so that he could salt her away in the Richmond for the duration, with no one to miss her. So he had a hand in the cover-up. What I needed now was a link from Grover to Mina Goulding.

Huge weeds with sharp thorns and purple bell-flowers grew everywhere in this end of town. They were twice the size of a man, and thick as a brier patch. They had complete control of the streets, we were continually forced to find alternate routes around the tangle.

Finally we stopped in front of a building that looked as if it had been a fast-food restaurant at one time. The big plate-glass window spaces had been boarded over, the only attempt I'd seen in all of Old Town to try and preserve the inside of one of the buildings.

A group of flagellants stood around the entrance to the restaurant. They were chanting and moaning and whipping each other with stalks of that thorny weed. Blood flowed freely from cuts all over their bodies, and untreated, festering sores from other beatings oozed infected pus.

It all passed dreamlike before my wildly running mind, the agonized moaning sounding something close to an angelic dirge. I felt as if I were in a bullet that was humming out of control, ready to crash. I was horrified by the activity, but fascinated by the scenic rush. It would all crash down in a minute, but why not enjoy the ride in the meantime?

We were led inside the restaurant. Since the windows were boarded, it was dark in there, the illumination eerily provided by hundreds of thin candles placed all over the room. There was no air circulation at all, and the boxed heat was a physical, suffocating presence. Breathing was a chore. Three-fourths of the place consisted of booths and tables, although in slightly less than mint condition. A building-long counter made of stainless steel described the rest of the room. This was where people had once ordered food. There were large brownish red stains all over the counter that looked almost like dried blood. Men dressed in what was apparently the official vigilante uniform lined the walls like a Parthenon frieze—silent, stoic, deadly serious.

My arms ached and were cramped from holding them up so long. I asked Bank if I could lower them, and after checking the room's security, he grudgingly let me.

The three of us were pushed into a large booth. The once-padded seats were slashed and torn up, so I was sitting mostly on plywood splinters. Corman sat across from me, immersed in pain, his hideous grin riveted to his face, his cracked lips bleeding all over his chin. The other man sat next to him, his head darting back and forth like a cornered animal.

Leaning across the table, I looked them in the face and said, "Now here's my plan."

They didn't find that humorous.

I turned to my right. There was a red telephone for taking orders with a plaque menu above it. Through the cracked, yellowed lamination I saw that the special was a jumbo soyburger with cheese, large fries, and a triple thick shake for $4.95. I wondered what a shake was.

The man with my frump stood near the table guarding us. I asked him for a smoker. What he gave me tasted like burning zoo dust and looked like what dogs leave in the gutter. I had to put it out.

I briefly considered the clothes everyone was wearing. As I'd earlier noted, without exception, it was stuff that hadn't seen the light of day for more years than I would ever spend on this planet. I figured that the government must have kept a factory in business since the initial quarantine just making clothes for the welfare drops. They never saw the necessity of changing styles with the times. The Old Towners were living in a world that hadn't changed appreciably in a century, so they didn't care. It was odd to me, but I guess it really didn't make any difference.

"The Judge," someone said, and I turned toward the counter. An almost normal-looking man stood behind the counter, leaning against it on stiff arms. I said almost normal-looking. He had an extremely triangular face, culminating in a pointed chin. His ears were pointed also, and his eyes . . . his eyes blazed fiery red. His mouth seemed to be set in a permanent scowl, and when he glared across the room at us, I knew that I had come face to face with the devil. He was dressed in gray: a gray shirt tucked into belted gray pants and a zippered gray jacket draped around his shoulders and fastened around his neck by a high button. The name Mel was embroidered over the jacket's left breast-pocket. He wore a gray, peaked cap with a black bill. Braided filigree wound around the base of the cap, and an emblem of a running dog, a greyhound, decorated the front of the cap.

"All rise," bellowed Bank, and seeing as how me and my two friends were the only people seated to begin with, we thought it opportune that we stand up. The entire room watched us as we struggled to our feet.

When we were up, Bank began talking. "This here vigilante circuit court for upholding justice and administering punishment thereafter is now in session, the Honorable Duncan A. Donut presiding."

"What are the charges?" asked the Judge in a voice that could only be compared to feeding-time in a monkey cage.

"These here fellas are charged with illegal entry into our town for the purpose of spiriting away one of our citizens, namely Michael Grover, with the intention of doing bodily harm to beforementioned citizen.''

"Are the defendants represented by counsel?" the Judge asked.

"No sir," Bank said. "Ain't no one wanted to stand up for them."

The Judge brought a heavy fist down on the counter top. "Damn it! You can't have a trial without a defense attorney." He glared around the room, then pointed to one of the guards lined against the candle-flickering wall. "You're the defense attorney," he said.

Our champion stepped out of the shadows. He wasn't hairless like the rest of them. Quite the contrary. He was covered with hair, matted with it. He looked like a mohair suit with lips and eyes, if you could call the glassy marbles stuck in his head eyes. They were coated with a fine mucous film that continually ran down his cheeks, wetting the hair of his face. When he opened his mouth to speak, I saw that he had sharp, jagged teeth.

"Do I hafta?" he asked in a clear-as-a-bell tenor that didn't fit his features at all. "I've got a reputation to uphold."

"Listen, S.C.," Bank said. "When we go ahead and convict these fellas, everyone will think you're the best thing since radiator juice for helping us out. Shoot, they might even elect you to be the bull in the rodeo this year."

"Do you really think so?" the human hairball asked.

Bank flapped his lip. "Why not?"

"By golly, I'll do it," S.C. answered, and tromped apelike to the center of the room. "I'll be the defense attorney."

Somehow, I didn't think that we were going to get a fair trial.

Judge Donut raised his arms in supplication. "Let the record show," he said pompously, "that Mr. Slow C. Playing has kindly consented to defend these heinous criminals."

I looked around; there was no one keeping any records.

"The defendants have heard the charges leveled against them," Donut intoned. "How do they plead?"

"Guilty," said S.C.

"Not guilty," I said.

"Shut up," said Bank, lip quivering with rage. He looked at the Judge. "This man is out of order."

"Out of order," S.C. repeated. "Definitely out of order."

I strode up to the counter. "I'm here to help Michael Grover," I told Donut. "I was a friend of his brother. I used to work for him."

The Judge's face turned a deep, flushed crimson. "Strike that last remark from the records!" he screamed. He was breathing heavily—hyperventilating. He looked past me to my "lawyer."

"You'd best restrain your client from any further outbursts, Counselor, or I'll hold you both in contempt of court."

S.C. plodded up and jerked me back by the jacket collar. He got right up in my face; his breath smelled like dead fish. "Now you've done it," he said. "Got the Judge mad at me. Keep your lousy mouth shut, troublemaker." He growled, showing me even rows of incisors.

"If you want to keep yourself out of a jam," I answered, "plead me 'not guilty.' If you don't, I'll start in again."

He snarled, drooling, and turned away from me.

It took the Judge several minutes to regain his composure. When he finally did, he spoke to S.C. "How does your client plead?"

"Not guilty," S.C. answered, to a chorus of jeers and catcalls from the rest of the room. The humiliation must have been too great for the hairy man, for he squatted on his haunches in the middle of the floor and began crying.

The Judge leaned way out over the edge of the counter, so he could see his defense attorney down there on the floor. "Counselor," he fumed. "You are making a mockery of this court. I have no choice but to hold you in contempt. Take him away."

Four of the vigilantes came and physically picked up the now hysterical S.C. Playing and carried him out of the building, much to the delight of the flagellants outside. They sent up a round of cheers when the doors opened.

Donut watched S.C. until he was all the way out of the room, then turned to look at Bank. "The plea is 'not guilty.' Call your first witness."

Bank nodded, blinking his puff eyes. "The State calls Mr. Bill Ding."

I went ahead and sat down, motioning Corman and the other guy whose name I didn't know down with me. Ding came up from somewhere. I guess he'd been there all the time. He walked past me without a glance and strode right up to the counter.

The Judge climbed up on the counter and crawled, on all fours, until he was nose-to-nose with Ding. From an inside pocket of his jacket, he produced a small, boxlike object. It was about the same size as a pocketcom, but instead of a readout screen, its front showed a numbered dial. The back was gone and wires and parts of a circuit board were hanging out. Donut held out the machine.

"Raise your right hand," he said, "and place your left hand on the worship box."

Ding did it.

"Now, repeat after me: I Bill Ding . . ."

"I Bill Ding . . ."

"Swear by the terminals of the Great Transistor . . ."

"Swear by the terminals of the Great Transistor . . ."

"To do what must be done."

"What must be done."

Donut pulled the box away from Ding and, kissing its dial, placed it carefully back in his pocket. He looked at Ding in bewilderment for a minute, then his eyes widened. Anger flashed across his face and he grabbed Ding's hat right off his head and handed it to him.

"This is a court of law," Donut said, ignoring the fact that everyone else in the room was wearing a hat.

"Let the record show," Bank interrupted, "that the witness for the prosecution has removed his hat."

"The record so states," Donut said with dramatic flair.

Bank paced the shadow-jumping room, hooking his thumbs in his belt loops, apparently searching for the proper words. He walked right up to the witness, turned his back on him, and tugged his lower lip with his left hand. Suddenly, he wheeled around and pointed an accusing finger at Ding. "Let the record show," he said, "that the Prosecutor is pointing at the witness."

"The record so indicates."

Bank walked up to Ding and put his arm around the man. "How long we known each other, Billy Boy?"

Ding looked uneasy, and kept gently writhing in Bank's grasp. "Well, after my daddy cut his arm off and had to be put up in one of the rooms, you started to come around and help my mother mud the floor. That was about a meter ago." He indicated with his hands how small he had been. "I didn't trust you at first, but . . ."

"That's fine, Billy. Now, I want you to tell me true, are those the food-droppers who came here to kill Mr. Grover?"

Ding nodded vigorously. "They're the ones, no doubt about it. Never did trust them, always knew they were spies. They said they wanted to kill Grover, said it was something big and that they'd start a war on the outside. Can you imagine—a war. What an adventure!"

The Judge jumped down from the counter and ran up to me, grabbing me by the lapels. "What's this about a war?" he demanded.

I looked at him and shrugged, giving him my best angelic smile. I almost asked if the records would indicate my expression.

Donut was breathing heavily again. The excitement was too much for him. He stood there for a minute, his eyes darting, looking at nothing in particular. Then he climbed back over the counter and took his place. "Let it be known," he said officiously, "that this court deals harshly with war criminals. I will show no mercy in meting out the proper dollop of justice when the time comes."

The courtroom burst into spontaneous applause. Ding cracked a grin that could have done serious damage to the bone structure of his face.

"Are there any more questions of this witness?" Donut asked.

"Is there anything else, Billy Boy?"

"Well, there's the matter of those oriental people who hide in the alleyways waiting for me all the time. Now I can handle it every . . ."

"That's fine," said Bank. "We'll talk on it later. Goodbye."

"Good-bye," Ding said, waving at the court. Then he walked out of the flagellants' door, to be greeted by a low, hissing moan.

"Next witness," the Judge called.

"That's all, Duncan," Bank answered, showing empty palms.

Donut nodded. He took off his cap and placed it somewhere behind the counter. He replaced it with one that looked just the same, except that it was all black. "By virtue of the facts presented here today . . ."

"Wait a minute," I said, jumping to my feet. "Is this a court of law or isn't it?"

"It most certainly is," Donut answered righteously.

"Well in a court of law, the defense gets to call witnesses before the verdict is given."

Donut's eyes widened as if he'd just discovered he wasn't wearing any pants. "I knew that," he said with a trembling voice. "I was just waiting for the proper moment."

"But who would be a witness for these sidewinders?" mocked Bank, and the entire room echoed the taunt.

"The Defense calls Michael Grover," I said, and waited for the explosion.

Bank walked over and shoved me back in my seat, shaking his hairless fist in front of my nose.

"This isn't a circus," Donut whined in his monkey house voice. "I won't stand for this behavior. Let the records show that."

"I've called my witness," I said, loud enough to get over the din that had broken out in the room. Bank slapped me hard across the face. It snapped my head around, but I didn't even feel it.

Donut was wiggling a finger at me, his face as red as an Italian's politics. "This will go hard with you, young man," he managed between gulps of air. "Calling your intended victim to testify . . . what do you think we are?"

"If I answered that question, you'd hold me in contempt," I answered.

"Silence that man!"

"Call the witness if you're a real judge," I shouted.

Bank slapped me again; I still didn't feel it.

"Bring him up here," the Judge ordered.

Bank and my toothless friend with the frump pulled me out of the booth and forced me to stand before Donut, within touching distance. "It's going to be the firehouse for you," he rasped pleuritically, and his blood-filled eyes glowed like tracers on a moonless night. "No bonfire either. We'll stretch it out until dark, let everybody get their barter's worth."

"Call my witness," I demanded.

"I will not call your witness!" Donut screamed and he was completely out of control.

"Was someone looking for me?" came a voice from behind. I slowly wheeled around and found myself face to face with a dead man.

"Hello, Swain," he smiled.

"Hello, Phil," I returned, and couldn't think of even one snappy comeback.

24

I guess he'd put it over on everybody. Not even the Old Towners knew that he wasn't his brother Michael. I wondered if the killer knew whom he'd gotten.

I waited quietly while Phil got us out of our courtroom difficulties. He then had Corman and the other man escorted back to the DMZ with word that I would be along in a while. His curly hair was wild and tangled, and he was dressed in faded blue overalls and a checkered flannel shirt rolled up to the elbows. I guess he'd gone native.

When the others had gone, he took me silently and directly to the area of the original meltdown, just for a look. There was no vegetation at all at Ground Zero, just green-veined black earth. There were bugs, though. Ugly black and red things that were almost cat-sized and somehow fed off the ground as if it were a sheet of chocolate cake. Grover told me to look out for those bugs, but I was doing that already.

We were about two hundred meters from the actual reactor buildings, and the remnants of the giant cooling towers jutted like dulled lances into the guts of an already darkening sky. There was building rubble around the towers—stone and steel, pooled and fused like melted wax, resembling nothing so much as a mud-caked anthill. Maybe that's what it was.

"They didn't know what would happen when the core melted down to the earth's hot center," Grover told me. "There were a lot of people, reputable people, who thought that it would cause a chain reaction that would destroy the planet. Nobody could say that it wouldn't, and still they built these damn things."

"They thought the same thing would happen with the first atomic bomb," I answered, "but they blew it anyway. Humans are a gambling species; it comes with the territory."

"Almost two hundred thousand died within weeks from the radiation. Another half million lives were cut short by radiation-induced diseases. And then the genetic damage . . . ."

"Ancient history, Phil. We do have other problems at the moment."

He looked at me the way a teacher looks at a pupil who hasn't done his assignment. "I think that everyone should be made to come out here at least once, just to see what fools we are." He moved his hands a lot when he talked. It was a habit that I could tire of very quickly.

"We think," I answered with a shrug. "Thinking includes the possibility of error. Why didn't you come back? You could have straightened out this whole mess."

He gave me that condescending look again, and I found that I was beginning to dislike Philip Grover. "I thought you, of all people, would understand this," he said.

"What I understand, is that I'm living here today, right now, and that the things that happened a minute ago or a million years ago are just so much toilet water being flushed away. Can we go somewhere else to talk? This place gives me the creeps."

He took me to his place. It was within spitting distance of Ground Zero. He was set up pretty well in an old church. It was one of those small-scale Gothic things with tall spires and rosette windows and buttresses that were useless appendages to a steel-girdered building. We climbed the twenty or so cracked stone steps that led to the heavy wooden doors with the big wrought iron hinges. We creaked the door just wide enough to slip through and went inside, just as the pigeons were returning to their overhanging cubbyholes to roost for the night.

We walked down a wide aisle that was lined on either side by rows of pews. "This comes in very handy," Grover said over his shoulder, "when we move large groups out. We can brief them here en masse before sending them on."

Aside from the pews, the high-ceilinged place was devoid of ornamentation. There was one Madonna and Child statue near the front, but the baby's head was missing, and the fingers were gone from the Virgin's hand, raised in blessing, making it look like she was shaking her fist. We went up a small set of steps, past a marble altar that had been set as a dinner table, and into a series of small rooms at the back of the building. These were Grover's chambers.

We entered a windowless room that was totally dark, and Grover had to light several tree-sized candles before we could see. It was a small chamber, marginally furnished. There were several cots against the bare walls, and a writing desk between two of the candles. A filing cabinet stood in the corner, and various supplies of food were stacked next to a wood-burning stove in another corner. Metal folding chairs were stationed wherever there was room, so I grabbed one of those and sat down.

"Never thought I'd see you again," Grover said, pointing to his eyes. He pulled a chair directly across from me and sat down.

"I knew I'd never see you again," I replied. "You don't happen to have a cigarette, do you?"

He reached into the front pocket of his overalls and pulled out a pack. Smiling, he handed them over to me. "One of the few luxuries I still allow myself," he said.

I took the fag and gave him back the pack. Miraculously, I had managed to hang on to the lighter that Corman had given me when he rescued me from Charon's people. I lit the thing and sucked on it gratefully. Thank heavens for simple pleasures. I let the smoke anesthetize my lungs for a few seconds, then let it out. "At the risk of being redundant," I said, "why didn't you come back?"

"I didn't see any reason to."

"My best friend is dead on account of you. You're going to have to do better than that."

"We all die, Swain."

"Not good enough."

"All right," he said. "That's why I took you out to Ground Zero first. I thought that maybe you'd see what was happening here. I can't allow anything to happen to myself. If I did, my work here would come to an end, and that's unthinkable."

"What exactly is your work here?"

"Helping these poor devils get out of the hell they've been forced to live in all these years. You saw what it's like out there. This earth should be free to everyone."

I didn't see an ashtray, so I flicked my ashes on the checkerboard-patterned floor. "I may be simple-minded," I said, "but by putting these people into the mainstream of society, aren't you helping to propagate the genetic damage you talked about earlier?"

"You're just like the rest of them," he fumed, angrier, I thought, than he should have been. He began waving his arms around. "You're eaten up with prejudice."

I put up my hands. "Just asking questions. That's what I'm paid for, remember? Your mother was a mutant, wasn't she?"

"Who told you that?"

"I figured it out all by myself. Now suppose you tell me the rest of it."

He leaned his chair back on two legs and linked his hands behind his head. "You seem to have it all worked out, Sherlock. You tell me."

"All right," I answered, "and you fill in the blanks. Your mother was an Old Towner who somehow made it to the outside. She married your father, probably without his knowing her background. Then she had children. Your father turned out to be a terrible husband and a worse father, but she stayed with him because, under the circumstances, she had nowhere else to go. Everything rolled along until Angela was born, and she was just too strange to pass off as normal. After your mother died in that plane crash, your father tried to hide Angie from view and keep his knowledge to himself. But it didn't work with you. You visited Angela and she told you, with that second sight or whatever the hell it is, about your mother. That's where Mina Goulding comes in. Somehow, you knew that she was a passer and could link you up with your brother in Old Town where he'd gone after your mother's death. I found her, and you used her to get to Michael. Then for some reason that I so far have been unable to determine, you switched clothes with him, and sent him to your apartment where he was killed. You decided that it was okay that everyone go on believing you dead, so you could carry on with your 'work,' and coincidentally protect yourself at the same time. I figure that Rick Charon killed your brother, maybe because Michael found out about the slave labor he was working in his factories. How am I doing?''

"About half-right,'' Grover said, and wiggled his hand around. He stood up and began walking around the room, gesturing continuously. "First of all, my mother didn't die in the plane crash. After Angie was born, dear old Dad figured out the truth and sent my mother away . . . back to Old Town.''

"There was no plane crash?''

"Oh, there was a crash all right. That's how my father got so screwed up. But the part about my mother being on board was something he made up to tell the world, so there wouldn't be any questions. My brother was smarter than me, I guess. He hunted around and discovered the truth, then came here to find her and help care for her. That's how he got involved in the underground railroad.''

"How come he didn't tell you what happened?''

"My mother wouldn't let him. She was afraid that my father would throw out the rest of us if he thought we knew.''

"But Angela told you.''

"She had been telling me for years, but it took me a long time to understand.''

I finished the cig and stamped it out on the floor. The pieces were all beginning to fall into place. "How did you find Michael?''

"Have you forgotten that my sister is going with Rick Charon? On one of my infrequent visits home, she told me that Michael had been doing business with Charon. After that it was easy. My brother and I were twins. I simply walked into Old Town and everyone thought I was him. I checked around until I found him.''

"And what about your mother?''

"She was dead. She had died in childbirth.''

I heard myself grunt. "Mina Goulding?''

"My sister. Father dear had turned Mother out even though she was pregnant. Mina was the first child Michael ever placed. When I found out I had a sister, I went to find her, but she had disappeared. That's when I got in touch with you.''

"You could have saved me a lot of work if you'd have told me about the Gouldings right from the start.''

"Couldn't do it. If you had known any part of it, you would have figured it all.''

"So I found Mina for you. Did you talk to her?''

He stopped pacing and leaned against the chair. "Tried to, but she didn't want to have anything to do with me. She was Charon's mistress and didn't want to jeopardize her position. Lousy little bitch.''

"That's why the tracks were completely covered when I went back. Charon had taken care of it. Does Sheila know the truth?''

"I wanted to talk to Mike first. Telling her the story was one of the things he was going to do when he went back to the city.''

"One of the things?''

"He had always done his business right from here, using Maria Hidalgo's people as paid emissaries back and forth. When I joined him, he decided to go back and take care of some business himself. So I lent him my clothes and gave him a key to my apartment. The guards let him pass on visual recognition alone.''

"What did he go back to do?''

"Well, the underground railroad is a fine organization, but it takes money to run it. We get that money through . . . donations from our former placees who have made a success on the outside.''

"By donations, you mean extortion.''

"Call it what you like. You'd be surprised how many former Old Towners are pillars of the community.''

"Like Rick Charon?''

"Small world, isn't it? Charon was placed by the organization that preceded Mike's, but we've got his files,'' he walked over and patted the cabinet, "and he's been very generous over the years.''

"So your brother went back to the city to put an even bigger bite on Rick Charon.''

"Crudely put, but not inaccurate.''

"And Charon finally saw red and killed him. Rather than come back and straighten it all out, you hid here and sent your vigilantes to protect you."

"I told you the reason I stayed behind. Someone has to look after these poor devils."

I shook my head. "Your problem here, Phil, is that you can't kid a kidder. Your altruism has left a pile of bodies that would string from here to the Pacific, and it'll probably cost more lives before this is all over. Here's the way it looks to me. You had twenty years to find your brother, but as long as the gravy train held out, it just wasn't very important to you. Then you found out that your father's money was almost gone and that your brother had a pretty good little business going for himself in Old Town. So you decided that you'd rather live like a king here than get a job in the city. I think you always knew what you were; those doctors must have told you something in the booby hatch."

I stood and rubbed my weary face. "God, I'm sick of people lying to me. You're slick, Phil, but you're just a punk. I'd be willing to bet that you wanted to find Mina so that you could work some kind of scam with her, and, I'll tell you the truth, buddy, I wouldn't be half-surprised if Charon didn't know in advance that your brother was coming to put the touch on him."

He jumped on me, knocking us both to the floor. When we hit bottom, he was on top and his hands were tightening around my throat. "Bastard!" he yelled. "Bastard!"

He was stronger than I thought he'd be and as he choked the life out of me, his eyes were wild, popping, his teeth bared like fangs. I tried to kick free, but his weight had me pinned down. Desperately, I scrabbled for his face and was able to stick a finger in his eye. He instinctively grabbed for the eye, and I rolled him off and pinned him. I hit him, probably more than I should have, but the last couple were for George, and they felt the best.

I got up and left him whimpering on the floor. I'd broken his nose for sure and done some real damage to his jawbone. No one would ever mistake him for his brother again.

Moving on to the filing cabinet, I opened the top drawer and thumbed through the folders until I came to Charon's. It contained records of his birth and detailed records of his entrance into straight society and his subsequent life. It was pretty hot stuff. I stuck the folder under my arm and left the office, bidding adieu to a man who would have the unique experience of dying twice.

25

I walked out the door and kept on walking, right out of Ground Zero, right out of Old Town. Phil Grover was still alive, a fact which technically put me out of a job. But the Grover thing had ceased to be a job the moment Charon's apes had so judiciously taken George Wesley's life away from him.

I had a lever against Charon now. Even if he controlled the law, even if he had half the damn state on his payroll, he couldn't escape his past. He had lived his life under the death penalty, cheating the hangman all the way down the road, and now it was going to catch up with him. Charon was through. The moment that his ancestry was revealed, his world would begin to crumble under its own weight. I was playing the game by the dirtiest of rules, but it was Charon's game—Charon's rules.

There were still things that bothered me about the case. Charon's obsession with stopping my investigation made more sense now—he had far more to lose than I could possibly have realized. But keeping that in mind, the murder itself began to make less sense. Considering the outcome, the actual killing was a sloppy job, not at all the sort of thing that a supercharged hustler like Rick Charon would come up with. Even if he farmed the murder out, he wouldn't hire people who would leave such a messy trail. The clincher, of course, was the thing that bothered me from the first—the murder weapon. Why would he commit a murder with something that could be so easily traced back to him? I suppose it could be ego, a deliberate flaunting of the law, but somehow that didn't seem to be the man's style. It looked to me like a murder done in the heat of anger with the sophisticated cover-up coming later. I didn't think Charon capable of such irrational rage. The further I went with that thought, the more confused I became.

Maria's people were waiting for me at the red line. They put me in another of those fancy bullets and took me back to the war bunker. On the way, I took my three remaining pills and knew that the next few hours would have to tell the tale. It was night again, my third without sleep, and the fatigue was battling with my mind for control of my body.

Maria was waiting for me in the war bunker, still dressed in her exo. The tiny room was filled with gray-suits, reading from pocketcoms onto vis screens or bringing messages back and forth. It was like the stock market on the day that the GNP is announced. The benches were empty; I walked over to them and stretched out. Maria pushed through the crowd to stand over me.

"You look like shit," she said.

"Thanks," I answered and placed my arm across my eyes. "I thought that I'd passed that particular plateau yesterday."

From somewhere under the desk she produced a bottle, and poured me a tumbler half-full of the good stuff. Returning to my makeshift bed, she took my hand and wrapped it around the glass. "Drink this," she said.

I leaned up on my elbows and took the glass gratefully. Turning it upside down, I drained it in one gulp. The speed had set my tongue on edge, giving the whiskey an acrid, metallic taste, like licking a tarnished silver fork. I handed the glass back, and for the first time noticed the bandage on Maria's neck.

"What happened to you?"

"Later," she said, and her voice held a degree of urgency. "Another drink?"

I shook my head. "But when this is over . . ." I rolled my eyes. I always promised myself a major blowout when I finished a rotten job. I very rarely ever did it, but it gave me something to look forward to anyway.

"What happened in there?" Maria asked. She was kneeling next to me, trying to see right through my eyes into my skull. People kept bumping into her, or asking her questions, but she just waved them away. She was ministering to me, gently, lovingly, yet there was a frantic feeling behind it—a casual demand that I remain usefully in the present. I felt as if I were being beaten to death with a bag full of feathers.

I sat up. I didn't want her to see how bad things were getting for me. Guess it was a jab to my ego to have her bringing me along, like a high-dollar whore with a senior citizen. I told her my story. She listened quietly and attentively through the whole thing, her only reaction being a demonic smile when I got to the part about Charon's heritage. When I was finished showing her the file, she gave me a kiss—a real one this time—and began pacing through the midst of the confusion.

I watched her for a time, knowing how useless it would be for me to try to influence whatever charges were clicking through her brain relays. Maria had an empire to run; I was just hard knuckles and a soft head.

After a time, she went and sat at her desk, folding her hands on the one spot that wasn't covered with transmission equipment. "I'll listen to advice," she said over the noise of the room, "but don't preach to me."

I got up and walked over to her desk, both of us knowing that I'd probably preach to her anyway.

"It would be unrealistic for me to think that I could defeat Charon with force of arms. He uses more money to light his cigars than we see in a year out here. But I can sure as hell sting him pretty good."

I sighed, wondering if she had been listening to what I had said. "There's no need for any more killing. We can break him without it."

"While you were gone," she said. "There was an attempt made on my life." She tilted her head so that I could get a good look at the bandage. A red stain showed through the gauze. "Several of my 'trusted' lieutenants saw my failure to retaliate immediately after Charon's raid as a display of weakness on my part. They felt that the time was right to shove me aside and take over. It was a close one, Swain—too close."

"I'm sorry."

She swiveled her chair around to stare at the map on the

side wall. "Things work on a very elementary level here. I either strike back, or step down. There are no other choices."

I watched her for a minute. She had a proud face, I guess it could be called aristocratic. I tried to picture what in the world she would be doing if the option of warlord hadn't been open to her. I couldn't think of anything. "So what are you going to do?"

She swiveled back to me. "We're going to hit Charon's factory tonight. Bounce it good. Right after that, you're going to drop your bombshell on the public."

I couldn't help but smile. "That way, your operation will have public sanction, and Charon's power will probably disintegrate before he can strike back." Then I frowned. "If you go for that factory, you're going to lose a whole bunch of people."

"You think I don't know that?" she asked, and her face betrayed no emotion.

"Do you know where Charon is?"

Maria shook her head, her ponytail sliding back and forth on the smooth contours of the exo. "He's been in hiding for the last two days. With the possibilities open to him, he could be on the moon for all I know."

I turned and watched the bustle around me. There was an excitement charging the air that I just couldn't relate to. I was beginning to feel too removed from the operation. I suppose that it had ultimately gotten a lot bigger than me, but I sure wanted to spit in Charon's eye just one time for George.

"This doesn't appeal to you, does it?" she asked.

I looked at her over my shoulder. "No it doesn't. It all feels half-baked, incomplete. Things don't slot together right, and I'm starting to feel that they never will."

"Swain, you're a romantic. Nothing resolves itself in a clear-cut manner. We just have to take the cards as they're dealt to us."

"Yeah," I answered. "I guess you're right." I walked over to the wall map. A tall, thin woman was marking on it with a red pen. The area where Charon's plant was located was circled, with hand-drawn arrows pointing down major avenues toward that section of the city. "So, where do you want me?" I called to her.

She came over and joined me at the map. "I've got a 'safe' house in the city. Right here . . ." she moved the woman aside and pointed to a section of the map just a few blocks off Tremaine, near all the vis stations. "It's protected and unknown. I'll get you there and look out for you until it's time for you to do your part."

I agreed. I could have refused to cooperate, but that wouldn't have stopped Maria from doing what she felt she had to do. At least my collusion would, perhaps, insure an end to the craziness.

I sat down and rested a bit while she arranged for my transport. By this time, most of the wall vises were juicing away like socialites at a dinner party. The room was a tangle of disjointed conversations all, I suppose, important for one reason or another. None of that mattered to me anymore. I sat back and closed my eyes and let the staccato rhythm of the tangled dialogues beat aimlessly against me like the hard summer rain. I thought about what I was going to do, then I removed the pertinent info from the file folder and tucked it away in my breast pocket.

I was aware of crowding all around me, and I opened my eyes to see a room totally jammed with gray-suits. It was so bad now that no one could even move. They were loud, excited people, charged with anticipation and adrenaline. They moved and talked quickly, energized by their nervousness. I watched them for a time, feeling like a sleeper whose dreams are being taken over by the things he dreams about. I shook my head and tried to gear my brain. I needed to get it up one more time, take one more lick, and then it would all be over. I could go home and feed Matilda, sleep for five days, and visit Virginia Teal in her home away from home.

Maria appeared out of the crush. She walked up and tousled my hair. "You going to make it?"

"Hell yes," I answered. "Never felt better." I briefly considered getting up and doing some jumping jacks to prove my stamina, but that thought quickly went the way of all good things.

"Your bullet's waiting upstairs," she said. "You probably don't need to go just yet, but . . ."

"But I'm just in the way here," I finished. I got up and

pulled her close. "I feel responsible," I said into her hair. "I didn't want to involve you in . . ."

"Shush," she whispered. "Fall of the cards, remember?"

"Yeah," I said, and pulled her back to arm's length. "Good luck."

"Good luck yourself." She looked at me strangely for a minute, those wide-set eyes jumping with life. "If only . . ." she began, but turned before she could complete the thought and walked back into the confusion.

I unwheeled the door and walked through the barrack, which was filled with little electric carts hauling away the magnificent arsenal that was cached there. One of Hermanita's men was waiting for me by the outer barrack door to lead me through the maze. Even though I'd walked it several times now, I still didn't have it down yet, although in my own defense I have to say that I guessed right a lot more than I guessed wrong this time.

The climb up the ladder was really tedious this time around. By the time I got to the top of the damn thing, I was totally exhausted. One of those souped-up bullets was waiting for me outside the rubble pile. There was another one in front of it. Protection, I supposed. A hand through the front window pointed me into the back door. I climbed in, and my maze-guide climbed in beside me. I was sandwiched between two gray-suits in the back and there were two more in the front.

The two cars took off as soon as I was settled in. I sat back and took the ride in silence. My companions made small talk, and I listened to that for a while just to keep my brain from drifting away.

We made our way through Maria's decay, then crossed into the city's lighted tenement district. We were just getting through the cracked streets and onto the smooth paveways when everything felt all wrong. There was no other traffic at all on the streets. I started to say something when the bullet ahead of us flared angry orange, then erupted in a huge ball of black-smoking, yellow-red fire and disappeared. Our driver hit his brakes and swerved, and the street in front of us came apart in a sheet of fire, and we were lifted physically and thrown.

We started rolling—over and over and over—and I remember thinking just how dreamlike it really was. Then everything got drippy brown with off-white fuzzy dots. Then a curtain of the blackest night descended on my little head show.

26

It was still dark.

It was still dark and the street lights made everything glow blue-white and my eyes tried to take it all in and I thought that I had never known the street lights to cast such a deadly pallor before and wasn't it a strange thing for me to be thinking, considering all the trouble I was in.

I was all twisted up. There were heavy things pressing against me. I tried to move my eyes around, but my environment seemed surreal and unrelatable. It crossed my mind that I was dead, and then it crossed my mind that nothing inside me worked anymore because I couldn't move. That thought was unsettling and made me decide to go to sleep again.

I was vaguely aware of muffled voices and beams of light slicing through my twisted sarcophagus. I even thought I heard my own name being called. Then I was being jerked, my rest disturbed. I tried to tell them that they were hurting me when they pulled me that way and thank you very much but I'd just as soon stay here for a while, but it was just too much effort and I went back to sleep instead.

27

My first conscious thought was of pain, like maybe there was some little gnome that had snuck inside my head and was in there playing with matches where Mommy and Daddy wouldn't see him. Other parts of my body hurt also, but not like my head. I took that as a good sign.

My head was resting on something soft, like a pillow only a bit firmer. Despite the negative warnings from my smarting brain, I opened my eyes to check out what was going on. Through layers of agony, a female face was staring down at me.

"Mina Goulding, I presume?"

"The name's Helen Trent, and who the hell are you?"

"I'll have to think about that for a while." I stared down at my body. I was lying on a couch, hog-tied. My arms and feet were bound behind me and strung together by a rope between them. My head had been resting on Mina . . . Helen Trent's very comfortable thigh.

I twisted my head around. The woman was handcuffed to the arm of the sofa.

"Well, if you're awake now, you can get your filthy body off me." She began jiggling her legs, bouncing my head up and down like a hairy basketball.

"No, wait, I . . ."

She gave her hips a severe jostle and dumped me off her, and off the couch in the process. I hit the carpeted floor on my stomach, cursing womanhood in general when I was able to get my wind back. After the symphony inside my head stopped for intermission, I looked up at the girl.

"I think that you're getting our romance off on the wrong foot."

"Suck eggs," she said matter-of-factly.

"Where are we?" I asked.

She leaned forward and peered at me over her knees. "What's it to you?"

I struggled up into a kneeling position. My nose itched like crazy, so I bent my head down and scratched it on the couch. "Look, lady," I said. "This really isn't any time to be cute. Your lover boy is tying up all his loose ends, and that includes me and you. Now unless we can figure some way to get out of here, we're going to be dead very shortly."

"Rick wouldn't . . ." she began.

"You know damn well he would."

She stared straight ahead for a moment, her thin face pale, her green lipstick making it look paler. She had really beautiful hair. It had a kind of auburn glow that made it stand out. I could see why Charon had kept her around so long.

"We're in one of the waiting rooms at Bermax Corporation," she said. "Rick's office is right through that door."

I closed my eyes and sighed. If there was one place that I didn't want to be right then, one place in the whole screwy universe, it was in one of the waiting rooms at Bermax Corporation.

"Where's Charon?"

She nodded in the direction of the door.

"Is he alone?"

"There's a woman with him, a long-haired bitch."

"That's Sheila Grover," I said. "Your sister."

Her eyes flashed at me. "I don't have a sister."

I tugged at my bonds; they were well tied. "We can play all the semantic games you want after we get out of this," I told her, "but right now we need to worry about staying alive."

I knee-walked over to her hands. "I think there's a lighter in the front pocket of my jacket," I said. "See if you can fish it out."

She could barely move her hands, chained as they were to the sofa arm. I leaned as far forward as I could and tried to direct my pocket toward her hands. I felt her long, slim fingers snake down my chest.

"Got it," she said.

I scooted around and pulled my restraining rope as tightly as I could. Wiggling her fingers, she managed to ignite the coils and place them on the rope. It was a solar lighter, so I hoped that it would have enough charge to do the job.

"I don't know what's going on," she said. "I had this really nice thing going with Rick, and then this crazy man comes to me with this wild story about being my brother and me being a mutant and all the money we could make together. I got rid of him and told Rick, and everything's been downhill ever since."

"You told him about Phil Grover?"

"Who? Oh, the crazy guy. No, I was afraid to tell him that story. I just told him that some people I used to know were bugging me. He likes to keep his affairs to himself, so he erased my life, as if I had never existed. Why did you people have to stick your feet in things? I was set like cement."

"Set to spend the rest of your life in the Richmond Hotel," I answered.

"So what?" she said sharply. "I had a roof over my head, three squares on the table, and all the dope and vis that I wanted. That's survival in my movie, honey. And in case you haven't noticed, that's about as much as anyone can look forward to in this lousy world."

The rope burned through with a snap. I was able to stand to give her a better target for the ropes on my hands. She got them about half-burned through when the lighter gave out, but they were loose enough for me to slip my hands out. I went to work on my feet and soon I was free, although the pain in my head told me I'd better lay off acrobatics for a while.

"Well done, Swain. You're a real trooper."

I turned to the sound. Charon's smooth, expressionless face was staring at me from a wall vis. "Hello, berserker," I said, and thought I detected a slight flinch at the corners of his mouth.

"I just had to see you in action one more time," he said, those gray eyes staring myopically. "You'll find the keys to

Helen's handcuffs on a table by the screen. Why don't you let her loose and come down and join us by the pool?"

"I don't feel much like a swim," I said, as I searched my pocket unsuccessfully for the documents salted there. "I have this sinus condition."

He grinned lethargically. "Then join us for a drink. It will certainly beat the alternatives if you try to leave without paying your respects."

I didn't have to wonder about Charon's ability to control the situation. "I could use a drink," I said.

"Good," he answered. "We'll be looking forward to seeing you . . . and you too, Helen."

"Thanks," she said and sighed in surrender.

I retrieved the key and released the girl. I stretched out my hand to help her up, but instead of her hand she gave me a look of pure hatred, which I accepted without comment.

She stood and we walked to the door. She was wearing sleeping robes, so hurried was her departure from the Richmond. I leaned as close to her ear as I could and whispered, "Stall him for as long as you can."

"What for?" she returned.

"No, no," came Charon's voice from out of nowhere. "No secrets."

I opened the connecting door and found myself looking down from the top of Charon's grandiose office. The pool lay far below us, down an incredibly long flight of stone steps. A tiny figure waved from poolside.

I went down the steps like an old man. I was exhausted, physically and mentally, and my head hurt so much I couldn't think straight. I had some bad pain in my ribs; my left leg was tender from a cause that I hadn't determined yet, and I was forced to limp. Aside from that, I was in the peak of health.

We made it to the bottom of the steps and crossed the wide expanse of marble floor. The frankincense atmosphere was thick down there, but was eventually overcome by the unmistakable odor of swimming pool, which hit us about ten paces before we got to the thing.

Sheila was splashing around in the water like a little kid. She looked up at me and giggled. She was as naked as a jail-cell light bulb. Charon sat at a lightweight patio table with a red- and white-striped, fringed umbrella shading him from an invisible sun. A large glass of distilled water was in his hand; he toasted me with it as I came up. A bottle full of same sat on the aluminum tabletop. There was a glass of what had to be bourbon and rocks sitting on the other side of the table.

I sat down and took a sip of the drink. It was Black Jack.

"Why don't you take a swim, my dear," Charon said to Mina Goulding. She looked at him once, then turned to stare down at the water, her arms folded across her chest. She probably would have sat, but Charon and I occupied the only chairs.

"Why am I alive?" I asked him.

"So typical of you, Swain. Right to the point . . . a man of action." He almost smiled. "You retrieved something that belongs to me. I just wanted to thank you."

He got up from the table and went to a rack set off to the side. Charon was dressed in a loose black swimsuit. He was leaner than I remembered, nearly all skin and bone. His body was pale, the color of porcelain and showed little musculature. He took a robe off the rack and put it on. When he resumed his seat, he pulled the blackmail papers out of his pocket and waved them in my face.

"Isn't it strange the way the game has turned out?" he said. "I tell you, life is full of surprises. I never would have thought you could have put up the fight you did all the way down the line. I'll tell you a secret, Swain. You really had me going for a while there."

"Well, I hope I didn't make things too hard for you."

"Not at all. It was the most fun I've had in years. And what a prize . . ." He waved the papers again. "Do you know how long I've been trying to get these? And now you drop them right in my lap . . . the last thing in the world you wanted to do. Quite a twist, wouldn't you say?"

"Sure," I answered. "I'm enthralled by the wonder of it all."

"Come on, Swain. Don't be a sore loser. You made a good showing, and haven't got a thing in the world to be ashamed about." He stuck the papers back in his robe.

208

"Actually, I had several reasons for letting you stay alive for a little while longer. I wanted to get hold of these first," he said, patting his pocket. "I also wanted to know who else is privy to this information."

"The whole world," I answered. "I beamed it down over all the satellites."

He took a drink of his water. "It doesn't matter. I'll just have to deal with things as they come up. The other reason is a bit more selfish. This has been a game to remember, and I thought it only appropriate that we end it on a truly ironic note."

He reached into the pocket of his robe and pulled out something that looked like a set of brass knuckles with a coaster stuck on the end. A cord dangled from the underside of the thing and disappeared into Charon's pocket.

"I've got a feeling that thing chops people up," I said.

"An ingenious conclusion, don't you think?"

Sheila climbed out of the water and padded over to where we sat. She really was well put-together, but I was in no condition to appreciate it.

"I'm cold," she said, hugging herself as she dripped puddles by my feet.

"It's a cold world," Charon answered.

"So that's the machine that killed Mike Grover," I said.

For the first time I saw shock on Charon's smooth face. "Mike Grover?"

"Well, well," I smiled, polishing off my drink. "Rick Charon doesn't know everything after all. Why didn't you tell him, Sheila?"

"I'm cold," Sheila said again.

Charon glared at her; his mouth tightened like a vise. "Sheila," he said, low and cold as ice.

She stood there pouting, the goose bumps all over her body making her look like a plucked chicken. "It was Mike," she said, pushing wet hair out of her face. "He called me at home. Told me . . . things about the family. Said that he wanted me to help get money out of you, or he'd let the word slip out. So I went to Phil's apartment and took that . . . thing you gave me and got rid of him. I did it for you, Rick."

"You did it to keep Sheila's name clean," I said. "Let me

see if I can guess the rest. You go to Sugar Daddy and tell him that you killed your brother because he was going to tell the police about the slave labor used in the Bermax factory. Sugar Daddy says, 'that's all right, honey. I'll take care of it.' Is that about right?''

Charon shrugged. "More or less. It doesn't really matter who did it," he said. "I would probably have killed him anyway, as soon as I knew he was in the city. That little piker had been draining me for years." He turned to Sheila. "But why didn't you tell me it was Mike?"

"House of cards," I said. "Everyone immediately assumed that the dead man was Phil, and Sheila went along with it. You wouldn't have believed her story if she'd have told you it was Mike, because Mike's financial success depended on Bermax remaining intact. And she couldn't tell you the truth, because then you would know something that she wanted *nobody* to know, the fact that she was a mutant. I have a question for Sheila, though. How were you able to get into the Marmeth that night without leaving a record?"

She looked slowly from one of us to the other. Then her face took on a defiant look. "I screwed the door guard," she said, not sounding very much like a little girl.

I sat there and watched Charon come apart. "You what!" he screamed. "No one touches my women, no one!" His face contorted with spasmodic rage. "You've defiled both of us, you disgusting whore."

She moved to touch his arm. He twisted away from her. "I did it for us," she said.

"Us? There's never been any us." He shook his head violently and slammed his fist down on the table. "I only kept you around because I figured you might be a hook into your brother's operation, a way to get at him. I wouldn't marry you if you were made out of solid gold."

Sheila's face turned dark and angry. "You mean that I killed my brother for . . ."

"Nothing," I said. "And while we're revealing secrets, Sheila, did you know that your fiancé also comes from mutated parents? That's why *he* worked so hard to cover up your dirty deed. He was protecting his reputation." I couldn't help myself. I leaned back and laughed. "This is really rich," I said. "What do you people do for fun anyway?"

Sheila tried to move toward Charon again. "Rick, I'm sorry about . . ."

"Don't touch me," he said in a voice that came up from a deep, dark tunnel.

She backed up, petrified.

"By the way, Sheila," I said, "have you met your sister, Mina Goulding? She's also been sharing Mr. Charon's bed."

Mina ran up to the table. "Rick, please let me out of this," she pleaded in a quaking voice. "I'm not involved in any of it. Send me back to the Richmond, and you'll never hear another word out of me."

"Nice try," Charon replied, "but you outlived your usefulness long ago. Think of it this way: You had your chance in the stable. Now it's time to step aside and let some other poor unfortunate girl have her day."

I looked across the table at him, as he sat there with his plaything in his fist, getting ready to plunge out some other lights and delighting in his ultimate game of life and death. He was a man only in the most basic definition of the word. The gnawing, festering disease that made up his insides wasn't recognizable as anything human. He was going to have to work for my life; I knew that much.

"Well, it's time to clean house, I guess. Who wants to be first? Don't be shy. This beam is really remarkable. I can set it to take you apart a tiny bit at a time, so that you can watch yourself die, or I can set a wide beam and slip you right off to dream land. We'll make a game of it," he said. "The first volunteer gets the easiest death. What do you . . ."

The lights went out. I jumped immediately, knocking over the table as I went. There was no grunt on the other end. I leaped on the spot, but Charon wasn't there. The lights flickered back on. Charon was several feet away, smiling at me. It was the first time I'd ever seen him smile.

"That was the generator," he said. "Something's happened to the main power."

"The game may not be over yet," I said.

"What do you mean?"

There was a sound behind me. A door about fifty meters

211

from us had burst open and a man came running in. It was Jumpstreet Harry Jenkins. He was talking as he ran. And for once, he looked wide-awake.

"The plant is under attack," he gasped. "Hidalgo's people." He was gulping air. "They got the power on your defensive fields."

He got right up to us before he recognized me. "Swain . . ."

"Hello, Captain Jenkins," I said. "You playing messenger boy now?"

"How many?" Charon asked.

Harry threw up his hands. "I don't know. Couple of hundred I guess."

Charon snorted. "We'll hold them."

Harry was looking at me. His face was contorted.

"Stick around, Harry," I said. "This is your opportunity to see a triple murder, live and in-person."

"You can go, Jenkins," Charon said.

"What are you going to . . ."

"I said, you can go. Go see to your people. And don't screw up this time."

I looked him dead in the face. "Yeah, run along, Harry. Maybe you can help Mr. Charon dispose of the bodies later."

"You can't kill these people," Harry said.

"I can do anything I damn well please, Captain. This is my game."

Harry was shaking his head. "No," he said. "No. I've turned my face . . . too many times. Done your dirt for you because I thought it was a fair trade for the protection of the city. But this . . . this is crazy."

Charon leveled his machine at Harry's head. "Leave this office," he said slowly.

Harry turned and took two steps. Then he swung back around and there was a laser in his hand. "Put that thing down, Charon. Put it down on the floor."

Charon laughed, high and shrill. "My game," he said. "I make the rules."

"Put it down or I'll kill you."

Charon juiced his machine in Harry's direction. Jenkins dove and rolled and came up with pink light flashing from his fist. The beam came up at an angle, entered Charon's throat and came out just above his right eye. The man fell and died—just like that. Just like everybody else.

Mina Goulding screamed and threw herself, crying, on Charon's body. I guess she was all out of opportunities.

Harry moved up to me, while I righted my chair and sat down. A big swatch was missing from his meticulously groomed hair where Charon's beam had taken it away. "I think it's over," he said, "and God help the department."

"It's over," I repeated. "You're a hell of a cop, Harry. I just wish that you'd have realized it sooner."

He rolled his eyes. "Why do you have to make everything so goddamned simple?"

"I'm simple-minded," I answered. "I'm also very tired."

I got out of the chair and splashed myself with water from the swimming pool. Harry ran out, I supposed to try and stop the fighting outside. I didn't care. I was out of it. I knelt there by the water for a minute, watching the ripples expand from my hand. A reflection joined mine. It was Sheila.

"You didn't tell the cop that I killed Mike," she said.

I just shook my head.

"So what am I supposed to do now that you've messed everything up?"

"Have you ever tried acting like a human being?"

"What, like you?" she spat. "Should I stumble around making a big deal out of everything as if it really mattered?"

I stood up and looked at her. "I'm going to tell you this once, then you'd better get out of the way because I'm going to take a poke at you. You go home and care for that broken old man and make whatever time he's got left in this world worth living. I'm going to keep my eye out, and if I ever find that you're not doing what I said, I'm going to put the word out on you and your troubles will really start."

She quickly moved away from me; she had that much sense.

I could hear explosions off in the distance, but they sounded far away and infrequent. I needed some sleep, and I needed it right away, so I wandered off leaving the whole mess behind me and looked for a quiet corner.

I could have been harder on Sheila, but what the hell, she was crazy. I guess we're all crazy when it comes right down to it. We all have our own personal bloodsucker that drags us down and eats us up and makes us see a world that exists only to our minds. We believe what we want to believe, then convince ourselves that everyone else is playing the rear end of the horse. And what does it come to? In everything we do, every day of our lives, we're playing the death game, charading our way to its always-open door. It frightens us in its awesome infinity, and fascinates us in its inevitability. We flirt with it, we run from it, and we try to insulate ourselves from its sting. We take it to our beds and hold it close to our beating hearts. We kiss it on its cold, deep mouth and taste the bittersweet nectar of our own folly. And ultimately we complete the game, regardless of our station or disposition. We lose the stakes that we gambled with, but ultimately win the greater prize. For the dead don't worry about power, or glory, or . . . usefulness. That's for the living, the ones like me who are running scared; the ones who are trying to bottle it all up and put a lid on it, like a jar with a fetus inside. The dead just lie there with blank eyes and unthirsting lips and savor the taste of their victory.

The cannon fire stopped outside.

What a crapshoot. What a goddamned crapshoot.

ABOUT THE AUTHOR

MIKE MCQUAY teaches a science fiction writing course at Oklahoma Central State University. A graduate of the University of Dallas, he has served with the military in Vietnam, Thailand, Japan, and the Philippines. McQuay is addicted to watching B movies on television late at night. His previous Bantam book was *Escape from New York*.

Swain is back in October, 1981

Read this stunning preview of his next adventure

MATHEW SWAIN:
WHEN TROUBLE BECKONS

by
Mike McQuay

The trip up was awful. Going to the moon is probably a lot like picnicking in a wind tunnel—a new experience, but you're anxious to get to the apple pie so you can go home. I was already worried about Ginny, and the claustrophobic atmosphere of the gouger just made it worse. On top of that, they didn't allow cigs, and the only kind of booze they had was champagne. Champagne, for God's sake. Those bubbles gave me so much gas that I kept floating out of my seat.

We came down in a place called Lunar Depot One, but everyone called it Loonie One. It was a huge complex, consisting of a series of domes formed of clear tetrahedral segments. Looking up, I could see black night and bright white and blue-white stars shining like mirrors in the sun. The moon was nongovernmental, a corporate playground for whatever mining companies had the resources to get up there and the military power to hold their claims. Each mining company had its own army to defend it, and holdings apparently changed hands through skirmishes more often than a hooker changes her pants.

They gave us heavy shoe weights when we got off

the ship, and those took some getting used to. Trying to walk in them was like sloshing through knee-deep yellow mud. Everything was slideways, so a lot of cumbersome maneuvering was unnecessary. I was directed down a long tunnel that pulsed neon blue along its length in spider-web patterns before terminating at the baggage claim area. I was I.D.'d and hand-printed for my bag, and then turned loose on my own.

Grabbing my suitcase, I slid down another tunnel, exiting in the main bubble. The place was jammed with Spacers, many in uniform. They represented a lot of different countries, and languages bounced in and out of earshot like hailstones on a tin roof. They pushed their way in groups through the chamber. The air crackled with the sound of an electrical storm, for Spacers yelled and warbled at the peak of their form like inmates in the monkey house. They pressed in around me like a fleshy vise, and I nearly drowned in the smells of ozone and sweat.

"English," I said quickly. "I didn't know what the . . ."

"Hey, English!" he yelled, cutting me off.

A woman slid off a metal stool and came over to me. She had short copper-colored hair, and was small without appearing small. She had a face that told me she had been all the way down the road and back, but somehow, on her, it was appealing. She was chewing snuff and carried a small tin can around that she would stop and spit into from time to time. Her faded tan one-piece had a tiny brown stain lacing its front.

"You need a lift?" she asked, giving me the once over. She had cat eyes, one gray and one green. I couldn't peg her accent, which was usually the sign of someone who had spent a great deal of time moving around.

"I need to get to Freefall City," I told her.

She turned up her nose. "What the hell do you want to go out there for?"

"Heard the surfing's good," I answered. "Can you take me?"

She spit into her cup. "Cost you three blues," she said.

Not knowing how much three blues were worth, the price sounded just dandy. "You've got yourself a fare."

She held out her hand. "Let's see the color of your plastic first."

Unclasping my pouch, I sifted through its innards until I fished out three triangular blue chips. I counted them into her hand. She spit into her can and counted them again. Then she lost them in her pocket. "Freefall City it is," she said. "Follow me, good-looking. And carry your own bag."

We went through a door set behind the line of cabbies, stepping into a dimly lit hallway of cement and metal beams. The hall was narrow, and cold as a tax man's heart. I felt as if I had walked into the meat locker at the Chicago stockyards.

We had to walk single file on the metal grates in the floor, our weighters clanging with every step. She spoke to me over her shoulder. "We don't get too many out to Freefall anymore," she said. "You surprised me."

We were passing a series of round wheel-lock doors marked with consecutive numbers. "Why's that?"

"They raise the young ones to stay, I guess," she returned. "And they don't take too well to outsiders. Got their own ways of getting along."

"What do they do?"

I could hear her spit plop into the can. "Beltel owns the place, has for about a century. It's the best gravity pocket in the whole damned orbit. They build and repair communications satellites and do a lot of manu-facturing for some of the other cities. Here we are."

She had stopped in front of number 17. I came up beside her just as she was getting the wheel unscrewed. It groaned loudly as she pulled it open. The thing was damp and rusty, as were the walls. The door opened to a clear tube. The cabbie hopped up and started crawling through the tube—that's how small the space was.

As I watched her fanny wiggle along the tube, her face turned to me. "My name's Porchy Rogers," she said. "How about you?"

"Swain," I answered and hopped up myself, pushing my suitcase in front of me.

"Just follow me," she called.

"Yeah, I wouldn't want to get lost."

We crawled through the clear tunnel, suddenly away from the buildings, into the lunar landscape. It was bleak, but almost compelling in its stark contrasts of light and dark. I had been in worse places. The tube hissed loudly in my ears. Other tubes fanned out on both sides of me. Those, like mine, terminated in round metal spheres that sprouted porcupinelike protrusions all around. The spheres were dark-toned and heavily riveted.

Porchy Rogers stopped ahead of me. She unwheeled another door. This one was connected to her sphere. The door pushed inward, and she tumbled through the opening. I could feel my knees starting to stiffen as I hurried to get through the door. Pushing my bag through, I fell in on top of it, sliding rudely to the floor.

"That first step's a killer," she said, and didn't even flinch.

I lugged myself to my feet, arching my back to loosen it up. Inside, the place was about as large as a good-sized bathroom. It was straight steel, cold and unornamented, like a round paddy wagon.

She closed and locked the door. The only light in the ball was a red one that showed when the oxy flow was operational. After wheeling the door shut, she went to a small control panel and flipped some switches. White cabin lights came up and the air hiss got louder, and I got a little better look around. There was a worn, flowered carpet on the floor that looked as if it had been old when the world was young. Four used bullet-seats were bolted to the floor. One of the seats had controls wrapping around it in a semicircle. There were several windows of porthole size and shape placed around the sphere, but most of them were so dirty that it was impossible to see through. Food wrappers, plates and cups, and other bits of garbage lay on the floor and bulkheads. They were wedged between things to keep them from floating. Pictures of naked weight lifters with oil-slicked bodies were tacked onto the walls and ceilings. The place needed a woman's touch.

"Are you bonded?" I asked her.

"Only my whisky," she returned and spat into her cup.

"Whisky?"

She turned to me and smiled like a Fancy Dan with a new gun. "Would you . . . yeah, you would." She began rooting through a metal tool box that was set into the floor, coming out with a bottle of Black Jack. She handed it across to me. The bottle had a nipple on the end, just like a baby bottle. I put it to my lips and milked the thing, and I'm proud to say that zero gravity didn't affect the quality even a little bit.

I handed it back. "No charge," Porchy said, and took a big pull herself. "You're a man after my own heart."

I took the bottle back and had another drink. "People of distinction always manage to search each other out." I was happy to know that pioneer life retained at least a modicum of the genteel pleasures.

Porchy put the bottle back in her tool kit and strapped herself into the control seat. "Park it anywhere," she said, wiping a drop of brown juice off her lower lip. I took the seat next to her. "I like you," she smiled, letting her eyes frisk me again. "You remind me of my ex."

"Divorced?" I asked.

Her eyes softened just a touch, sagging like bread dough. "No," she answered softly. "Dead."

"Tough luck," I replied, and moved on because I could see that she wanted to move on. "What's the chances of getting a smoke?" I asked.

She winked and started flipping toggles on her control board. The sphere began vibrating, a low whine filling the cabin. She juiced a small vis on her board and a set of numbers started reading across the screen. She punched another button and a sucking sound joined the whine. "You can smoke now if you want to."

Gratefully pulling a fag out of the pocket of my waistcoat, I stuck it in my mouth. "What's that sound?" I asked.

"I opened a hole to the outside, so you wouldn't smoke up the place."

"You mean we're leaking air?"

"Don't worry about it."

I shrugged and lit the cig, watching the smoke scoot at an angle and quickly disappear through the hull.

Porchy pulled a blue baseball cap out from under her seat and stuck it solidly on her red hair. She hooked earphones and throat mike over that. She spoke to the mike. "Control Charlie, this is Shuttle 17, over."

"Shuttle 17, this is Control Charlie. Over." The

voice had a metallic ping to it that could get real distracting.

"Request undocking and flight space permission," she said casually, while her hands danced across the board, running preflight.

"Permission granted. Request terminal coordinates."

She reached next to the control panel and took up a tattered black book that was attached by a small chain to the floor. The book was bloated and mildewed. She opened it and flipped through the worn pages. Finding her place, she quickly ran a blue-nailed finger down the page, pausing midway. "Terminal coordinates: 2Q2-1719."

"Repeat coordinates please."

She haunched down closer to the book. "2Q2-1719."

"Permission denied to those coordinates."

"Are you saying no?" She gave me a sidelong glance.

"Permission denied to those coordinates."

"Request reason for denial."

"To file a complaint or request, grievance form 47D must be filed in triplicate for a period of thirty Earth days in the office of the air controller. A copy of this form may be obtained . . ."

"Never mind," she said, and shut down communications. She looked at me. "You heard it," she said.

"Is there anything you can do?"

"What are you asking me?"

I took my plastic pouch and dropped it in her lap. "It's all I've got," I said. "But it's yours if you can get me to Freefall."

She hefted the pouch, then gave it back to me. "Listen, good-looking. They don't make enough of this stuff to buy my ass," she said, then looked at me, those eyes sagging again. "You really want to get there bad, don't you?"

"Yeah."

She was looking at me, but I could tell that she was thinking about someone else. Her face pulled against itself for a while, then she just shook her head.

"I guess you just found yourself a sucker," she said and rejuiced communications. "Control Charlie, this is Shuttle 17. Request permission for direct flight path to coordinates 8P-517."

"Purpose of flight?"

"Sightseeing."

"Permission granted for flight, but landing permission must be granted by ground control at coordinates."

"Roger, Control. Out."

"Thanks," I said. "You okay."

"I'm a fool, and you know it," she replied, and unplugged her headset. Reaching out, she pounded the undocking lever with a closed fist. There was the sound of a hydraulic swoosh, a rocket thrust, and I saw the ground leaving us through the porthole. It tilted crazily off at a gray, pitted angle, then it was upside down. Porchy punched our coordinates into her computer, flipped to auto, then sank back heavily into her seat. Rocket thrusts blurted from several different locations, then we were back in proper perspective to the ground. I finished my smoker, ground it out in my hand, and stuck it in my pocket for lack of an ashtray. It made me feel better when Porchy shut down the sucking sound.

"Where are we going?"

"Well, eventually we're going to Freefall, but we're going to have to go through the back door."

"The back door," I repeated.

"I hope you don't scare easily."

I wanted to ask her about it, but decided that maybe

I didn't want to know. As we floated across the surface at skyscraper height, I stared out the window at the mining sites that scarred the surface like thorns on a rose bush. There was activity all over the surface— moving machines, pumping diggers, and ugly bulbous freighters that fed off the lunar bowels like metal ticks. This went on for a time, until the light gave way to a line of total darkness. We were losing the sun.

"Dark side," Porchy said. "We'll be there soon."

After that, ground operations could only be seen as camp lights, shining brightly in the unatmosphered night. It began to get cold in the cabin, and Porchy turned up the heat. "Darksiders are crazy," she said, and drew in her eyebrows. "Confinement and darkness, not many can handle it." She shivered. "Even the pros hate them."

Up ahead, we could see a series of unrelated flashes brightening the perpetual night. As we got closer, tiny laser streamers could be seen zipping pink-hot lines through the cold, bleak landscape.

"Battle," Porchy said. "It looks like someone is going after Marseilles, a big Frenchy company."

"Who?" I asked, as I watched buildings explode in brilliant flashes that lasted only an instant before the vacuum sucked up all their air.

"Germans, maybe. I don't know."

"Does this happen often?"

"All the time."

"Who's going to win?"

She chuckled low, and gave us a little height to avoid the carnage that was now directly below us. "I don't know who will win," she said. "But the Frenchies will lose. They always lose."

We left the battle behind us, and floated in silence for a time. All at once, she sat up straight and cut off the auto pilot. "Here's where it starts getting rough," she said.

A huge mine was coming up rapidly in front of us. It was vast, far larger than any of the others we had seen. Its lights stretched out, defining a vast plain like a field of stars ready for harvesting. "Western Mining," she said. "The oldest and still the biggest."

She hit the port and forward thrusters and turned us sharply. "Western does all of the mining for Freefall. We're going to hitch a ride with some titanium."

"What?"

"Just watch."

We were coming up on a large, well-lit area. A round building sat in the area of orange light. It was painted red and tilted at a slight angle. Train tracks led up to the building from all around, and then tracked backwards into the night.

"Gas gun," she told me, and as I got closer, I could see what she meant. The thing was shooting ore out of its open end at an incredible rate of speed, spewing large chunks into the darkness. "Compressed hydrogen shoots the metals out of here and they catch them at Freefall. If we handle it just right, we can travel the ore path and avoid the radar."

"Is that good?"

"This is the frontier, Swain," she replied. "Vehicles found in unauthorized air space are shot down on sight."

"Wonderful." I took a deep breath and thought about my friend the bookmaker.

"Ready?" she asked, as we closed in.

"No," I answered. But she took us in anyway. We swooped in close to the gun, then she goosed her reverse thrusters for all they were worth. No sooner had we cleared the lip of the gun than we were caught in a tooth-cracking turbulence. We started vibrating like a fat man with a jackhammer.

"Hold on!" she hollered over the sound of my body shaking to pieces. But I had already figured that out for myself. Porchy's hat came off her head and hung in the air of the cabin, her hair dancing a samba around her head. Loose plastic and cigs went around my head like visions of sugar plums, and the naked weight lifters came off the wall and gyrated through the cabin.

Then the rocks.

Mammoth and frightening, they raced silently past our portholes, blocking out everything for a few seconds, only to leave us quietly behind.

"Is this safe?" I yelled.

"Hell no!" she returned, hands shaking wildly on the thrusters.

"Don't tell me that!" I hollered back.

"What?"

"Lie to me!"

"It's perfectly safe," she returned, and then ruined it all with a wink.

We rode the rocks for nearly an hour, the trip getting easier the farther we went. We stayed on the ore trail until making visual contact with the huge collection net that hung in the sky like the king of the wind socks.

"We're close enough for local traffic now," Porchy said when contact was made, and it was with obvious relief that she took us out of the fast lane.

"That wasn't too bad," I said proudly, then realized that my hands were cramp-locked onto the chair arms. "Is Freefall near here?"

She pointed to a small cluster of stars out the front port. "There it is," she said.

"That doesn't look like much," I told her, and fished one of my cigs out of the air.

"It will," she responded. "Where exactly do you want to go?"

I stuck the smoker into my mouth and chewed on it. "It's a private home. She calls it Miss Lily."

Porchy looked at me and almost smiled. "Rich girl, huh?"

"Yeah."

"Friend of yours?"

"Sometimes."

The city was no more than bright pinpoints of light for a long time. Distances in space are impossible to judge, so I had no idea how far we actually were from the place. The light became brighter the closer we got, then divided itself off into a sequence of light rings.

"What's that?"

Porchy was busy laying city grids onto her vis, looking for Ginny's place. She answered without looking up. "The city gets its light from the sun," she said, as if she had said it a thousand times before. "They do it by orbiting reflecting mirrors between the sun and the wheels. What you're seeing is the reflection around the edges of the mirrors. It bounces light onto the wheels where other mirrors reflect it back and forth before letting it into the habitations, so that they can get the light without getting the cosmic radiation." She spat loudly. "I found your friend's house."

I looked down at her city grid, and saw a flashing pinpoint of green light in the corner. She jacked the thrusters until we had bull's-eyed the flash into the center of the vis.

It was a while before the city came into clear view. It was a strange sensation moving up on Freefall, like flying into the innards of a cosmic watch. There were spoked wheels of various sizes rotating slowly. The outer circumference of the wheels was nonrotating, a dirty gray and black band made of moon rubble that acted as radiation shields for the various wheels. The reflecting mirrors orbited at an angle to the wheels, like open-mouthed clams, and their reflection was too brilliant to stare at directly.

There were hundreds of satellites within the city proper. Most were wheels, many were balls or tubelike affairs or even corkscrew ships. Most of them clustered around the Beltel wheel, which was the matrix of the city. It was startling in its size—something that I was unable to appreciate until we were close up—and it housed the Beltel headquarters and homes for all but its upper management employees. All of the agriculture was done on the main wheel, called Papa Bear by the inhabitants, as was the raising of animals. Papa Bear was the focus and lifeblood of Freefall City.

The city looked used, like an old bullet or a worn-out coat. The radiation shields had a lot to do with that; they made the wheels look like dirty snowballs. But it was deeper than that. There was a trail of garbage and refuse that tagged along after the city like a process server on a child-support case. The trail was miles long and wide and contained enough scrap metal and other junk to fill the Grand Canyon. I bet *that* never showed up in the postcards.

We kept closing in for what seemed like forever. It was like we were right there, and yet the place never got any closer. Then, suddenly, we were in it. Mammoth rotating wheels turned the clockworks and clicked out some uniformity in a place that had no natural rules. I felt like a virus invading a body, skipping erratically amidst the eternal machinations. There was something else, too. From the first moment we entered the city, I knew that I didn't belong there.

Read the complete novel, MATHEW SWAIN: WHEN TROUBLE BECKONS, on sale October 15, 1981, wherever Bantam Books are sold.

"The most important horror collection of the year."
—*Locus*

DARK FORCES

Edited by Kirby McCauley

(14801-x) $3.50

**Including a complete new short novel
by Stephen King**

This new volume of 23 chillers contains new works by a star-studded roster of authors. You'll find spine-tingling tales from Davis Grubb, Ray Bradbury, Edward Gorey, Robert Aickman, Joe Haldeman, Dennis Etchison, Karl Edward Wagner, Lisa Tuttle, Ramsey Campbell, T.E.D. Klein, and many other masters of horror.

Get ready for terror as you encounter slug-like creatures who inhabit New York City's sewers, zombies who become all-night store clerks in California, a young boy who is kidnapped in his very own bed, and a multitude of horrifying beings and events.

Available in September wherever paperbacks are sold or directly from Bantam Books. Include $1.00 for postage and handling and send check to Bantam Books, Dept. DF, 414 East Golf Road, Des Plaines, Illinois 60016. Allow 4–6 weeks for delivery.

FANTASY AND SCIENCE FICTION FAVORITES

Bantam brings you the recognized classics as well as the current favorites in fantasy and science fiction. Here you will find the beloved Conan books along with recent titles by the most respected authors in the genre.